W9-BNI-547

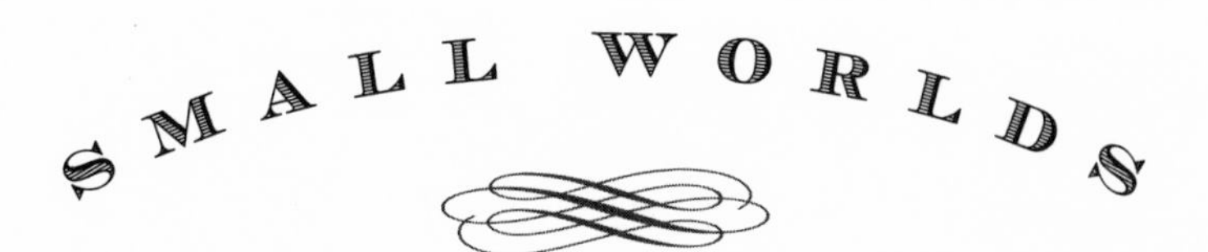
SMALL WORLDS

# SMALL WORLDS

ALLEN HOFFMAN

ABBEVILLE PRESS
PUBLISHERS
NEW YORK
LONDON
PARIS

*For Stefani*

Jacket front: Boys' *kheyder*, Lublin, Poland. YIVO Institute for Jewish Research/Alter Kacyzne/Raphael Abramovitch Collection.

Editor: Sally Arteseros
Designer: Celia Fuller
Production Editor: Abigail Asher
Production Manager: Becky Boutch

 Inquiries should be addressed to Abbeville Publishing Group, 488 Madison Avenue, New York, N.Y. 10022. The text of this book was set in Minion and Chevalier. Printed and bound in the United States of America.

First edition
2 4 6 8 10 9 7 5 3 1

Library of Congress Cataloging-in-Publication Data

Hoffman, Allen.
Small worlds / Allen Hoffman.
p. cm.
ISBN 0-7892-0129-1
1. Jews—Europe, Eastern—Fiction. I. Title.
PS3558.034474S58 1996
813'.54—dc20 96-5768

*Small Worlds*
is the first novel in the series SMALL WORLDS

*Even man's eye is a small world: the orb is the globe, the white is the encircling ocean, the iris is the dry land, the pupil is Jerusalem, and the image reflected in the pupil is the holy Temple, may it soon be rebuilt in our days and in the days of all Israel. Amen.*

Tractate Derech Eretz Zuta

# RECOLLECTIONS

The Russians called it Krimsk; the Poles called it Kromsk, but it was mainly the Jews who lived there. They called it whatever their hosts preferred. Krimsk—so it was named in 1903—had hills and valleys, forests not far from town, pastures and fields close by. The railroad was a day's wagon ride away in the more fortunate town of Sufnitz, whose railroad spikes firmly held the rails onto the heavy wooden ties and also kept its name firmly rooted. Sufnitz managed to avoid changing its name every time the border shifted.

Krimsk had no railroad with its fixed spikes mating metal to the wood rooted in earth, but it did have a flowing river whose name remained constant—the River Nedd. In his famous and disastrous Russian campaign, Napoleon had crossed the River Nedd at Krimsk. Unfortunately even such a remarkable and lustrous fact was slightly tarnished, for no one knew in which direction he had crossed: on his way from Paris to Moscow, or on his return from Moscow to Paris. It was clear that he had crossed it only once, his arrival or departure having occurred fifty miles to the north, where the river turns to flow east-west. So there was something slightly senile about the town's historical recollection. Napoleon was on the tip of the town's tongue, so to speak, but not sufficiently fixed in mind to risk uttering the great man's name. To make matters worse, Napoleon had arrived in victory and departed in defeat.

Coming and going were worlds apart, and no one who had seen the crossing was alive to tell about it—with the possible exception of the Krimsker Rebbe, who believed that he had witnessed it. But this had been in a previous existence as a young frog, perhaps even as a mature tadpole, and try as he might, the sum of his recollections of Napoleon yielded only a short man with hairy tufts protruding from his nostrils—and this through several feet of water. Much what one would expect from a frog on the riverbed with his smooth-skinned envy of the hirsute.

So the town didn't speak much about its illustrious past. Not even among themselves. It was a shame, for although there were many goyim, there was but one Napoleon. A fact not lost on the rebbe, who used to compare him favorably with the great pharaoh in his hasidic parables. Even that was no more; for the past five years the Krimsker Rebbe had hardly spoken at all. Yaakov Moshe Finebaum, the Krimsker Rebbe, had withdrawn to his study. Although everyone knew why Napoleon had departed, no one could fathom the rebbe's reasons for his retreat; but it threatened to be as permanent a withdrawal from the life of Krimsk as Napoleon's had been.

# KRIMSK, RUSSIA
# 1903

## TISHA B'AV

*(The ninth day of the Hebrew month of Av)*

*When the holy Temple was destroyed [on the Ninth of Av, Tisha B'Av] . . . men of faith ceased to exist.*

—Mishnah, Sotah

*Rabbi Yitzhak explained that "men of faith" are those who used to have faith in the Holy One for it has been taught: Rabbi Eliezer the Great declares that whoever has bread [for today] in his basket and asks, "What shall I eat tomorrow?" is none other than one of those of diminished faith.*

—Babylonian Talmud, Tractate Sotah

*Rabban Shimon Ben Gamliel declared in the name of Rabbi Yehoshua: From the day [Tisha B'Av] the holy Temple was destroyed, there has been no day without a curse.*

—Mishnah, Sotah

# CHAPTER ONE

THE KRIMSKER REBBE HAD RETIRED TO HIS STUDY. FOR five years he had not emerged. His devoted hasidim believed that their rebbe immersed himself in Miriam's well, which miraculously materialized in the small book-lined room. They thought they heard splashing behind the double doors on the eve of every Sabbath. This was one of the well's few appearances in Europe, although the wondrous spring had a distinguished supernatural tradition, having accompanied the Jews during forty years of wandering in the desert. The non-hasidic Jews of the town didn't go so far as to believe in Miriam's well appearing in Krimsk, but they did believe in the purity and force of the rebbe's lonely mission although they couldn't imagine exactly what that mission might be. In Krimsk only his rebbetzin, his wife Shayna Basya, doubted the merit of his endeavor. She was confident that she understood his saintly withdrawal. Shayna Basya believed that he was slightly cracked.

And she believed that she knew why. Inheritance. At their marriage feast she had asked her mother-in-law to pass the water, and the old lady, who looked even more like a frog than her husband—she had smooth, flat eyebrows, not her husband's prickly brushes—handed her the horseradish. Shayna Basya had incorrectly assumed that her mother-in-law was merely delineating the traditional course of their relationship. Shayna Basya, herself the daughter of a great rabbinic family and possessing awesome respect for the age-old familial arts of her people, received the call to combat and seized every opportunity to discomfit, shame, and insult the older woman as penance for the twin sins of bearing Yaakov Moshe and permitting him to welcome Shayna Basya under the wedding canopy. The old lady received the abuse with the tolerance and appreciation of a woman who loved the rewards of family. Or so Shayna Basya had thought until the old lady lay dying from a burning fever and repeatedly begged for another glass of horseradish. Shayna Basya went into the next room where Yaakov Moshe was reciting from Psalms and told him that his mother had asked for a glass of horseradish. He had wearily arched his eyebrows in query. So? She means water, Shayna Basya explained. What's the difference? her husband remarked and went back to his Psalms.

The awareness that Shayna Basya had married into a family of dubious sanity chilled her; it floated around her like a cold, clammy fog from which there was no escape. If only some way could be found to protect her child; but even there she felt unequal to the task. Half the girl's inheritance was from the Finebaum side, where they believed that Moses hit the rock and horseradish flowed forth. There were distressing inclinations in Rachel Leah, who worshiped her father. The more absurd his actions, the more she worshiped him. Rachel Leah resembled Shayna Basya's own sainted grandmother, the rebbetzin of Bezin, and even that created problems. How could saints be around madmen and recognize them for what they were, plain *meshugoyim?* They needed either other saints or benign cynics. It was the latter role Shayna Basya hoped to play. She knew it wouldn't be easy. After all, she was genetically only one-fourth her sainted grandmother and never felt terribly benign. The cynicism, she had in abundance.

The last week her husband had been acting strangely in his self-imposed exile, and Shayna Basya, as a good wife, was disturbed. He had been eating everything that Rachel Leah brought in to him and on several occasions had even requested seconds. This, from an ascetic of five years who used to fast every Monday and Thursday and eat no hot food except on the Sabbath. He had eaten more last Monday than he usually ate in a week, and he had wanted to know why the coffee was cold. Something was happening, and now was not the time for it. What disturbed Shayna Basya most was his talking at length to Rachel Leah. The girl emerged from his study with her eyes shining and a flush on her face. When Shayna Basya asked her daughter what they talked about, Rachel Leah's eyes sparkled like the most fervent hasid, and she declared, "How father loves God!" The girl seemed positively feverish. What were the two of them doing in there, drinking horseradish? They certainly weren't bathing in Miriam's well.

Shayna Basya brought her husband fresh linen every day. She had no illusions about his bathing. She had very few illusions. With a husband who withdrew from the world, leaving her with a household and a young daughter, she couldn't afford many. Men like her husband, his virtues notwithstanding, simply shouldn't marry and have families. Who would have arranged for Rachel Leah's match if not Shayna Basya? Through the discreet offers of Reb Yechezkal, of course, Yaakov Moshe had had the good sense or the good luck to choose a fine, reliable man as his sexton. Almost as fortunate as he was in choosing Shayna Basya herself for a wife. It was remarkable how such an unworldly man consistently could make such excellent choices. Occasionally it made Shayna Basya suspect—and she wasn't admitting anything—that there might be more to the world of the Krimsker Rebbe than met her jaundiced eye. But even if there were, a family isn't a book that you can put on a shelf and reclaim five years later, unchanged and unused.

Rachel Leah was now privately engaged to Yitzhak Weinbach, an important match manufacturer, and they were to be married following the Succos holiday. The rebbe knew nothing of this; Shayna Basya didn't want him to know until after the ceremony. Rachel Leah herself didn't know about it for sure. In spite of her childish spiritual notions, Rachel Leah would have the financial security and stability that Shayna Basya had never had. Enough of precarious Torah and the privation of loving God; let someone else lead the hasidim for a few generations. Their family, father and grandfathers, uncles and even her brothers, had done enough. Let someone else lead the Jews into a closet if they wished. Frankly, Shayna Basya was at a loss to understand how the Krimsker hasidim could remain followers, much less devoted admirers, of her husband. Thank God for superstitions. Shayna Basya had her share of them, but a chandelier couldn't be expected to fall on his enemies every day. In their old age it might be a very healthy thing to have a wealthy manufacturer for a son-in-law. If the rebbe stayed in his study all day, what difference should it make to the rebbe whom Rachel Leah married? But it would, of course. He was the Krimsker Rebbe, and she was an only child. And the Krimsker Rebbe, disturbed or not, was not one to compromise principles. Shayna Basya found herself wishing alternately that she had had a dozen children or that she had not even been married; either way the monstrous fate of an only child would have been avoided. Shayna Basya didn't want to send Rachel Leah in to her father with the meal of ashes that he would eat before the start of the fast. She would prefer to keep them apart. On the other hand, she had no desire—no, that wasn't quite right, she had a fear of going into his study herself. If he realized what Shayna Basya was doing at night, that would be a disaster for Rachel Leah and for everyone.

# CHAPTER TWO

Boruch Levi had risen early and had been traveling all day to arrive home for the fast day, Tisha B'Av. As with all Jewish days, the fast day would begin at sunset. He knew that the Temple in Jerusalem had been destroyed on the ninth day of Av, but that was long ago and far away. The Talmud and the other holy books that told of such things remained closed to him, for he was no scholar. He barely had had time to learn to read and start the Book of Genesis when his father died and he left the classroom for a trader's life. He was never one for study and for veneration of the past anyway.

He was on the road home this afternoon because Tisha B'Av was a day of calamity and suffering for the Jews. He didn't want to be with the peasants on such a day. You didn't have to be a scholar to know what the goyim were capable of doing to the Jews. Pity the peasant, however, who started up with Boruch Levi: large and well muscled, surprisingly quick, he was probably the toughest Jew in the district, but still, it was better to be home on a day of ill fortune. So he had hitched his horse to his wagon long before sunrise. Through the hot morning he slowly drew closer to his native town, where he would rest, eat the feast before the fast, meager though that be, and go to the study-prayer hall to hear the Book of Lamentations.

As he rode along in his wagon on the road back to Krimsk, Boruch Levi held the reins so loosely they nearly fell from his hands. Although he appeared lost in reverie, he was intently studying his horse. The two hemispheres of Thunder's rump seemed to be trying to tell him something. Boruch Levi leaned forward. The afternoon sun was behind them and wrote on the twin mounds of horsehair-parchment with a single stylus of light. First one haunch rose to tear the sparkling letters from the sun's bright luminous tongue, only to erase them in shadow as the hoof touched earth—and the opposite hemisphere rose to flash its brilliant message. Back and forth the mystic alphabet flew, and Boruch Levi stared as if in a trance. Were the two sides arguing or agreeing? They were definitely talking to him. Such an astonishing communication did not surprise him; he had had a feeling about this horse.

A year ago Boruch Levi had cast his quick, stubborn glance on the lean, aging beast and had mistaken it for the solution to his economic plight. It wasn't a bad horse; it had dragged him and his rebuilt wagon around Volhynia, but that was not the reason he had bought it. He had had a feeling that fate wanted the horse to enter Boruch Levi's life and dramatically change it—for the better, of course. So Boruch Levi had a horse and waited for his fortunes to change, but until today he had been just one more Jewish peddler with a horse.

Such a horse! The creature's name was Thunder, even though its most explosive moments were mere piffles. Boruch Levi came to call him Piffle Fart. Today he felt that Thunder, alias Piffle Fart, would not disappoint him. He felt it as the certainty of truth, for Boruch Levi believed in the evil eye (you shouldn't know from such things), Satan—heaven forbid—spirits, witches, the power of salt, the magic of the color red, and, of course, the propitious powers of saying "pooh, pooh, pooh," accompanied by expectoration for a good measure of extra prophylactic precaution. Everyone in Krimsk—except for the "enlightened heretics," who believed in nothing—believed in the Other Side and its pervasive powers. As superstitious as Boruch Levi was, however, he did not believe only in the Other Side. Those who did were passive and fearful, mainly women and tailors.

Boruch Levi also believed in himself. He had the massive confidence that he was going to succeed in life. He knew in the depths of his hard, strong bones that he was not going to fall prey to the snares of ill fortune, nor to the machinations of defeat. Since his belief was rooted in the marrow, it was every bit as convincing and beyond question as all his basic premises: God, his family, the Jews, the goyim, the active power of evil itself. For his sake it was fortuitous that the basis of such beliefs about himself was beyond question, because he did not possess those attributes that Krimsk recognized as blessings. Not learned, not wealthy, not wellborn, Boruch Levi managed to believe in himself with a cocksure stubbornness and pride that defied reason. Certainly the reason of Krimsk—but Boruch Levi knew he was right. The Torah itself recognized the magic powers of clouds, bones, the dead, and heaven knew what else. Why not a horse's posterior? Even uneducated Boruch Levi knew about the precedent of Bilaam's ass. He stared at his undeciphered message. What was the sun telling him through this horse's backside? Boruch suspected the rising and falling hemispheres were in opposition. Old world, new world; old world, new world. Should he leave his widowed mother and orphan sister to join his older brother in America or not? Krimsk, America; Krimsk, America. He squinted to discern if one side were brighter than the other, but he could not detect any difference.

Frustrated, he looked around at the ripening fields of oat and rye standing silent in the golden late-afternoon heat. He looked up toward the majestic green oak trees bordering them but took no solace in their cool vernal grandeur as he usually did when he came back to Krimsk. Gevalt! What was he to do? Who could interpret such signs? Boruch Levi sat up. That reclusive saint and tzaddik, the Krimsker Rebbe; that's who! He had predicted the future more than once. His words lived. His thoughts worked miracles. Miriam's well materialized in his study on Sabbath Eve! Boruch Levi had not seen it, but he had heard the splashing; it sounded like a small animal leaping by a stream.

There was a problem, however—the rebbe had run away from the world. No doubt he had his reasons, but down deep Boruch Levi, uneducated though he was, knew that God didn't want his servants running away. You had to try; that's what the world was for, and if God couldn't tolerate an honest mistake, who could? Now when it came to honesty, the Krimsker Rebbe was a true tzaddik. He didn't care about money. Boruch Levi couldn't stomach the other rebbes in the district. How could he call such men tzaddiks? With their grand courts, silver canes, gold snuff boxes, thick fur coats, bejeweled wives and daughters, shiny carriages, and sycophantic cultivation of the very rich, they were more like Polish counts than Jewish rabbis. Blessings for the rich; crumbs for the poor when they managed to gain entry. The Krimsker Rebbe lived plainly, almost in poverty, and he refused to accept gifts. And not just the small trifles that the other rebbes sold themselves for. About twenty years ago the rebbe had refused something truly magnificent. Boruch Levi had been a child of two or three, but he had heard the remarkable story. A rich hasidic lumber merchant who controlled great hardwood forests had arrived in Krimsk and, desirous of honors befitting a man of his stature, had sent several large, bulging envelopes to the rebbe. The then young and brilliant Krimsker Rebbe wouldn't permit them to stay overnight in his house and immediately returned them unopened. The great merchant remained at the most distant end of the table from the rebbe in the stuffy, crowded little prayer-study hall. The merchant offered the rebbetzin a new carriage with two handsome chestnut horses; he even wanted to send the rebbe's ailing mother to a spa in Switzerland. All blandishments failed. With all his money intact, he remained so near to the door that every time it opened the knob kissed his beard. How long could a man who bought and sold entire royal forests have a love affair with a simple plank door?

The lumber merchant invited an architect from Lodz,

and using only the finest oak for beams and the most graceful birch and maple for planking, he constructed at the marketplace a majestic building in which three hundred Jews with all their shuffling and rocking could pray comfortably—and in the very latest fashion there was an airy balcony for a hundred women. The brass fittings glowed with rich brilliance, and the massive chandelier held over two hundred candles and provided so much light that if it were lit during the day no one praying anywhere in the synagogue would know when the sun set. The holiest scribes in Warsaw wrote the synagogue's holy Torah. Next to the holy ark, he had a massive chair built of specially matched pieces of walnut. It was as if God himself had grown a tree in the shape of a chair. This was to be the Krimsker Rebbe's throne. The donor, in what he was sure was overwhelming modesty, planned to occupy a more modest chair on the eastern wall where the notables sat, closest to Jerusalem.

The week that the building was finished, the merchant went to the dilapidated small study hall. When the rebbe presided over his table, the merchant assumed his usual seat by the door. The third meal of the Sabbath went late into the night. When it ended, the merchant rose from his place on the simple bench and invited the rebbe to accept the newly built synagogue as his own, even to name it whatever he wished. The hasidim glowed with pride and pleasure. All eyes turned to the rebbe. The rebbe thanked him kindly, but said that he must refuse. Stunned, the merchant stood with his mouth softly opening and closing like a fish; there were those who said that his eyes began to roll. He fell back down onto the bench, and if Yonkel the tailor had not caught him he would have tumbled over backward into the corner.

The merchant recovered and jumped to his feet. "Is it a sin to build a synagogue?" he demanded. "No," the rebbe answered. "Then why in heaven's name won't you accept it?" The rebbe paused, and then said very precisely, "The Talmud teaches us that a man should not enter a synagogue alone, for that is where the Angel of Death stores his tools." "Alone? Alone?" the merchant mocked. "I'll bring in half the province." And he did, too. Half the province and almost all of Krimsk were present on the inaugural Sabbath; the donor stood blessing the Torah when the great chandelier fell from the ceiling and killed him. From then on, it was a ghost synagogue—except for Reb Zelig, all feared to enter. The town referred to the synagogue simply as the Angel of Death.

That's a rebbe! Boruch Levi reflected. No doubt the rebbe could glance at his horse and tell him Thunder's secret. But what hope did Boruch Levi have of speaking to the rebbe when not even the tsar himself could get in to see him? Boruch Levi begrudgingly admired the egalitarian ethic that equated him to the tsar of all the Russians, but it didn't solve his problem, and Boruch Levi was one to solve problems. Thunder's lightning message ceased, and his owner realized that his horse had stopped. Boruch Levi looked up to find himself at the final fork before Krimsk. The horse certainly knew the way, and there was no reason for him to hesitate. To the right lay Krimsk; to the left lay the peasant settlement of Krimichak—and—"Grannie Zara!" said Boruch Levi aloud, and as he did so his horse cut a fart like a cannon.

"Thunder, my boy, you should live and be well!" Boruch Levi called as he snapped him into a trot in the direction of the cat lady of Krimichak. Boruch Levi knew that he was on the right path now. Grannie Zara possessed dark powers. The Krimsker Rebbe had forbidden such visits, but not one pregnant woman dared not visit Grannie Zara lest the baby fall from her womb long before its time, or worse, lest she give birth to a cat. All the Jewish women went except for the rebbetzin, and she would have gone, too, had she not had her Minsker nose tilted high in Krimsk. In the distance Boruch Levi saw a wobbling black line inching toward him. Good, he thought, a funeral; Grannie Zara is sure to be alone in her hut. As he drew closer to the procession, he could make out the red-faced priest at its head, staff in hand. The staff played rhythmically across the wobbling creature's path like the single antenna of a soft, crippled insect that carried death inside. To avoid kicking up hot, heavy dust, Boruch parked under a leafy tree by the roadside. When the procession finally reached him, he stood and removed his cloth cap. The funeral was different from the usual one. Behind the priest no family wailed and sobbed, yet everyone in the entire procession marched distressed, quiet, and fearful. Staring fitfully about, anxious eyes acknowledged the bareheaded Jew, and he respectfully nodded. As the corpse passed the wagon, Thunder fired a parting salute. Dizzy, Boruch Levi sat down. Wotek, the herdsman, turned aside from the tail of the procession.

"That's how it is, friend. A man dies and a horse farts—even for a witch."

Boruch Levi nodded blindly.

"A witch for sure," Wotek said. "The cats camped on the body and wouldn't let anyone come close. They had to drive them off with torches."

The peasant turned back to the procession. Boruch Levi, not knowing where to turn, just sat, but his horse continued toward Krimsk, gently loosing piffle farts all along the way.

# CHAPTER THREE

SQUIRMING IN DISCOMFORT, REB BERYL SOFFER SAT behind the large hardwood desk in his magisterial office. He felt the treacly, clutching, sweaty grasp of his collar in the summer heat and was tempted to remove his jacket just this one time. Heat or no heat, however, today was a business day, and the master of Soffer and Company would not succumb. Still, he was only human, even if he did own one of the greatest match factories in the province. True, Reb Beryl wasn't unchallenged as Volhynia's match king. And the challenge came from his own former assistant, Yitzhak Weinbach, who had founded the rival firm of Weinbach and Company. Unlike Reb Beryl, "Mr. Weinbach" resented being called "Reb Yitzhak" in the warm, personal Yiddish idiom with which Krimsk's Jews had bestowed honor upon one another for generations; rejecting the genteel tradition for the modern, secular world, Yitzhak preferred the cold, impersonal "mister."

Whatever Reb Beryl called him, Yitzhak Weinbach was a bright young man, and very ambitious, too. Reb Yitzhak had already offered twice in the past year to buy Beryl out. Reb Beryl had no doubt that Yitzhak could do it, too, although the devil only knew where he could raise that kind of capital; but Mr. Weinbach—he said the name more in sorrow than in bitterness—would certainly do it if he said he could. Reb Beryl admired bright young men; once Reb Beryl had been one himself, but Reb Beryl had known enough to keep his jacket on, and Reb Yitzhak didn't. No, on very hot days he would strip down to his undershirt—like a wagon driver. Reb Beryl kept his shirt, tie, and jacket on like the governor, a duke, or even better like a rebbe, except for the fact that a rebbe doesn't wear a tie, but if he did he clearly would never take it off, and that was the point. Reb Beryl might not know how to learn a folio of Talmud, but he could make a point. There were those who dressed like leaders, and there were those who didn't.

It was as simple as that, and the world knew the difference, too. In the bathhouse on Sabbath Eve who could tell Rothschild from a wagon driver? The butchers were, maybe, a little stronger; the yeshivah students were, maybe, a little paler. Nicholas II himself might pass for a tailor in the Krimsk bathhouse, provided the tsar was circumcised, of course. In fact, nobody looked better in the altogether than the Angel of Death's beadle, Zelig. Zelig stood straight, moved without the afflicting self-consciousness of his body's shame. No more concerned about exposing his genitalia than his earlobes. Not that Reb Beryl was preoccupied with such things, but it was striking the way such a bearded Jew strolled about the bathhouse like a Cossack. Of course, Zelig didn't seem to let the evil eye bother him anywhere. How else could he serve as a beadle in the Angel of Death synagogue without congregants? How else could he arise with alacrity, plunge into the ritual bath—on the bitterest freezing days—and scurry to open the great wooden doors when he knew that no one was coming to pray? Only his footsteps would echo off the hard, reflecting varnish of emptiness. Reb Zelig would soothe tempers, but there were none. He could keep honest accounts, but there were no numbers. He treated everyone with kindness and warmth, but even the poor would not go inside. For all the good he did the Jews, Reb Zelig might be a gypsy strumming a mandolin.

Staring off into the summer heat looking for a gypsy, Reb Beryl turned his thoughts back to the matter at hand. He, Beryl Soffer, was going to secure the contract to provide Nicholas II's armies west of Minsk with enough matches to burn down half of Russia. Wasn't he the match king of Volhynia? Yes, yes, but the dark shadow of Yitzhak Weinbach crept across his cushioned throne. It suddenly seemed very hot in the office of Soffer and Company. But not hot enough to remove his jacket or loosen his collar. An itch came welling up to plague his bottom like the insidious challenge of his former employee. As Reb Beryl scratched, he had the itch of an idea. The general of the Quartermaster Corps should be made to understand that it was in the Holy Tsar's interest to deal with a conservative loyalist—that is to say, the match king—rather than with a grasping pretender, an upstart with no respect for tradition. A man who flings off his jacket at the slightest discomfort and plunges into things with a brazen rashness—almost, God forbid, a revolutionary fervor. Not a Communist, but perhaps a social revolutionary. Or at least the tsar's army might think so.

Reb Beryl, like any good conspirator, loosened his tie. Could he do such a thing? Say such a thing about a fellow Jew? If only he had his rebbe to talk to; but his rebbe wasn't speaking to anyone. Reb Beryl would be in the beis midrash tonight for Tisha B'Av, but the Krimsker Rebbe wouldn't. Why did that holy man have to punish the Jews, too? Didn't God and the goyim do enough between them? That was the story of Tisha B'Av. Reb Beryl wondered if the Jews were so much worse than everyone else. Immediately he was ashamed: to have compared his people, who were His people, to "them," the gentiles, who belonged to those ugly little wooden statues, blocky, dry, and dwarfish, that they were forever parading through the unpaved streets with such violent reverence. The Jews flew from the marketplace faster than a beggar stuffs himself at a wedding. Of course, blockheads or not, they did own Krimsk, Volhynia, Russia, and all of Europe. The Jews once had a land, but that was lost on Tisha B'Av, along with the holy Temple. Now the Jews had the World to Come, where Reb Beryl couldn't conceive of the angels needing matches. Here, in this world, the owners needed tons of them—if only the tsar would give him, the worthiest recipient, the man of jacket and collar and loyalty beyond question, the contract.

# CHAPTER FOUR

MANY THINGS BOTHERED YECHIEL KATZMAN, THE talented young talmudist, as he followed the dusty path that morning from the study hall to Reb Gedaliah's house, where he had promised to teach the primary class. Had the pious Reb Gedaliah the least hint of the heretical notions flooding Yechiel's head beneath his black scholar's skullcap and long side curls, he never would have permitted him near his young charges. Yechiel had been his prize pupil—favorite one, too. The young man—only eighteen years old—already far surpassed Reb Gedaliah in his knowledge, not to mention his overwhelming intellectual acumen. Honest and conscientious, Reb Gedaliah felt no pangs of conscience when he left his students with Reb Yechiel. Yechiel, he believed, would one day become a great communal rabbi or even a Rosh Yeshivah, dean of one of the great talmudic academies. He had a brilliant future.

As luminous as his future might be, however, it did not illuminate the present, for he had just come in from the brilliant morning sunlight; he blinked as his eyes fought to adjust to the heavy shadows that did nothing to cool the dark room. As he took his seat at the head of the table, the small nondescript forms that were his pupils emerged into familiar detail. Waksman's skullcap perched precariously to one side as usual, but Waksman sat so still there was no danger of it falling. The Berman boy huddled forward as if it were the coldest day in winter; Yechiel wondered what he would do when winter came. All of them so still and quiet. Why didn't they leap up and flee into the sunny fields? Here they sat in half-darkness, sweated, and observed their nine-year-old bodies becoming as unfeeling and crooked as the wan, warped benches they sat upon day after day.

Yechiel could see them all now, and as he looked over the long table at his young charges he felt as if he were inside an ancient tomb. He thought that this was how pharaoh's commander, the captain of the Ship of the Dead, must have felt as he gazed over his crew, plucked from life to serve a lifeless master. But no, he spied a hint of motion. Matti Sternweiss was sneaking candies one by one in his fat, stubby fingers from his stuffed, bulging pockets into his stuffed, bulging cheeks. After appropriate digestive activity, his circulatory system would return the overabundance of chemical sugars to his fingers so they would remain stubby and fat when he plunged them into his bulging rich-man's-son pockets. Sternweiss was too active for an occupant of the tomb, yet he participated in his own burial. It is the much-vaunted Jewish genius, Yechiel thought bitterly, that we can bury ourselves. The whole world is striding into the twentieth century, and Krimsk can't even manage to stand still. No, it has to burrow deeper and deeper into the past.

Yechiel Katzman was supposed to teach them the laws

concerning the *terumah,* the priest's portion of all produce. All Jews who were not priests set aside a portion of their produce exclusively for the priests. According to the Mishnah, the *terumah* became holy as the priests' property; the *terumah* had to remain ritually pure; and it could be consumed only by priests or members of their families who themselves were in a state of ritual purity. The matter quickly developed great complexity, as it involved two populations (priests and nonpriests), two categories of produce (holy and profane), and even two states (pure and impure) that applied to both populations and to both categories. Once these complex, precise laws had guided the Jews' daily behavior, but no Jew in Krimsk had ever offered a priest his holy portion of *terumah* because no priest had received an offering of *terumah* since the destruction of the Temple in Jerusalem almost two thousand years ago. Yet Yechiel was about to teach these ancient, intricate rituals as defined by the Mishnah, the oral commentaries on the Torah. Codified in writing about the time of the Temple's destruction, the Mishnah served as the basis for further oral commentaries, the Gemara, which were committed to writing several centuries later. Together the Mishnah and Gemara form the Talmud. Two thousand years ago the Jews had their temple destroyed, had lost their sovereign state, and had even been exiled as slaves from their very land, but in spite of such catastrophes, their ancient, arcane library had continued to grow and grow and grow.

Why didn't Yechiel himself flee? That was the real question. Perhaps he would, taking his forbidden books with him. For the moment he sought temporary refuge in the promise that he had made to Reb Gedaliah to teach his class today. After all, this ship, any ship, even of the dead, couldn't be left without a captain. Yechiel looked around, felt the suffocating heat, and began the daily funeral oration.

"What does the Mishnah say?"

In dull expectation, the little heads slowly turned toward Matti Sternweiss. Avoiding responsibility, Matti continued to chew his sweets behind fat-smothered eyes.

"*Nu?*" Yechiel urged.

Matti gamely swallowed the thick, sweet mass and leaned forward to the table. His fat, stubby fingers rooted themselves on the open page like fleshy tree stumps in a small, flat field where the rain has dried long ago into little black memories.

"The Mishnah says," the boy began in his singsong chant, "that a barrel of ritually pure, priestly *terumah* wine has broken in the upper chamber of a wine press and begins to flow down to the lower chamber, which is filled with profane, nonpriestly, impure wine. If you can save a liter of the pure *terumah* wine in a ritually pure vessel, then both Rabbi Eliezer and Rabbi Yehoshua agree that you should run and get a ritually pure vessel to collect the pure priestly wine; and if you cannot save that minimal amount in that way, then Rabbi Eliezer says that you let the *terumah* flow down to the lower chamber even though it will mix with the impure, profane wine."

"Very good, Sternweiss, that's what the text says. What's so bad about the priestly *terumah* wine flowing into the impure ordinary wine?"

"Even plain, ordinary, impure wine is valuable in that it can be drunk by any ritually impure Israelite. No one, however, is permitted to drink the new admixture in the lower chamber of *terumah* wine and impure, profane wine. This forbidden admixture is called impure *medumah.*"

"Yes, that's right. Very good, Sternweiss." In spite of his earlier hostility, Yechiel found himself liking the fat little *fresser.* He consumed the Talmud as effortlessly as he consumed candies, even if his appetite wasn't quite as strong. Eight years ago, he, Yechiel, had sat at the long table giving exact answers, and Reb Gedaliah's eyes would light up as he entered into a dialogue with Yechiel. But Yechiel's eyes didn't light up now; he felt them grow heavy.

"So according to Rabbi Eliezer, all the wine is lost because the *terumah* and profane impure wine become a forbidden impure admixture," Yechiel mourned.

"Yes," answered Matti, "but not through any act of ours."

"Through our inaction," Yechiel suggested.

"Yes, but for that we are not responsible," Matti responded.

"According to Rabbi Eliezer," Yechiel rejoined.

"Yes, according to Rabbi Eliezer," Matti repeated, and then he continued with the Mishnah as he knew Reb Yechiel was inviting. But Reb Yechiel interrupted him by crying out, "And is there a different view?"

The nine-year-olds looked at him in astonishment. Reb Yechiel was not given to strange cries of passion. Yechiel, one of the best young talmudists in Krimsk, was always so kind, direct, and warm with them. Others in the study hall gave strange outbursts of humming, singing, shouting, pacing, as though they were fleeing the devil himself—but not Yechiel. Matti fingered the sticky candies in his pocket for security.

"Yes," Matti answered, "Rabbi Yehoshua disagrees."

"Yes," Yechiel exulted. "What would he have us do?"

"If we cannot maintain the purity of at least a liter of the priestly *terumah* wine by collecting it in a pure vessel, Rabbi Yehoshua permits us to collect it in an impure vessel. Through our direct action, the pure priestly wine becomes impure priestly *terumah* wine, but we save the ordinary wine in the lower chamber from becoming the forbidden impure admixture."

"Yes," said Yechiel aloud to himself. "Rabbi Yehoshua considers the final result. Rather than let the profane, impure wine be lost, he permits us to cause impurity to the priestly wine by catching it in impure vessels. Why would he do such a thing?"

Matti was confused. "As you said, to save the profane, impure wine below."

"But, Matti, that alone wouldn't be enough. You see, in any event, the priestly *terumah* wine's purity will be lost either by falling into the lower chamber or by our catching it in impure vessels."

Yechiel felt himself being drawn into the process of conceptual analysis. The joy of examining problems and developing concepts exercised a narcotic effect upon him. He was becoming absorbed in that self-contained world where the sun never shone and darkness never reached because it was lit with the light of Torah. But he hadn't slipped into that realm completely, and it was Rabbi Yehoshua's fault.

"Even Rabbi Yehoshua recognizes a case where we should not cause impurity," Yechiel declared.

Matti responded, "The Mishnah teaches that if a Jew is walking along with several loaves of pure *terumah* bread for the priests and encounters a goy who says to him, 'Give me one loaf and I shall make it impure by eating it, because if you do not give me one, I will most assuredly touch them all and thereby make them all impure,' Rabbi Eliezer says that even though the goy will make them all impure, you must not give him any. Rabbi Yehoshua, however, says that you may put one loaf down onto a rock, but you may not hand it directly to him."

Yechiel stood up and began pacing back and forth behind his chair. Rabbi Yehoshua, he thought, doesn't quite have the courage to give it directly to the goy. Put it on a rock for the goy to pick up, and if that doesn't satisfy the goy then the Jew and all his *terumah* are in danger. Still, Rabbi Yehoshua permits you to give it to him indirectly. Yes, but what about the final Mishnah in the chapter?

"Nu, Sternweiss, what about the final Mishnah; it's late."

Matti found himself unnerved by Yechiel's strange, agitated behavior. He swallowed thickly even though no candies dwelled in his sheltering mouth.

"The final Mishnah in the chapter teaches that the same applies to Jewish women; if the goyim say, 'Give us one of yourselves and we make her impure, otherwise we will most assuredly make all of you impure,' the goyim must make all impure, for you must not surrender to them one soul of Israel."

Yechiel spun around.

"What does Rabbi Yehoshua say?" he asked.

"They both agree in this case," Matti answered softly.

"Why?" Yechiel demanded.

"You must not surrender one soul of Israel." Matti cowered, fearful of Yechiel's passion.

Yechiel stood leaning on the chair. Yes, that's fine, he thought sarcastically. You can save the plain, impure wine according to Rabbi Yehoshua, but not the Jews. In all the other cases, there was a solution. Rabbi Yehoshua seemed to look ahead to the final results: in any event the priestly wine becomes impure; therefore make it impure in a way that saves the ordinary wine. In any event the loaf of priestly bread will become impure, so put it on the rock for the goy, to save the other loaves. In any event, the woman will be raped by the goyim, so . . . but no, here Rabbi Yehoshua lets all be lost. What happened to his concept? He seemed to have been developing some idea of preventive destruction. Yes, call it that, you are permitted to destroy a little to prevent the destruction of a larger amount. But the Jews—no concept.

As he mused, Yechiel heard some of the students coughing—self-induced coughs to attract his attention. He sat down and looked at the students. They were hoping to be dismissed, since all Torah studies had to cease at noon. Sunset inaugurated Tisha B'Av, the day of calamity, the day all the priests had ceased to receive *terumah* and the goyim began to make the Jews impure with a vengeance. Yechiel looked at the students; they seemed frightened and sat very still. The only motion was Sternweiss's train of candy consumption. It galled Yechiel. Sternweiss thought he had all the answers. Just let him meet Spinoza, Darwin, and Graetz.

"Sternweiss, you were brilliant today," Yechiel said.

Sternweiss nodded in modest agreement.

"You have selflessly shared your sweet Torah with your fellows."

Sternweiss looked a little uneasy at hearing this strange compliment.

"I have no doubt that you will be equally quick to share your lesser gifts with them."

Sternweiss didn't answer. His fat little eyes shifted about. He looked like an animal about to be slaughtered. His gaze was hopeless, for he knew that he was too weak, too slow, and too afraid.

"Empty your pockets!" Yechiel commanded harshly.

Slowly, Matti Sternweiss emptied his pockets, until they were no longer fat and no longer bulged. A considerable pyramid of hard, sticky candies graced the table in front of him.

"Students, that is very generous of Reb Matti to share his gifts so willingly. On your way out please help yourself. Don't forget to make a blessing . . . and don't forget to thank your benefactor. You are excused."

A dozen eager hands shot toward the candy and dismantled the pyramid. "Thank you, Reb Matti," they mocked. "Blessed art Thou our God, King of the Universe." And they raced, howling, into the sunshine.

A mutiny of the Ship of the Dead, thought Yechiel with satisfaction; but his sense of triumph died abruptly as he watched Matti Sternweiss waddle outside with tears streaming down his face. Yechiel felt ashamed. After all, it wasn't socialism that interested him, but people. He couldn't make himself get up and apologize, and the mutiny of the Ship of the Dead seemed a very small triumph. Yechiel the captain was still sitting in the darkness. And the pharaoh; the pharaoh really was entombed. The Krimsker Rebbe hadn't just planned his burial like the pharaohs of old, he really had entombed himself alive.

Sitting in the darkness, Yechiel turned toward the sunlight, and it blinded him. In his dazzling blindness, he heard his students gleefully shouting, "Itzik Dribble!"

# CHAPTER FIVE

BY THE TIME THE SUN WAS SETTING, THE KRIMSKER Rebbe's hasidim had gathered in his beis midrash, the room that served both for prayers and for study. Although the large, low-ceilinged room was much larger than the house to which it was attached, the beis midrash's ramshackle architecture made it clear which structure provided the essential support. Indeed, the room the beis midrash leaned upon was the Krimsker Rebbe's study. The door remained closed, as it had for five years. The hundred and fifty hasidim had ceased long ago to look at it in expectation. Awaiting *maariv,* the evening prayer, most of them stared out the numerous windows, which were so close to one another they seemed to run around the walls, giving additional proof of just how little structural support the walls provided.

The hasidim watched the white light fading into the dark slate-blue fingers of dusk. The heat remained; it would not let up for several more hours, but with the superior ventilation, it was tolerable. A few latecomers walked swiftly to their places. Boruch Levi had led Thunder to his stall, curried and fed him. Only then did he go inside his house to eat. In silent despair, he had come to the beis midrash and taken his seat. In observance of the Tisha B'Av mourning rites, he had removed his leather shoes, and he aimlessly explored the surface of the rough floorboards with his stocking feet.

Yechiel Katzman stared at the setting sun with the feeling that he had lost another day. He, too, had run through the accepted rituals, all of them. As befitted a scholar, he had dipped his bread into ashes to symbolize the verse in Lamentations, "He pressed me down into ashes," but he had felt that he was eating ashes not just for the Ninth of Av but for the entire year.

Beryl Soffer sat waiting with his son Itzik. He wanted to watch the sunset, but he was afraid to take his eyes off his boy. On the way home from his office, he had been mourning the prohibition against bathing during the nine days of Av—how he could use a visit to the bathhouse!—when he heard the children taunting his son with the name that so painfully stabbed the father's heart—Itzik Dribble.

Itzik Dribble didn't dribble, although his mouth hung open more than it would have had he been more intelligent. Not just his mouth. From his neck up, everything seemed to be slightly slack. His dull blue eyes lacked focus. His pale blond hair lay limp on his head. His ears appeared to droop; the cartilage was a little too soft, as if when the Creator had breathed a divine soul into Itzik's nostrils, one of them began coughing and turned away too soon. In any event, Itzik was left without a full measure; his divine image, not fully inflated, lay slack and limp at the edges.

Hints of the divine emerged in his shy kindness and sweet engaging smile.

These humane traits were variously interpreted. The adults thought that teasing Itzik—practically the town pastime—was all the more sinful. The youthful teases, not all so youthful, pointed to his charming smile as vindication. See, he likes it; he's smiling. And of course Itzik Dribble smiled when he proffered a lit cigar to the cat that, supposedly, loved to smoke cigarettes, and the cat scratched him. He even smiled after he licked the fresh cow turd that did not taste anything like the brown clotted cream that they said it would. Perhaps he was not so foolish as those who teased him, but foolish enough to lick turds and smile.

Twisting his earlocks, Itzik Dribble rocked back and forth, a gentle smile playing over his loose lips. Sensing his son's impatience, Beryl's own face twisted with concern. The boy was too quiet, too agitated, and he was winding his earlocks around his finger in such a mad whirl that it was a wonder the hairs didn't come out at the roots. Reb Beryl fingered the candies in his pocket and debated whether he should give one to Itzik. Once the sugar began to dissolve on Itzik's tongue, his attention would melt with it; calmed, his energy would collapse into the hollow of his mouth, where he would fight to liberate the sweetness from the rock in hissing swooshes of air. When Reb Beryl heard the air rushing into his son's intently sucking mouth, he could relax. Today, however, there was a problem; today was Tisha B'Av, a fast day. Itzik was still two years from his bar mitzvah, when he would be obligated to fast. But no other eleven-year-old would be permitted candy on Tisha B'Av. What kind of Tisha B'av was that? Reb Beryl decided not to begin dispensing the candies to Itzik so soon. He placed a comforting hand on his son's shoulder. He had the sensation of patting a puppy that was about to pounce at a grasshopper. He reached into his pocket for a candy but was distracted by the whispering in the room. Reb Beryl immediately stood up. He reached to pull Itzik to his feet, but discovered that his son was already standing.

# CHAPTER SIX

THE KRIMSKER REBBE ENTERED THE CROWDED BEIS midrash from his study as casually as if he had been doing so several times a day for the past five years.

The Krimsker Rebbe was of medium height, but there was a squatness to his stance that kept him from drawing himself up to his full measure. This squatness made him appear to be sitting when he was standing. Indeed, the effect was of stability and potential. These characteristics offered differing interpretations. The adult hasidim saw them as representing enthronement: the rebbe seated upon the throne of Torah, of good deeds, and of divine service with the wondrous potential of standing, that is, rising, to—heaven, the state of an angel, might one dare to whisper to oneself the messianic rumor? The children, however, whispered among themselves that the Krimsker Rebbe looked like a frog: the stable seated stance with the potential of performing the most remarkable leaps at the slightest provocation.

The rebbe's distinctive face reinforced both interpretations. Above a full black beard, the skin, smooth and dark, drew tightly about a strong, equally smooth—almost streamlined—bone structure featuring high cheekbones and sloping forehead. His brushy eyebrows, somewhat incongruous with the smooth skin and bone structure, did not appear as striking as they might have because his eyes did not sparkle. On the contrary, his wide hazel eyes did not make any immediate statement. At first glance they seemed impassive. Only when coupled with the face and stance did they generate force. And the nature of that hazel statement, neither brown nor green, remained ambiguous. It was difficult for any observer to guess what the rebbe was thinking as he steadily observed his surroundings. For the hasidim, the Krimsker Rebbe seemed to have the slightly weary air of concerned royalty who, while in close touch, remain masterfully above the common world around them. For the children, his impassive wide-eyed perception and smooth appearance suggested the uncompromising phlegmatic nature of an amphibian. They would not have been surprised to see his two large eyes move independently of one another. The two views were not as contradictory as they might have seemed, for more than a few of the hasidim under the age of twenty, who now saw the rebbe as royalty, affectionately remembered him as a frog.

This evening, of course, was neither a Sabbath nor a holiday—far from it, it was a time of catastrophe and calamity; the rebbe wore a simple black skullcap and his "weekday" long black gabardine coat. In preparation for the Tisha B'Av rites of mourning, forbidding the wearing of shoes made from the hides of living creatures, he crossed the threshold in his stocking feet. Although the hasidim gaped in astonishment and felt their hearts pounding in amazed, fearful delight, he merely noticed that the benches were still standing upright. He calmly motioned to his sexton, Reb Yechezkal, to turn them over in accordance with the mourning custom of sitting on overturned benches or on the floor itself.

The supercharged silence was shattered by Reb Yechezkal crying, "Jews, the benches!" as if he were sending the hasidim into battle with the solid, worn furniture.

With greater alacrity than the beis midrash had ever seen, the congregation attacked. Reb Yechezkal himself, as captain of the host, supervised the overturning of the rebbe's place; the rebbe sat on the eastern wall next to the holy ark, behind a long, heavy table. There was no room to turn over the chairs without moving the table, and since there was no room to move the table with such a crowd, the custom had always been to turn over the table. There (lower than anyone else) the rebbe would sit mourning the destruction of the Temple. The rebbe nodded to Reb Yechezkal that everything was in order. The white-bearded old man accepted the rebbe's confirmation by looking down at his feet in modest confusion. He was the Krimsker Rebbe's sexton once again, God be blessed! He frantically motioned to Reb Muni to begin the evening service.

Reb Muni, who had been witnessing the events in fearful amazement, fought to control his trembling knees as he threaded his way toward the lectern. He reached out and grabbed the reading stand to steady himself. He was fortunate that he did so, for at that instant he was almost upended by a small boy bullying and squirming his way toward the rebbe, who stood facing the east with his back to the congregation. Reb Muni's outrage turned to alarm when he saw the pale blond boy head directly for the rebbe. Out of the corner of his eye, he saw Reb Beryl Soffer, the boy's father, in futile pursuit, but Reb Beryl was too rotund and the beis midrash too crowded. The hasidim stepped back to let him pass, but it was too late; Itzik Dribble was already tugging insistently on the Krimsker Rebbe's coat sleeve.

The rebbe turned and looked down at the boy with his usual apparently impassive attitude.

"Are you really a frog, Rebbe?" Itzik Dribble asked, anxious and insistent.

Reb Beryl, his florid face filled with shame and horror, took his son's hand. His other held a large quantity of candy.

"Itzik," he pleaded softly, and not without love.

The rebbe, without taking his eyes from Itzik, flicked his hand in a clear gesture that neither Reb Beryl nor anyone else was to interrupt Itzik.

"Yes, I am a frog," the rebbe answered, as matter-of-factly as he might say "good evening."

Itzik's anxiety melted into his sweet, soft smile.

"You really pray by jumping like a frog?" Itzik asked in infectious delight at having had his expectations fulfilled.

"How else should a frog pray?" the rebbe responded.

"Show me! Rebbe, please show me!" Itzik demanded in a joyful squeal.

The rebbe turned to his sexton and motioned him to right the table. Reb Yechezkal and the hasidim quickly turned the table to its more conventional position. The rebbe took Itzik's hand and, stepping onto his chair on the eastern wall, led him onto the table.

"Let us pray together," he said simply.

The rebbe began to jump, and Itzik jumped, too. The

rebbe jumped in spasmodic, graceless, propelling leg thrusts that kicked his rigid body into the air from its squat stance. Itzik's jump, however, in no way resembled a frog's. With his mouth hanging open, his face radiated pure delight and his leaps were so fluid and graceful that he seemed almost to float in an upright position. The rebbe's stocking feet pounded the table at irregular intervals; Itzik's softly tapped a smooth, even rhythm. The two devotants were so out of phase that the rebbe dropped Itzik's hand. After eight or nine jumps, the rebbe stopped. Itzik Dribble continued until the rebbe again took his arm and guided him to rest. He turned Itzik so they were facing one another. "Itzik, now you must pay attention," the rebbe said.

"Far away in the land of Israel, the Holy Land, lived a very rich and very religious man. The man knew all the Torah by heart. He had a son named Rabbi Chanina. When the man sensed that death was near, he called in his son, Rabbi Chanina, and told him to study Torah day and night, to do all the commandments, and to be a good friend to the poor. The father announced that he and the mother would die on the same day and that Rabbi Chanina would get up from sitting shivah on the eve of Pesach, Passover. He told his son that he should not mourn too much—and that he should go straight to the marketplace and buy the first item that he saw, no matter how expensive. If it was food, he was to prepare it for the Pesach seder. His father told Rabbi Chanina not to worry, for he would surely be rewarded for all his expense and effort.

"Everything happened just as the father said. The father and mother died on the very same day, and Rabbi Chanina arose from his mourning on the eve of Passover.

And Rabbi Chanina did just what his father told him to do. He went straight to the marketplace, and an old man offered him a silver dish. Although the price was much too high, Rabbi Chanina quickly bought it. When he put the silver dish on the seder table it began to sparkle with great beauty. Rabbi Chanina opened it, and inside he found another silver dish. He opened this dish, too, and inside he found a frog jumping joyously about. He gave food and water to the happy frog. He treated the frog very, very well, and by the end of the Passover holiday the frog had grown so large that Rabbi Chanina had to build a special roomy cage for him. In the comfortable cage the frog grew and grew. After a few more weeks the cage was too small, and Rabbi Chanina built a special room for him. The frog's appetite grew with him, and Rabbi Chanina gave him enormous amounts of food because he wanted to do just as his father commanded. The frog grew and grew, and it ate and ate. It ate Rabbi Chanina out of house and home; Rabbi Chanina and his wife sold everything to feed the frog, and finally they had nothing but the bare walls. And when there was nothing left to eat, the frog opened his mouth and began to talk. 'Good Rabbi Chanina,' it said. 'Do not worry. You have been so very good and kind to me that you may ask me for whatever you want and your wish will be granted.' Rabbi Chanina said, 'The only thing I want is for you to teach me all the Torah.' And the frog taught him all the Torah and the seventy languages of the world by writing a few special words upon scraps of paper that Rabbi Chanina then swallowed. By this method, Rabbi Chanina learned even the language of the animals and birds. Then the frog turned to Rabbi Chanina's wife and said, 'You have been so very kind to me, too, and I shall reward you, also, before I leave. The two of you must accompany me to the woods.'

"They went with him to the edge of the forest, and there the frog began to croak majestically in great loud cries. All manner of birds and beasts came running. He spoke to them and they swiftly departed, only to return moments later with the forest's most wonderful treasures: diamonds, rubies, emeralds—and special medicinal roots and herbs. He taught the wife their use, and with them she could cure all diseases. As Rabbi Chanina and his wife were turning toward home with all their gifts, the frog said to them, 'May the Holy One have mercy on you and reward you for the trouble you went to because of me without even asking me who I was. Now I shall tell you who I am. I am one of the sons Adam fathered during the one hundred and thirty years he was without Eve. God has given me the special power of assuming any identity I wish.' Rabbi Chanina and his wife returned home and lived in great wealth and happiness. The king himself respected Rabbi Chanina and visited him often."

The rebbe paused and then said, "Now, Itzik, say Amen."

Itzik fervently said, "Amen!" and then asked, "Rebbe, where is the frog now?"

"Come," the rebbe said as he led him down from the table. "Let us now pray as men, for we are all many things."

The rebbe handed Itzik to Reb Beryl and said, "He is a very good boy. I am proud of him."

Reb Beryl smiled with paternal pride, even though he knew the remark was more to the rebbe's credit than to his son's, but he was after all the father, and he loved what God had given him. He offered Itzik the candy, but the boy was still too excited even to notice. Reb Beryl led the boy back to their places. He, too, felt the warm flush of deep happiness. "Such a tzaddik," he sighed aloud.

"From heaven," Reb Yechezkal whispered to him, and Reb Beryl nodded his head.

"From the highest heaven," he agreed.

His praise of the rebbe was interrupted by Reb Muni's chanting the evening service.

"Bless the Lord who is blessed," Reb Muni called out in a powerful chant.

"Blessed is the Lord who is eternally blessed," sang out Reb Beryl and every other Jew. He even heard Itzik's sweet, thin soprano in the resonating wave of affirmation, for at that moment every hasid there truly felt that blessed is the Lord who is eternally blessed.

Since there was no comfortable place to sit, the congregation stood through the evening prayer. It was a service of the heart that most of those present would recall in later years as the spiritual zenith of their lives: a moment of communal religious ecstasy. In future days they would find that their certainty about it increased, although they could not recall any specific details. It was impossible to explain to others. They could only smile sweetly and somewhat dumbly—not unlike Itzik Dribble—and say that to understand you had to have been there. Even to one another, they could not articulate what they had experienced; it was beyond words. When two or more would refer to "that *maariv*," they would roll their shoulders slightly and lift their heads on thrusting necks as if they were mutely recalling some physical sense of exaltation they had once experienced.

When the daily evening service ended, however, and everyone lowered himself carefully onto the improvised mourning stools, they suffered a parallel descent of the soul. As they opened their books to Lamentations, they felt the poking, sloping (always in the wrong direction) boards inflicting their annual aches, and fought to maintain their precarious perches without tumbling onto the floor. They squinted in the half-darkness—half of the kerosene lamps had been extinguished to increase the sense of loss. They realized it was still very hot even though the sun had set. They looked at each other and envied one another's leg-room, more ample light, or wider part of the bench. The Jews of Jerusalem had been sent into exile—uprooted and discomforted in a strange land. In the synagogues the Jews discomfited themselves by sending their own small world into exile. It was as if the hand of God had smacked the beis midrash, and everything was upended but the Jews themselves; their punishment was to sit without chairs, to read without light, to mourn a distant Temple's destruction while mourning the loss of elbow room. And no one felt guilty at such petty thoughts; they were present every year. No one even realized at the time or even later that they were remarkably incongruous with the heights of ecstasy that they had reached moments before, because in all fairness they had fallen into dark, disheveled, wretchedly crowded discomfort. What was the distance from Jerusalem to Krimsk? In great Jerusalem the Temple burned, the land was desecrated, the Jew flung into exile as Rachel cried by the road near Bethlehem. In tiny Krimsk, the interior withered in dislocating spasms, for the Jew flung his benches, shoes, light, food, drink, into exile—and in Krimsk the rebbe cried.

Yes, the rebbe cried. The Krimsker Rebbe cried on Tisha B'Av, and suddenly every hasid forgot his own pain, no one felt inconvenienced. No one begrudged his neighbor any comfort. Everyone listened to the strange gulping sobs of their rebbe. No one had ever heard the Krimsker Rebbe cry. Never. Not on Tisha B'Av, not in the cemetery, not even when his son died, not in the closing moments of Yom Kippur. Never. Anguish, fear, and affection touched their hearts, for their rebbe was crying, and their rebbe was not a man of tears.

Yet no one knew what to do. The rebbe's whole body convulsed with each sob. The hasidim instinctively wanted to comfort him. These were the cries of a man suffering intense pain, a man altogether inside himself with his suffering. Although they wanted to reach out and hold him, or at the very least touch him and tell him that he was not alone, they just sat dumbly. One just didn't go over and touch a rebbe, much less cradle him. They feared he would not stop crying.

Reb Yechezkal bent toward the rebbe, paused, then returned to his place. And if he is mourning the Temple, what can I do to console him, the sexton thought. We are taught by the Talmud not to try and console a mourner when his dead lies before him, and if the Temple is burning before him, what can I do? Reb Yechezkal considered crying with his rebbe; after all, a rebbe's sexton must accompany his rebbe everywhere. Reb Yechezkal realized, however, that he himself was not a man of tears—perhaps that was what once drew the rebbe to choose him as his sexton. The rebbe's faithful staff—so he liked to term himself—had not served the rebbe for five years. He had thought that the rebbe had no need for a faithful staff because he was sitting in a room. When the rebbetzin had sent him on missions "at the rebbe's request," Reb Yechezkal had always doubted if the rebbe knew anything about it. Except for those occasions, he had faithfully guarded the entrance. He realized now that the rebbe, indeed, had been on distant journeys, had learned to travel alone, and had learned to cry. Left so far behind, what could the sexton do? True service was selfless; the once-faithful staff must be a quiet stick in the corner. Reb Yechezkal was the Krimsker's sexton once again—only the Krimsker no longer needed a sexton. God be thanked, he thought softly, and had he felt a warm tear in his eye, Reb Yechezkal would have known that it was for himself and not for the Temple. He saw the hasidim looking at him for guidance. He did what the day called for; he bent over, placed his arms on his knees, rocked slowly, and mourned—the way the Krimsker Rebbe used to.

The hasidim began to rock slowly, almost cautiously, to and fro.

Itzik finished the last sweet suck of candy and swallowed. He had been enjoying the gentle rocking motion on all sides. It was like cuddling in the thick quilt, with warmth all around him. Now that the candy had dissolved, however, he heard the Krimsker Rebbe's anguished sobs, and he leaped to his feet with a deep-throated cry that startled everyone. He tripped across the low, swaying congregation until he reached the rebbe, the lowest of them all. Itzik bent over and tapped him on his shoulder.

When the rebbe looked up, Itzik Dribble cried, "What happened to the frog?"

The rebbe looked at him in bewilderment and asked, "What frog?"

"The big talking one. Now I'll never get to see him."

Itzik collapsed onto the table next to the rebbe and started sobbing.

The rebbe lifted the boy's head and hushed him.

"Nothing happened to the frog, Itzik."

Itzik looked at the rebbe with the deep distrust of someone who has been fooled too often. "Then why are you crying?"

"I am crying because of what happened to the frog's world."

"You mean his forest with the jewels?"

"Yes, that, too. When the Temple in Jerusalem was destroyed on this day, the Ninth of Av, the world changed. The sky the frog looked up into was no longer so pure as it once was. The rain that fell upon his pond shriveled. The dew that cooled the forest at night was no longer a blessing. The fruits of his forest lost their fullness and taste. Honey was not as sweet as it once was. Each day has a curse, and the curse of the following day is greater. And that's very sad for everyone in the world, including the frog."

"Is the frog crying now?"

The rebbe sat and thought. "No, I don't think so."

"Then why are you?" Itzik asked, confused.

"The frog prays by jumping, and he can always jump or croak or eat a bug in praise of God, but men have a problem with prayer since the Destruction. From the moment the Temple was destroyed, the gates of prayer closed—but the gates of tears remained open. And I shall tell you a secret, Itzik, today's tears are special. We know that the Messiah will be born on Tisha B'Av. A woman shrieks and cries in giving birth to the child; thus may our tears be the travail hastening the coming of the Messiah. This room is pregnant with him, and through our tears we must deliver him on the birthstool of our hearts."

Several of the hasidim started to cry softly. Itzik turned to stare into the semidarkness toward the source of the sounds.

"I know all about the Messiah," the boy said blankly.

"You do?" the rebbe asked curiously.

"The Messiah's an old joke," he said triumphantly. "The last time he came they had me licking cow shit and it didn't taste at all like clotted cream."

Itzik Dribble let burst a peal of laughter, climbed to his feet, and went back to his father with a half-smile hanging on his half-open mouth.

The Krimsker Rebbe turned to Reb Yechezkal and said, "Lamentations."

Reb Yechezkal looked toward Reb Muni, but Reb Muni had already begun the smooth, low dirge:

*How the city sits alone,*
*she that was once so full of people*
*has become like a widow . . .*
*She weeps late in the night,*
*and her tears are on her cheeks.*

# CHAPTER SEVEN

The Krimsker Rebbe had returned to his study enervated and depressed. He wandered over to a corner and quietly settled onto a small carpet in front of the leather couch. Using the couch for a backrest, he sat cross-legged on the floor and was reaching toward a book on a nearby stool when a low voice called to him, "Rebbe, I must talk to you."

The rebbe, assuming it to be a voice from the Other Side, didn't bother to look up.

"Rebbe, I must talk to you," the voice repeated, but the rebbe dared not look up, for he knew very well that Lilith of a thousand desires engaged him in many guises, only later to reveal herself in her sinfully sensuous splendor. He drew the book toward the light and stared at its title. He was pleased to see that he had picked up the talmudic tractate on divorce, for it contained the most famous passages on the destruction of the Temple. These were among the few talmudic passages one was permitted to study on Tisha B'Av. Strengthened by his reaching for the Torah, he casually opened the volume. To his satisfaction, the thick folio pages fell open to precisely the permitted material.

"Rebbe, I know it's late." The voice pleaded for an audience. The rebbe, determined not to listen, closed his eyes tightly to avoid looking in the direction of the bedeviling voice. He wanted to scream—"You are Satan! You are the Evil Inclination! You are the Angel of Death!"—but he knew the folly of such an outburst; once Lilith was addressed, even in furious anger or in hateful condemnation, the dialogue had begun, her entangling web started with such fragile thread. On this day, when the world withered, he hoped to avoid such a web. He glanced down toward the bottom of the page and began reading:

> *Rav Yehudah and Rav said, why is it written "And they oppressed a man and his house, a man and his inheritance?" It happened once that a carpenter's apprentice set his eyes on his master's wife. The master was in need of money and the apprentice said, "I'll loan you the money, if you send your wife to me for three days." The master agreed and the apprentice made the loan. Three days later, the master appeared and asked, "Where's my wife?" The apprentice replied, "I let her go immediately, but I heard that some of the young rowdies sexually abused her on her way home." The master said, "What shall I do?" The apprentice said, "If you'll listen to me, you'll divorce her." "But her divorce payment is very great." "I'll loan you the money for her divorce payment," the apprentice suggested. So the master divorced his wife and no sooner had he done so, than the apprentice married her. When the date fell due for repayment and the master defaulted,*

*the apprentice said, "Come and work for me to pay off your debt." The apprentice and the woman sat, ate, drank and carried on while the master stood and served them, refilling their cups as his tears flowed from his eyes and fell into their cups. And it was at that moment that the awful decree of the Temple's Destruction was sealed. And there were those who said the Destruction was sealed because there were two wicks in one lamp.*

The Krimsker Rebbe shuddered and closed the book. He feared that Lilith controlled the pages. It was like Lilith to offer him an escape into purity only to entrap him in sensuality. Although the Torah was not subject to impurity, the Krimsker Rebbe knew that he himself was; his seductive adversary knew him all too well. And as he sat in anxious consternation, the voice said, "Rebbe, I know it is late, but my horse was trying to tell me something today on the road to Krimsk, and I think it's something very important." In all the nights Lilith had disported in his study, never had there been any animals present; much less talking horses. The Krimsker Rebbe realized that he was not alone in the room. He looked up to see Boruch Levi sitting cross-legged in the shadows across from him.

"How did you get in here?" the rebbe asked.

"I came in through the door right after you did. It was open," Boruch Levi answered.

They both glanced up to see that the door was still open. The rebbe wondered why Reb Yechezkal had not closed it after he had entered. "Reb Yechezkal," he began to call, and then he thought better of it. Better to get this bumptious fellow out of here first.

"Reb Boruch, whatever in the world makes you think that I can help?" the rebbe asked with a hint of amazement.

"The rebbe is a tzaddik, and the rebbe knows how a frog prays. Is a horse so different?"

There was a certain logic to what he was saying. "Does your horse speak to you often?" the rebbe asked, not knowing where to begin.

"No, no. This was the first time," Boruch Levi answered.

"What did he say?" the rebbe asked.

"I don't know."

"What were the words?" the rebbe asked wearily.

"There weren't any. Just light. The sunlight shining off his—off his backside," Boruch said.

The rebbe leaned forward, thrusting his head into the shadows so that he could get a good look at the man across from him. To his surprise the man did not look at all crazy. Boruch Levy, lithe and powerful, slightly anxious, looked very, very sane, indeed. He looked like a man you would want on your side in a fight. Like a man you could rely on and whose word you would readily accept on pledges far beyond his means. The rebbe shrugged. "Reb Boruch, I am at a loss; it would have been, after all, a miracle for the sun not to reflect off your horse's—backside."

"Yes, I suppose so, but this was something different. It was as if someone were writing a message in light first on one haunch then on the other, almost like they were arguing." Boruch Levi paused, hoping that he had succeeded in convincing the rebbe that there had indeed been a unique communication.

"What do you think they were arguing about?"

"Whether or not I should go to America," Boruch Levi

said quietly with an apologetic tone; he knew all too well that the Krimsker Rebbe had never given his blessing to any Jew leaving for America.

"Even the stones in America are trayf," the rebbe replied succinctly with his standard answer, wondering why this horse peddler was bothering him with such a trivial question when surely he knew how all the rabbis felt about this matter.

"I know that, but"—here Boruch Levi paused—"but why all of this? If the Evil Inclination wanted to send one more poor, ignorant Jew to America, would he have to bother with all this?"

The Krimsker Rebbe looked at the uneducated man who met his own gaze with such resolute strength. Not at all intimidated, this horse peddler was a most surprising fellow. The rebbe suspected him of having a very good native intelligence. He was blessed in another way as well; he had come to the right rebbe with his question. If the Krimsker Rebbe was not one of the great experts on the Evil Inclination, then who was? This was, after all, a true hasid.

"Reb Boruch, my hasid, you are asking very well and I shall explain the matter to you, but you are not to tell anyone else." The rebbe saw Boruch Levi nodding in agreement. "These matters are not for the marketplace. There is no doubt that you received a special message through your horse. The message said that you should leave Krimsk very soon in no more than two weeks for America. The message of light came from the setting western sun. This means that your golden light is in the West, in America. You, however, were traveling east at the time behind your horse; as long as you remain in the East, you will be following a horse's backside and facing impending darkness. Since you are now in a state of change, neither here nor there, you can see both simultaneously, the horse's backside and the magic light."

"So I shall be leaving Krimsk," Boruch Levi said thoughtfully.

"God forbid!" the rebbe retorted. "This message is obviously Satan's work from the Other Side. You must pay absolutely no attention to it. Reb Boruch, the answer to your question is this: the Evil Inclination has to bother with all this, as you call it, because your soul is from a very elevated root—so high I dare not tell you—and to seduce it, he needs very sophisticated devices such as the sun's shimmering golden letters. You can not imagine, Reb Boruch, the wiles of the Evil Inclination in our day."

Boruch Levi knitted his brows in concentration and nodded. "Thank God she died," he whispered.

"The horse?" the rebbe asked.

"No, Thunder, may he live and be well, is not a 'she,'" Boruch Levi answered.

"Then who died?" the rebbe wanted to know.

Boruch Levi shifted his weight in discomfort by leaning forward and grinding the palms of his hands onto his knees. "Rebbe," he said in embarrassment. Then he sat up straight and answered, "Grannie Zara, the cat lady."

Upon hearing this, the Krimsker Rebbe sat bolt upright. "The witch of Krimichak?"

"Yes."

"Are you sure?" the rebbe asked.

"I watched her funeral go by," Boruch Levi answered.

The rebbe drummed his index finger on the floor with monotonous fury and began to hum. "So that's how it is," he said. "So *that's* how it is." He nodded his head in vigorous agreement with himself. The rebbe did all this in joy, almost in ecstasy. Boruch Levi, however, thought the rebbe was angry at him for having gone to consult the witch.

"I ask the rebbe's forgiveness," Boruch Levi said.

"Forgiven, you are forgiven, but next time please knock."

Boruch Levi cleared his throat. "Yes, of course, excuse me, but I ask the rebbe's forgiveness for having gone to Grannie Zara."

"What?" the rebbe asked. He continued to drum and hum.

"I was on my way to ask the witch to interpret my horse's message when I met her funeral procession, and the truth is I was very disappointed to discover that—" but the Krimsker Rebbe had stopped drumming and raised his hand to stop Boruch's confession.

"Enough, Reb Boruch, you are forgiven, and I ask your forgiveness."

"My forgiveness?" Reb Boruch asked in quiet astonishment.

"Yes, yours. If the shepherd does not remove the stone from the well, then the flock must drink where they can. Reb Boruch, I ask your forgiveness."

"A hundred times you are forgiven. A thousand times even!" Reb Boruch blurted, both embarrassed and delighted that the rebbe would ask his, a simple peddler's, forgive-ness. "Rebbe, I knew what I was doing was wrong. I take the responsibility."

Again the rebbe raised his hand. The rebbe found himself liking this man more and more. He was steadfast and honest, made of very strong stuff.

"You had a very narrow escape in the afternoon. Be on guard against the Evil Inclination day and night, Reb Boruch. With you it will try anything. And remember, the Evil Inclination has a great advantage over us. It has no Evil Inclination to make its job more difficult."

"Yes, Rebbe, I will be careful."

The rebbe pointed to the open door. Boruch Levi nodded and rose to leave.

"Thank you, Rebbe."

"Boruch Levi the son of Naftali, the place does not matter. You will always make a good living. For you the question is not what kind of a living, but what kind of a life. For now, forget America."

The rebbe returned to his book, and on his way out Boruch Levi shut the door.

# CHAPTER EIGHT

WORD OF THE KRIMSKER REBBE'S RETURN SPREAD SO quickly through the town that many were convinced that, quite literally, it flew on the wings of the twittering swallows that darted through the darkening evening. That the rebbe knew the birds' language, and that of all Creation, was beyond doubt after hearing his story! And indeed many hasidim hurried home with the news only to be greeted by the family massed in impassioned inquiry. Did the rebbe really dance on the table with poor Itzik Dribble?—Yes, like an angel. And did he cry for the Messiah to come?—Such tears can't be imagined; how the Holy One didn't redeem us on the spot I'll never know!

As the story was told and retold, lived and relived, everyone became more excited. Technically it was the wrong time for such feelings. They could neither eat nor drink, and how could hasidim celebrate without even so much as a small glass of spirits or a friendly little herring? Moreover, they couldn't very well talk jubilantly while sitting on the floor like dumb mourners. Yet the restlessness and high spirits—the thirst for song and the hunger for dance—could not be denied. Spontaneously they flowed into the streets, telling and retelling, discussing and marveling at the miracle that had occurred in the beis midrash. With one topic, with one attitude, with one voice, Krimsk was one great stream of conversation, sailing about the market-place, swirling through the lanes, and flowing reverentially quiet as it passed the very majestic fount of the Krimskian sea, the beis midrash and the study itself in which the rebbe once again was receiving hasidim in private audience.

Not all of Krimsk participated in the mass celebration. The Krimsker Rebbe's highly praised dance partner, Itzik Dribble, sat at home sucking serenely on a candy while his father, Beryl Soffer, paced back and forth retelling the amazing events to his wife, Faigie, a slight woman from whom Itzik had inherited his blond hair and the physical grace he had exhibited on the rebbe's table earlier in the evening. Very quiet, she sat shaking her head from side to side in amazement as her husband strode to and fro, either addressing her directly as he approached or indirectly over his shoulder, propelling his rapid words as he lumbered past. "Do you hear, Faigie? The rebbe delayed the evening service for all of Krimsk to dance with Itzik. The Book of Lamentations, too, Faigie! That's no small thing, the Book of Lamentations on Tisha B'Av, but it had to wait while he told Itzik a holy story." Faigie continued to shake her head from side to side. "And then he said that Itzik was a good boy and that, he, the holy Krimsker Rebbe, was very proud of him. Do you hear, Faigie?"

Faigie heard as she continued to shake in fearful amazement. As she looked at her little golden calf blissfully devouring the sweet, she was pleased that the rebbe had recognized and honored the divine spark in Itzik, but she was also afraid that nothing good would come of all this. Had she heard about Itzik telling the rebbe that the Messiah was an old joke—which, of course, her husband purposefully omitted—she would have been relieved, for Faigie believed that if the sun of good fortune shines upon you, it inevitably casts the shadow of sorrow. That was simply how the universe worked. In some way, Beryl's full bank account was paid for by Itzik's empty head. For her, unlike her husband, Itzik's failing held no mystery. She expected no miracles concerning Itzik. Quite the contrary, she dutifully expected disasters. Beryl believed that they were the innocent victims of fate. Faigie shared his belief that they were victims, because everyone was a victim, but she knew only too well that they were not innocent. When the sun shines, beware the shadow.

When she finally had become pregnant after two years of marriage, Beryl had commanded her not to go near Grannie Zara. The rebbe had said that a witch denies the heavenly host and that anyone who went to Grannie Zara was certainly denying the will of heaven. For a Jew to go to the witch of Krimichak was like worshiping the golden calf. But Faigie, so much of the time passive and accepting, had a streak of resistance, deep, stubborn, and not at all predictable. What did the Krimsker Rebbe know about giving birth? He was a great tzaddik who knew the holy Torah, but that was not the only one; there was another torah, another law. The everyday torah—the torah of the kitchen with its spilled salt, the law of the path with its black cat, and the way of the womb with life's dark beginnings. So when Faigie felt the first kick from the child inside her very own body, she threw a pinch of dough into the oven and went out the back door and through the fields to the stream path. She followed it past the wooden bridge to the stepping stones. Lifting her skirt to keep it dry—Beryl would never guess where she had been—she negotiated the mossy green rocks to the Krimichak side. All went well until she approached the clearing behind the witch's cottage. There, Zloty, the witch's great calico cat, appeared.

She calmly padded up to Faigie, arched her back, and rubbed her furry side against her legs. The soft nap caressed Faigie's still-damp ankles in luxuriant warmth. The witch's cats, especially Zloty—their feline queen—inspired fear in both Jews and peasants. Zloty's affectionate welcome would have driven most of Grannie Zara's visitors to absolute distraction, reducing them to sweaty fear. Not Faigie, however. She knelt down to pet the cat. Zloty responded with a loud purring and pushed herself more demandingly against Faigie. Faigie scratched the creature behind the ears, and the cat hunched up in furry delight. Faigie paused with her outstretched hand near the cat, and the feline lifted her great front left leg, white with an orangish brown patch near the paw, and placed it into Faigie's hand: a gesture of trust and affection. Faigie looked down at the outsized limb, large enough for a cat twice Zloty's size—and indeed it was twice the size of Zloty's other limbs. Everyone greatly feared Zloty's large left leg, for they ascribed the abnormality that lay in Faigie's hand to witchcraft. One version had it that Grannie Zara, using Zloty as a messenger, often enlarged her to various sizes, and after one such enlargement the reduction worked imperfectly; one paw did not return to its original size. The other explanation had it that Zloty was someone whom Grannie Zara had bewitched through a spell. The imperfection of limb resulted from technical failures in the otherwise successful transformation. Had Faigie been forced to choose, she would have preferred the latter explanation. There seemed to be something conspiratorial in the way the cat's paw lay in her hand, as if the cat really were someone in disguise. The cat seemed to be holding her.

It was then that Grannie Zara's voice had sung out in sweet clarity, "Who treads in my garden where no weeds grow?" Faigie wanted to stand up and answer; after all, she had come to see Grannie Zara, but Zloty would not remove her paw, and Faigie remained hidden. "I sowed the seed; there was no weed. Enter, my guest, and therein feed." Zloty shook her whiskers at Faigie, warning her not to reveal herself. "Who's there?" the witch demanded. Zloty, still holding Faigie's hand, answered with a clear meow. "Come out!" the witch called, "Lest you give birth to this!?" Faigie, still kneeling, looked up across the clearing to see Grannie Zara's golden straw broom waving high in her open window. She started to rise, but Zloty increased the pressure of her paw and Faigie stayed where she was. The cottage window closed; Zloty removed her paw, nuzzled against Faigie's knee, and bounded away into the woods. Faigie rose and returned home to await her fate. When the midwife brought her newborn child to her and Faigie saw the straw-colored film of wispy hairs lying limp upon the infant's head, she was not surprised. Grannie Zara had waved her gold broom, and sure enough, from Zaigie's womb emerged a blond golem.

Faigie loved the child as a mother should, putting his

needs above hers, but she did so with a calm detachment. Since there was no mystery in his faulty genesis, there was no hope. Nor was there the spontaneous joy that so often accompanies the miracle of renewal. She was calm; calmer than anyone she knew, for there was no depressing sense of guilt. Faigie believed that she had done nothing wrong. As for going to the witch, everyone did it—because they had to. After all, it wasn't as if Grannie Zara hadn't saved the Jews. She had. Twenty years previously, in the terrible pogroms of the eighties, she had singlehandedly stopped the Cossacks with an upraised broom. The marauders had swept into the country with license to plunder the Jews, but what Cossack could read a license, much less obey one when his saber dripped blood? They pillaged what crossed their path, all the while cursing the Jews and praising the tsar, to be sure. It was Krimichak and Krimsk's fate to lie in their path. They galloped up to Krimichak's outskirts and reined in their mounts.

Grannie Zara, her ever-present cats in tow, strolled out of her cottage, lifted the straw broom above her head in religious solemnity, and intoned, "You are wise to listen. For every sprig you see, one year of life less for you and your horse if you do not ride for one peaceful hour by the Mother of God—lest Black Mary do her work."

And they turned and rode on for a peaceful hour to heaven knows where to do heaven knows what. Of course the Jews flocked to Grannie Zara. Who else had saved an entire Jewish community? The Krimsker Rebbe, whom Faigie's husband worshiped, wouldn't consent to give blessings—until tonight he even refused to look at the Jews. At least Grannie Zara had invited her inside.

Faigie had enough confidence in the blind fortunes of destiny to imagine that Zloty had saved her from a fate worse than that of giving birth to her golden calf. Not that Faigie was pleased with the way things had gone, but they could have been worse. Had she not gone to Grannie Zara's, she might have given birth to a cat, and had she accepted the invitation to enter—against Zloty's advice—she might have been turned into one herself.

Faigie, not given to speculation, had followed her instincts. What else did she have? Others followed their passions. Even her own Beryl, sweet and unpretentious, had a passion that grasped his portly soft flesh in an iron vice. He didn't worship money or what it could buy, but such an otherwise decent simple man could neither eat nor sleep when he contemplated the possibility of anywhere in all Russia a forest in flames, a cigarette smouldering, a frying pan sizzling, or a kerosene lamp glowing without a match from Soffer and Company as the cause of it all. And her Beryl was a simple man!

The Krimsker Rebbe only wanted to be holier than God Himself. Even plain Gittel Waksman, her husband a shoemaker, has to buy her son Froika a violin. She can't carry a tune, the boy can't carry a tune. So dream that he fiddles at poor Jews' weddings? Never. No less than the tsar. Gittel Waksman won't be satisfied with less than the Romanov family for Froika's audience. And she won't! No compromise.

Where did they get such ideas? Faigie's instincts seemed more reasonable to her than the mad passions she saw blazing around her. Still, Faigie worried that something was wrong with her; she didn't fit in Krimsk. Every match in

Russia, God, the tsar himself! What was in their pillows that they dreamed such dreams? It was enough to make Faigie hold her head in her hands to keep it from bursting.

Faigie, no earth shaker, just wanted to avoid being hit by rocks that were forever sliding down the hill toward her. Now that Itzik had danced with the rebbe, she felt the rumbling of the earth moving toward her family. The Krimsker Rebbe had put the forces into motion, but Itzik, more properly, belonged to Grannie Zara. Faigie's instincts told her that she had to see both Grannie Zara and the Krimsker Rebbe to tell them the truth. What else could she tell them?

"Do you hear, Faigie? Rabbi Chanina listened to his father, and that saved him."

But Faigie wasn't listening to her husband.

"Who?"

"The son, Rabbi Chanina."

"Beryl, the rebbe is receiving people tonight?"

"Boruch Levi walked in just like that."

"I must see him, Beryl."

Reb Beryl's enthusiasm deserted him. "You?"

"Yes."

Faigie stood up, went to Itzik and gave him a goodnight kiss, then turned to leave. Beryl followed her toward the door.

"Why, Faigie?" His face had a foolish, pained look. "Haven't we taken up enough of his time tonight?"

"I want to talk to him about our children," Faigie said.

"But we have only one," Beryl protested.

"Yes," Faigie agreed as she stepped out into the soft, supple embrace of the warm night.

# CHAPTER NINE

YECHIEL KATZMAN'S ERSTWHILE STUDENTS DISAPPEARED from the beis midrash immediately after services. One moment each sat dutifully by his father's side, and one moment later each had vanished, fleeing barefoot beyond the boundary of Krimsk into the woods that lay on the road to Krimichak. Without pausing at the town's outskirts, they plunged into the dark, cool shadows. When the sturdy tree trunks and the impenetrable veil of foliage snuffed out the last faint lights of Krimsk, they dropped, panting, onto the soft, mossy ground. Convinced that the entire beis midrash must be in frenzied, vengeful pursuit, they gulped for air, and as they did so, their own wheezing gasps frightened them all the more.

Froika Waksman thought he saw particularly frightening specters in the surrounding darkness, for it was he who had convinced Itzik Dribble that the Krimsker Rebbe was a frog. Itzik had resisted the idea, but Froika had turned to the others and commanded, "Show Itzik how the frog rebbe prays!" Yonkel Berman, Alexander Bornstein, and

Shlomi Feldman began jumping in a stooped stance, and Itzik's resistance immediately collapsed. Froika then introduced him into the leaping circle, and Itzik practiced the prayer that he was to perform so successfully later in the day with the rebbe himself.

When Itzik asked the rebbe if he was really a frog, the boys knew they were in trouble. Their fears increased when Itzik informed the rebbe that the Messiah was an old joke and described the aromatic dish that accompanied this revelation. In fact the messianic turd belonged to a more mature, more fertile imagination. Older boys, with the assistance of the dairyman's helper, had executed the prank over a half year earlier, but now the younger boys were certain to be blamed for it.

They held Itzik responsible for their problems, and perhaps God, too, the God who looks after fools—for Itzik unfairly had turned the tables on them. Or so it seemed, because they did not at all understand the redemptive nature of Itzik's involvement with the rebbe. For acting the fool, Itzik was now the darling of the town, while they, who had suffered through innumerable hours with the Torah, were exiled into the dark forest reverberating with crickets and the other anonymous, menacing voices of the night.

"Do you hear something?" Froika asked in a whisper.

They reined in their wheezing and concentrated in silence. The sounds of the darkness seemed to swell into a great crescendo bursting about them in a chaotic roar.

"I hear them," Yonkel Berman said in quiet terror.

"It sounds like they're coming this way," Shlomi Feldman added.

Gripped by fear, they heard the Krimsker Rebbe, frog

turned tiger, and hundreds of hasidim charging toward them in a veritable pogrom of bloody, lusting vengeance. Aloft, they must be holding Itzik Dribble as their wooden-headed yellow icon. They sat in a nearly impenetrable thicket that the most skillful woodsman would have had trouble revealing, but to those sitting there, guilty victims of their own imagination, it seemed the most exposed and obvious hiding place in the world. Alexander Bornstein, the one most likely to cry, was frightened beyond tears. "What do we do now?" he asked in a tone so quiet and even that his friends understood it could have been ironed smooth only by terror.

"We have to get to Krimichak," Froika answered with a certainty that lacked enthusiasm.

His friends heard the logic. No matter how impassioned, no Jewish mob would dare enter the peasant town. Once in Krimichak, the boys would be safe—from the Jews at least. The goyim were another matter, but at this juncture they appeared very attractive.

"We can't use the bridge," Alexander said, sounding as if he were sitting in the back of a closet.

"Nor the stepping stones; that would be the first place to guard," Froika responded. He thought for a moment, then said, "We'll have to cross the pond."

Froika's suggestion met with a solemn silence. Where the stream slowed down and spread out to form the pond, they would have to swim across. The boys well knew that on Tisha B'Av no one was permitted to wash above the knuckles of the fingers, much less go swimming.

"They'll never look for us there," Shlomi Feldman said, giving his consent.

"It's *pekuach nefesh*"—Yonkel added the talmudic expression meaning to save a soul in a matter of life and death.

They began to thread their way out of the thicket toward the path that would bring them to the pond. Alexander scrambled to stay in contact with the vanishing figures and climbed onto Yonkel Berman's heels. "What are you doing?" Yonkel cried, more in fear than in anger. The younger Bornstein couldn't answer but managed to plant his feet onto the ground. Alexander felt somewhat better; Yonkel had yelled at him, and he still hadn't wet his pants.

The ground was soft underfoot with the hesitating springiness that comes from the combination of decay and growth. Treading on that fertile organic resilience, their steps seemed disconnected from the reality of the earth's surface. With the stinking, sweet aromas from the bruised turf flooding their nostrils in heady, dizzying swells, they had the sensation of traversing a distant dark land, foreign from Reb Gedaliah's hard, dry benches. Drunk on its perfumed mulch and moving quickly, they could barely understand such a world. Then as suddenly as they had entered it, they lost it. Crawling through a tangled vine, they emerged into low bushes beside the path. Froika crouched low. The others quickly did the same. Satisfied that no one was coming, Froika furtively approached the path. With a final pause, he looked in both directions under the large quarter moon that found its way through to bathe the cleft in the forest in its pale, still light.

Froika started to run stealthily. His three friends pursued him. As the boys ran along the path, they felt exposed and hunted, the hard-baked clay slapping mercilessly at the soles of their bare feet.

Froika halted at a small hill before the pond and led them into the forest. The ground was softer, and they entered a third world. Not as dark, not as soft, not as closed, not as suffocatingly pungent as the thicket, but darker, softer, more closed, and more fragrant than the path. They flowed silently up the small hillock like raindrops on a dark night—unseeing but moving together in a formation that the elements can affect but not violate. At the hillock's crest, they halted and furtively poked their heads above the bushes to observe the pond several meters down the forested slope. Bulrushes and reeds choked its shallows. Ten paces to their right was the path that led to an open grassy area, the easiest place to enter the water. The water itself lay smooth and dark like mildly stirring ink; the channel on the far side churned its way past the still water, which had the faintest haze hanging above it. Had it not been for the haze, the pond would have sharply reflected the trees and sinking moon. As it was, by looking down into the pond, the boys saw the moon already sinking into the sheltering fluid of some distant ether from unfathomable voids above. The Krimichak shore thirty meters away lay low, obscured by shadows. The boys searched for its outline. They could not detect it, but they could see the dark shape of trees lining the ravine walls above, and they could hear the distant crickets chorusing on the far shore—yet close compared to the silent celestial expanse clutching the moon.

When they heard voices, they instinctively pulled their heads below the bushes and waited, like very small children slipping under the blankets to hide from parental wrath. Even there, they scrunched their heads into their shoulders like turtles without shells and listened.

"She's dead. I told you so," a whispering voice argued.

That assertion met spirited shushing sounds.

"She was never this late," the same voice persisted.

Froika listened to the young Polish voices and realized that he and his friends had not been discovered. Quite the contrary, they had discovered the boys from Krimichak. Froika wondered how they could cross the pond. For Jewish boys to be caught between Krimsk and Krimichak was not very healthy.

Alexander was aware of these problems, but at the moment he was more concerned with the warmth suffusing the front of his pants and the disappointing awareness that he had wet himself after all. This brought him to despair. It wasn't enough that Itzik Dribble had maligned them and they had to flee for their lives, only to run into the boys from Krimichak in the middle of nowhere. Now this, too!

"And after the spell she ducks under again. What is she?" the same voice persisted.

"I don't know," a second voice answered. This voice sounded weary, but far from convinced.

"She's dead," the first voice answered with shrill insistence, "and whoever goes into that water tonight dies. There's death in the water."

This last assertion gripped Shlomi Feldman in terror, for he believed that the dark pool on the dark night of the dark moment of Tisha B'Av certainly held death in the rheum of its misty eye. He watched the quarter moon skewing in descent toward the shrouded depths like the eye of a dying man rolling upward into the skull of death. Shlomi wanted no part of the dark reflection of the water.

Death was not for Shlomi, and his soul asserted its right to live in a warm young body.

Shlomi's sneeze created a moment of quiet that was quickly followed by a flurry of whispering. Shlomi found Froika's ear and begged for him to flee. Froika pushed him away so that he could listen better.

"Let's get the priest," the assertive voice yelped in fear no less overwhelming than Shlomi's. "On three, we'll run all together toward the bridge path."

"One, two—" he counted.

"Wait a minute," Alexander Bornstein called out. "It's only us."

And he stood since he knew that, as short as he was, the underbrush would cover his urine-stained pants.

"Who are you?"

"Just us," Alexander said nervously.

And everyone stood up in the darkness that their eyes had adjusted to.

"It's the Yids," the assertive voice said with undisguised joy. The Krimsk boys recognized Casimir, two or three years older than themselves, a tall, strong, sinewy boy, stubborn and impulsive.

"What are you doing here?" Tadeusz asked. He was the quieter, more reasonable voice. Shorter, stockier, crafty and shrewd.

"It was too hot in town," Alexander answered, and his answer momentarily disarmed them.

"You're not here because of the naked lady?" Tadeusz asked.

The Krimsk boys feared his quiet, contemplative tone

more than Casimir's boastful taunts. Shlomi wished to answer, but he could only shake his head.

"We don't know anything about that," Alexander said weakly.

"A naked lady?" Froika respectfully queried.

"She comes when the moon is like this—from the Krimsk side, dipping naked in the moonlight. Then she covers her breasts and whispers a spell into the water." Casimir interrupted his telling to look around fearfully, casting a particularly careful glance at the pond. "*Barooka ta*," he said, quietly repeating the magic spell.

"That's not magic," Alexander piped in a squeaky voice, and as soon as he had, he realized that he should have kept his mouth shut. He fell silent too late. Tadeusz motioned for him to stand directly in front of him. The small boy with the wet pants complied.

"It's not?" Tadeusz asked.

Half glancing at his interrogator, Alexander nervously shook his head.

"Then what is it?"

Alexander didn't know what to say.

"What does this little drippy piss-pants Yid know?" Casimir taunted.

"What is it?" Tadeusz asked Alexander with a single-mindedness that demanded an immediate answer.

"It's a blessing," Alexander said softly.

"A Jewish blessing?"

"Yes."

"He's a lying Yid," Casimir spat fiercely. "Then where is she? Why isn't she here tonight?"

Casimir grabbed Alexander and began to shake him

as if the information were physically stuck in his throat and could be dislodged. Alexander began to cry in choking sobs. "What a crybaby!" Casimir said in angry frustration as he continued to shake him. Alexander's face contorted in pain, and his head snapped back and forth in futile pursuit of his shoulders. He was crying silently now, as if his voice within could not navigate the herky-jerky passage up to his mouth.

Tadeusz placed a restraining hand on Casimir's arm.

"Why would Grannie Zara run around saying Jewish prayers?" Tadeusz asked.

No one answered. Froika, fearful that Alexander might be choked to death, thought some response necessary and said, "Why don't we ask Grannie Zara?"

Casimir's mouth dropped open, and his hands fell from Alexander's throat. He turned to gape at Froika.

"Grannie Zara is dead," he whispered as if giving voice to such a statement could endanger all of them.

A moaning "ooooh" emerged from Shlomi, as if he were part cow.

"They had to drive the cats off with torches," added tall, ungainly Stefan, whose face already hosted significant numbers of red pimply splotches that seemed strangely dark in the moonlight.

Intimidated by the witch's life and terrorized by her death with its corpse-hugging cats crouched in defiance, everyone stood in silence.

Tadeusz broke the oppressive quiet in his even, authoritative voice. "At least we can find out if death is in the water tonight."

Casimir seized Alexander and dragged him toward the

open shoreline. The other Krimichak boys firmly grabbed Froika, Shlomi, and Yonkel, following after Casimir and Alexander.

Casimir flung Alexander out into the pond, and he landed with a whomping sound on the seat of his already wet pants and sank down to his waist. He splashed about and staggered to his feet. The water was barely above his knees. He walked toward the shore as if the danger were in the water, but as soon as he reached the shore Casimir lifted him above his head and threw him farther into the water.

"If there is death in the water," Tadeusz patiently explained, "you won't know it unless his head goes under."

Casimir's face flushed with the wisdom of his friend's suggestion, and he dragged Alexander deeper into the water near the reeds that reached up to the taller boy's hips. He thrust Alexander's head under water and forcibly held it there for several moments. Alexander sputtered, coughed, and gasped for air.

"It might take effect slowly," Tadeusz cautioned his impatient friend.

Casimir, exhausted from his unsuccessful experimentation, turned to listen to Tadeusz. As he turned, he dragged the half-dead Alexander by the hair. Slumped over on the water, the victim bobbed his head in faint attempts to get air.

Breathing deeply from his heavy exertion, Casimir stood still. Alexander, as if possessed, suddenly lurched toward the reeds. Casimir's grip on his hair pulled him short. Alexander raised his arms in entreaty toward the reeds.

"What is it?" Casimir asked curiously.

Alexander stood up with his arms outstretched and

implored in a desperate, strong voice. "Good Rabbi Chanina, save meeeee!"

As Casimir anxiously turned his head away from Alexander toward the reeds, he caught a glimpse of a large dark object that pounded into his head, tearing at his eyes, then fell with a slap into the water.

"Aieee!" he screamed in terror, letting go of Alexander and rushing to hold his wounded eyes. "I can't see! I can't see!" he cried.

Alexander, triumphantly chanting, "Good Rabbi Chanina, Good Rabbi Chanina," reached the shore as Casimir continued to wail in blind terror, "My eyes! My eyes!"

In fear the Krimichak boys, who could not see what had happened, let their captives loose. Alexander ran up to his friends, explaining, "It was Good Rabbi Chanina who sent the talking frog to save me." The Krimichak boys drew back from the Jewish boys in fright.

"I'm blind!" cried Casimir in horror.

"Let's go!" one of the Krimichak boys yelled. Tadeusz started into the water to lead Casimir ashore. The Polish boys broke into a headlong rush along the river path toward the bridge, screaming as they went.

The Jewish boys grabbed Alexander and lost no time rushing back along the hard Krimsk path. They could hear the wild screams of Casimir and the more distant hollering of those escaping toward Krimichak. They themselves were quiet, except for Alexander Bornstein, who kept murmuring, "Good Rabbi Chanina." The faint lights of Krimsk caused their souls to dance even though it was Tisha B'Av.

# CHAPTER TEN

In her father's home, Shayna Basya had followed her mother and widowed grandmother into a small room off the beis midrash to sit upon low stools and listen to the reading of Lamentations. She would watch the tears silently form in the corners of her grandmother's blue eyes until they overflowed into the deep furrows that creased her clear, pink skin. Softly and silently the tears welled forth into their long-established channels. Grandmother took little notice of them—dabbing her cheeks to keep her book dry—and in later years, when she could no longer see well enough to read, she sat quietly and let them splash upon the bodice of her dress. Shayna Basya had once leaned over with a handkerchief to pat the old woman's cheeks. "No, my darling, now there is no holy word beneath; let them fall," her grandmother had said, and she reached for Shayna Basya's youthful hand, which she drew to her lips. As she kissed the girl, the old woman's tears fell onto her granddaughter's hand. Shayna Basya refused to dry the drops. She watched them become smaller and smaller during the lugubrious chant of Lamentations—all the while reflecting the dim, flickering candlelight until suddenly they were no more.

Even in her own home in Krimsk, Shayna Basya had heard Lamentations, but now that her husband the rebbe had withdrawn to his study, there was no possibility of Shayna Basya and her daughter listening to any services at all since there was no other room adjacent to the beis midrash.

Forced away, Shayna Basya and her daughter, Rachel Leah, sat on stools in the sparsely furnished parlor, fingering their copies of Lamentations that they would soon read at their leisure. They had nowhere to go, no one to talk to, nothing to do. Shayna Basya was musing over more innocent and enjoyable days in her family's dynastic home in Bezin when she heard the jarring explosion of sound: the sudden, forceful simultaneous upending of every bench and table in the beis midrash. Rachel Leah looked up quizzically, but Shayna Basya, crushing the small book in her reflexive grip, leaped to her feet, for she had heard at the heart of the noise the raucous screech of snapping wood that told her something had irreparably given way.

As if a wooden rod had been splintered over her own back, she staggered out of the room and down the hallway. The study door stood open as if it had been blown that way by the explosion from the beis midrash beyond. She stood on the threshold to the empty room and saw the door to the beis midrash ajar and trembling. Crossing over to it, she peeked out to have her worst fears confirmed.

Her husband Yaakov Moshe was jumping on his own table with a fool. She could not bear the bizarre thumps of his senseless crashings onto the tabletop, and she stepped back to collapse onto the sofa. Looking up, she saw Rachel Leah watching the idiotic performance with a pleasantly curious smile on her lips. Shayna Basya had seen that the hasidim, too, reverently observed the tabletop thumping. As long as Yaakov Moshe was in the beis midrash, he sailed on waters beyond her reach, but where would it end?

Overwhelmed, she was unaware that the thumping sound had stopped until she noticed the rapt, radiant expression on Rachel Leah's face. Shayna Basya crept behind her to hear about Rabbi Chanina's sitting shivah with the large frog that ate him out of house and home on Pesach. Even in her distressed state, she was captivated by its simple charm and fairy-tale ending and touched by the poetic beauty of telling such a story to the poor, pitiful son of a rich, talented father. Of course the hasidim loved it, why shouldn't they? But as impressed as Shayna Basya was, she was not entranced, for she understood that whatever Yaakov Moshe was up to, he was pursuing it with all his remarkable talents and intellect. She and her plans were in serious trouble.

All the agony and travail of Reb Muni's Lamentations—ancient humiliations and sufferings, remembered and unending, chronicled and without number—assailed her weary, anxious heart. The Krimsker Rebbetzin cried. Even the quick, gentle touches of Rachel Leah's handkerchief upon her cheeks could not protect the holy words beneath. They became indistinct on the dampening page. Shayna Basya saw tears on her daughter's hands in the reflected light and sensed that for Rachel Leah the light would be extinguished before the drops would disappear.

After the reading, her silent tears still unchecked, she

led Rachel Leah back to the parlor. Enervated, she fell onto a low couch and passively permitted her tears to fall. Feeling no better, she sat up only to hear a strange murmuring surrounding the house. She sent Rachel Leah to find out what was happening. Flushed and excited, her daughter returned.

"All the Jews of Krimsk are parading in the streets, celebrating their rebbe's return. And Father is receiving hasidim in his study. Such devotion to Father—it is as if the holy Torah itself is at the center of their communal praise," Rachel Leah announced triumphantly.

"Are you sure?" Shayna Basya asked, referring to Yaakov Moshe's receiving supplicants.

"Of course, all these years Father has been giving his life for God and his Torah," the daughter confidently explained.

"And how do *you* know *that?*" her mother wondered.

"He told me," Rachel Leah innocently answered.

Shayna Basya remained silent, although she wondered about that, too.

"Isn't it amazing!" Rachel Leah said.

"It certainly is," her mother agreed wearily, "and if you don't mind, now I think I would like to rest."

"I couldn't possibly rest at a time like this," Rachel Leah declared as she left the room, closing the door.

"Yes, I can see that," Shayna Basya said quietly to herself.

Although Shayna Basya was concerned at the rebbe's behavior, she remained calm. Tisha B'Av didn't concern her. The day was full of lamentations, prayers, and mourning, thoroughly unique in its misery. On such a fearsome, difficult day, what rebbe's behavior could possibly be inappropriate? How could Yaakov Moshe's conduct be more outrageous than the day itself? Shayna Basya felt as if she were a holiday fish in the bottom of the bowl between strokes of the chopper's pounding blade. The next blow would not fall at least until tomorrow after sunset.

She was mistaken. Within half an hour, Rachel Leah returned with Reb Yechezkal, who informed Shayna Basya that the rebbe had commanded him to summon Yechiel Katzman, the brilliant young talmudist, to the study. Shayna Basya realized that Tisha B'Av was not only a distant, exotic repository for ancient tragedies but also a living calamitous magnet drawing forth new sorrows, momentous and overwhelming.

"I shall speak to the rebbe," she said. After Reb Yechezkal left, she turned to her daughter. "Darling, I am going to talk to your father. Please see to it that we are not disturbed."

Shayna Basya stood up and started toward the study. She felt at a loss in her cloth Tisha B'Av slippers, which flopped about on her feet. She yearned for her good, sturdy high button shoes, with which she could pace the study floor and stamp in fury.

# CHAPTER ELEVEN

SHAYNA BASYA KNOCKED ON THE STUDY DOOR AND received no answer. Her fist rapping on the door produced a hollow rumbling echo in her ears that sounded like the first clumps of earth falling onto the top of a coffin. From dust to dust, she thought, although she didn't quite know what she meant. She supposed she meant that the charade was about to end—and that a more permanent reality existed before the game had begun and would be there when it ended. She knocked again and still received no answer.

"Yaakov Moshe?" She called her husband's name quietly and, receiving no answer, gently opened the door and entered.

Her husband, sitting on the floor, his back against the couch, was dozing. Or at least he seemed to be. Shayna Basya knew that before he had gone into self-imposed exile, he often avoided hasidim by feigning sleep. This was one of the few pieces of her family's advice that Yaakov Moshe had taken. Her father and later her brother had used the technique sparingly in order to maintain some minimal amount of privacy and to keep themselves from becoming totally exhausted. Yaakov Moshe, however, had seized it early in his career and had expanded upon it until he withdrew for years on end from his hasidim and from his family.

Her scrupulously honest brother had quoted Genesis—"a heavy sleep came upon Adam"—and explained to Yaakov Moshe that when Adam awoke, he found a "helpmate," meaning of course that a rebbe, only human, would be more effective if he had some rest. Yaakov Moshe had laughed and asked, "Who has such creative energy that every time he closes his eyes, he can create a helpmate?" Even her brother, who worshiped Yaakov Moshe's talents, was shocked at such a blasphemous joke and quickly changed the subject.

Shayna Basya closed the door behind her and shuffled across the room to her husband. She stood above him for a moment and called, "Yaakov Moshe," so gently that even she was aware that she didn't want him to wake up. She bent over to tap him, but as a respectful wife how could she loom over her husband like a gross, vulgar creature? Perplexed, she found herself sitting on the edge of the couch. Yes, sitting on a couch on Tisha B'Av! Something she had never done before. Let it be, she thought, that's the least of it. She leaned over and gently tapped him on the shoulder. He turned toward her, and his eyes were open. It wasn't clear whether he had opened them in response to her touch or not. "Yaakov Moshe, are you awake?"

He blinked, and she knew from experience that he was listening.

"Yaakov Moshe," she began meekly. Slumped on the

couch, her scarf covering the side of her face, she dared not look at him. "Yaakov Moshe, I wanted to discuss Rachel Leah with you. She's all we have. Our only daughter. Her future is our future." Here she paused, hoping that her husband would say something, but he remained silent. "She is old enough to stand under the wedding canopy, and if a mother's heart is not concerned . . ."

"It is being taken care of," he said.

"Yes," Shayna Basya said, "that's what I want to talk to you about."

She could feel his eyes on her: the wonder of his wide open eyes, full of amazement at how a woman could prattle on. She flushed, and under his unequal gaze she felt the warmth springing to her face.

"Yaakov Moshe, I have already taken care of it." She waited for a reply but received none. "I couldn't consult with you. It wasn't my fault—and a match had to be made. I used Reb Yechezkal. She is promised to Yitzhak Weinbach, the successful young match manufacturer."

Expecting an outburst, she turned to face her husband. He didn't seem concerned; he seemed to be falling asleep. His eyes, still open, no longer focused on her.

Frustrated, Shayna Basya sat up straight. "I said that Rachel Leah is already engaged. She will marry Yitzhak Weinbach, God willing, after Succos."

Her voice was strong, and she spoke with aggressive determination. Her voice seemed to capture her husband's attention. He was looking directly at her. She returned his look.

"I shall make Rachel Leah's match," he said wearily.

"I have made it," she answered.

"Yitzhak Weinbach is a boor. Rachel Leah's soul will suffocate," he said matter-of-factly. He spoke clearly but as if he were addressing a trivial representative of hers. This secondhand conversation frightened her, because this was how he had spoken to her in the "best" years of their marriage, when he directed everything.

"Yitzhak Weinbach is not a scholar, that's true, but she will never starve—and neither will we."

Yaakov Moshe flicked his hand as he had in the beis midrash. There was nothing to discuss; her words were not worth listening to.

"Reb Yechezkal told me that you sent him for Yechiel Katzman, and I couldn't order him not to go, but he is on a fool's errand. Rachel Leah is engaged to Yitzhak Weinbach, and she will marry him," Shayna Basya said calmly.

"You had neither the authority nor my permission. Whatever you did was of no account. It is not your concern. You may return to your room." He remained perfectly passive.

"Yaakov Moshe, I want the child to be happy," she whispered. "Do you hear, happy?"

She leaned over to plead before him, looked searchingly into his hazel eyes, and saw a soft response. He was perplexed. A happy child was a foreign concept; as foreign as the streets of America. Shayna Basya saw that she was getting nowhere. She sat back.

"Let her have a normal marriage; she's an only child," she said.

"We're all only children and there are no normal marriages. Otherwise there would be no Tisha B'Av," he said.

Shayna Basya was shaken at how he had returned to

the world. It was such answers that had once enchanted her, but he had been gone too long.

"Let Tisha B'Av be one day a year for the child. That's enough," she answered.

He looked quizzically at her. "I have commanded Yechiel Katzman to come here, and I shall make the match."

"No," she said.

"Yes, these matters are for fathers to decide."

"Once every five years?" Shayna Basya asked, and as she did so, she regretted it. She didn't want to taunt and to nag. Such tactics had never influenced Yaakov Moshe; they only demeaned her.

"Yaakov Moshe, my husband," she said respectfully, carefully controlling her voice. "As your wife I mean no disrespect, but our married life has not been normal. Even if there is no such creature as a 'normal marriage,' how many can be as abnormal as ours?"

"You married a rebbe."

"Yes, but I wasn't prepared for my husband to disappear into his room for five years," she said. The petulant, hurt tone broke through again.

"Do you think I was?" he asked innocently.

"I don't know, but it has been no life."

Yaakov Moshe did not react. He seemed to accept, perhaps even to agree, with her assessment.

"Things change," he said.

She looked at him to see if he were joking. Shayna Basya knew how raindrops falling on granite must feel. The drop might flatten out as thin as a reflection or it might splatter into a hundred particles, but either way the water slid off the rock, leaving no trace of the encounter.

"How?" she asked with an increasing sense of futility.

Her husband shrugged casually. So casually, in fact, that one not familiar with his gestures would not have noticed any reaction at all, but Shayna Basya was familiar with the pattern of their encounters—really her interviews with the rebbe. A few sentences, then a few words, then a few gestures, then nothing, and after several moments of silence, Shayna Basya would walk out the door. His silence could be very effective. Shayna Basya had the contradictory feelings that she was alone in the room and at the same time intruding on his privacy, a visitor in a hibernating bear's cave. No, better, a fish in a sleeping frog's pool. Yes, Shayna Basya knew what the children thought of her husband's appearance.

"Yaakov Moshe, you can jump on tables until the Messiah comes, but Rachel Leah marries Yitzhak Weinbach. Do you hear?" Even Shayna Basya could detect no response. She began tapping her foot in frustration. She had been determined to do battle, but he seemed to have won once again by a strategic retreat. His eyelids were lowering like the setting moon, slowly and in response to the earth's irrevocable pull.

She reached over and poked him on his shoulder. She quickly repeated the act and his eyes reopened. To still her trembling hands, she held them tightly together.

"Yaakov Moshe, I have something to tell you," she said. She looked directly into his eyes as if eye contact were some kind of grip that could keep him from slipping away. "Yaakov Moshe, things are not what they seem."

His eyes closed. Her hands released one another and darted across to grasp his lapels. They still trembled as she pulled him toward her. His eyes casually opened.

"Yaakov Moshe," she whispered in selfless fury, "I am Lilith."

Yaakov Moshe made no response to her confession. He nodded faintly. She tightened her grip.

"The Lilith of your dreams!" she added with hot passion, shame, and confession.

"Not tonight, Lilith," her husband said.

"You don't understand. I am Lilith," Shayna Basya rasped.

"Yes, Lilith, of course," the rebbe said, but he did not register surprise.

"Yaakov Moshe, there is no other Lilith. I visited you in the night. I came here to your study."

She saw that her husband was very definitely listening. His hazel eyes stared at her.

"Go now, Lilith. We shall meet another time," he said, but not in boredom.

"No, Yaakov Moshe, it is not Lilith. It is Shayna Basya, and I'm staying to discuss Rachel Leah's match."

He looked slightly confused. "Were you discussing Lilith just now?"

"Yes, Yaakov Moshe, I was discussing Lilith because I have misled you. I let you believe that Lilith was visiting you here in your study at night. I ask your forgiveness for deceiving you, but you must understand that the world is not the way you think it is. Rachel Leah must marry Yitzhak Weinbach."

Shayna Basya turned away in shame. When she was visiting him in the middle of the night, she had enjoyed a sense of triumph at outwitting him. He needed madness, guilt, and passion. She had shared his need for the last and indulged him in the first two as well. All those nights when she returned to her own room, she had flushed with the keen thrill of triumph that comes with outwitting a strange lifelong foe.

Now, however, she had no sense of triumph, just shame. What she had done seemed mean and low. Her head told her that the world had forced her to do it, but her heart told her that it was wrong. She had deceived her husband by taking advantage of—of what? At worst his madness—and at best, his saintliness. Her heart felt like crying, but her head told her that if she did not succeed in rescuing Rachel Leah, she and Rachel Leah both would have the remainder of their days to cry. She turned to face her husband.

He was shaking his head in thought, a slight rocking motion that suggested he was literally weighing something in his mind. His ridiculous obtuse eyes registered a look of surprise that it could possibly have been his curious fate to have been seduced by his own wife. Yaakov Moshe stopped rocking. He did not believe it. The thought that his uninspired, pedestrian wife—so lacking in spirituality, even lacking that small amount that was a woman's portion—should prove to be Lilith struck him as nothing less than ludicrous.

"You were listening at the door when I—struggled with Lilith?" he suggested.

"No, I was lying with you. I was on you when you struggled. I was Lilith," she said.

"It *was* Lilith," he said.

"No, it was me," she said.

"I don't believe you."

Shayna Basya could no longer help herself. She began crying. She neither sobbed nor shuddered, but she should have: the copious tears flooded her eyes and poured down her cheeks. She put her hands to her face, and her fingers waded in the warm stream.

"Why do you think it was you?" he asked.

His question was one of intellectual inquiry, not sympathy. Tears to him—as his wife well knew—represented one more form of bribery. Envelopes stuffed with money, eyes spilling tears—all corrupted judgment. She was trying to confess, and he would not believe her. How could she prove that she had visited him in the night? His arrogance infuriated her all the more. On the nocturnal stage of his desires, no major role could be played by his mere wife. Nothing less than a demonic prototype would meet his expectations. She felt a suffocating wave of horror and had a desire to scream. A screeching blast that would bring all the town into the holy rebbe's study. But what good would that do? They would certainly believe their holy rebbe, not a frail woman. She buried her face deeper into her hands. Her hands knew that she told the truth.

"One should be careful not to slander oneself. One must guard one's tongue," her husband said gently.

"Guard one's tongue?" she mused to herself.

"Yes," he answered.

"It's a little late for that, isn't it? You are the one who starts with the tongue. Unless yours is caressing your 'Lilith of a Thousand Desires,' we could never begin." She said this aloud in lonely despair.

Shayna Basya's weeping face lay buried in the remorseful shelter of her hands and she was unaware that the rebbe had moved until she heard his voice, heavy in anguish and seething with anger. "You, woman, are Lilith!" he rasped.

The voice seemed to be above her. She removed her hands and opened her eyes to see that her husband loomed over her with a hazel feline fury blazing in his eyes. The ferocity of a cornered beast and the savageness of a humiliated man.

"You devil! You she-devil. It was you!" he spat through teeth frozen in fury.

All Shayna Basya could do was nod in agony. She shuddered and began to sob as she saw his hand spring forward toward her.

# CHAPTER TWELVE

Despite his apparent lethargy, the Krimsker Rebbe had been in remarkably good spirits when his wife had entered the study. Her visit had plunged him into angry despair. This was not his first sudden dramatic change of mood on this Tisha B'Av. As he leaped with Itzik Dribble, he had experienced an ease that he had thought lost forever. An ease based on honesty and kindness. Since the Destruction, prophecy had been given to fools and children. It was true that one teacher in the Talmud believed that prophecy had been given to the wise, but the Krimsker Rebbe, based on his own experience as a wise man, knew that to be absurd.

When Itzik Dribble dashed to his side, the rebbe welcomed the prophet. Itzik Dribble had all the necessary qualities: he was both a child and a fool. Hadn't the wispy blond dunce divined that the rebbe was a frog? Yaakov Moshe did not believe that a fool was divine, but he was convinced that a fool truly reflected the post-Destruction world. Certainly since the Temple burned and the Jews went into exile it had become a fool's world.

The rebbe believed that his foolish act of leaping on the tabletop was honest testimony. Since he believed that he had once been a frog, there was the added honesty of a public confession in front of his hasidim. How else could Yaakov Moshe have witnessed the Emperor Napoleon—that modern pharaoh—crossing the River Nedd? It was not a fish's-eye view; it had been a frog's eye that had seen so clearly through the blue waters and the blue air to the emperor's blue uniform. Fish could see only in the water, not in the air. The real proof was from the Torah. The delicate oblong fish was the silver-scaled symbol of good fortune, dwelling only in the water where the evil spirits cannot penetrate. The fish, too, his eye forever open, never falls victim to the evil eye. It was the blinking, croaking frog, one of the eight creeping impurities, who understood pharaoh's rapacious passion, and Lilith's, too. The amphibious hibernator, impure in two realms, asleep in the mud or hopping like a meshuggener.

As the rebbe hopped like a madman, he experienced a calm sense of fulfillment. This led him to tell Itzik the story of Rabbi Chanina and the miraculous frog.

Then the rebbe and his congregants soared in prayer. Yaakov Moshe carried them to great spiritual heights, and in response they carried him even further, as if he and his hasidim were two wings of one great, noble eagle. For the first time in his life as rebbe, he experienced a relationship with his hasidim as one between the loved and the beloved, each giving and receiving to create a union that went beyond their individual talents. From this heady nectar of exaltation, the Krimsker Rebbe tasted the bitter gall of Tisha B'Av. He realized what had been lost: Israel's holy union with the Divine Presence, and prophecy among the nobles. Those passionate worldly and divine unions that only the Holy Temple could effect. It was then that he sank onto his mourner's bench in tears.

The rebbe, who could not remember tears, found himself bawling and found it the most natural thing. Through the ease of his soul's outpouring, he felt comforted. Yaakov Moshe recognized the penitent source of his comfort. Then Itzik Dribble came to him for the second time and profaned the name of the Messiah. The rebbe had said Lamentations in response, and he had meant it. In spiritless lethargy he sat through the reading, and then he had dragged himself to his study.

He heard a voice and thought that Lilith, his old seductress of his lonely nights, was attempting to frustrate him further. When the voice spoke to him about a horse's backside, he finally looked up to discover Boruch Levi. And Boruch Levi brought the most wonderful news about Grannie Zara, may her name be erased forever.

From the moment he had arrived in Krimsk, the rebbe knew that he was involved in mortal combat with the witch of Krimichak. She ruled the Jews of Krimsk. Even among his own hasidim, pregnant wives furtively sought out the witch to forestall any miscarriage or birth defect. The Krimsker Rebbe struggled unceasingly to convince the Jews that the witch had no cures; rather, she herself was the disease. Grannie Zara, as representatives of the Other Side often do, masqueraded as a life force. Before the rebbe had arrived, she had saved both Krimsk and Krimichak from certain destruction. How could he convince the common folk that the legions she had dispersed had arrived at her command? How could he convince them that there is a fate worse than a Cossack pogrom? If we make ourselves impure by running to witches, then we lose both worlds, this one and the World to Come.

Losing the World to Come was a terrible thought. This depressing world of burdens and woe did not have much to offer the Jew. The rebbe understood that the reason for this lay in its very genesis. When God was considering creating man, the angels argued furiously among themselves. Mercy said, "Man will be merciful and act mercifully," but Truth said, "Man will be false and act falsely." Righteousness said, "Man will be righteous and act righteously," but Peace said, "Man will be quarrelsome." And what did God do? He took truth and flung it into the ground and created man.

The rebbe understood that man's very creation was posited on the absence of truth. If God had buried truth to create man, what hope did the Krimsker Rebbe have of persuading Krimsk that in Krimichak dwelled a Satanic illusion of life? The more he pleaded, the more quickly they melted into the forest toward her abysmal cat-filled cottage.

His very soldiers deserted to her camp. Her home itself was a very picture of deceit. Her cottage, neat and clean; her person, energetic and warm. The Krimsker Rebbe knew that he was a messy, fractious sort. How was he successfully to do battle against such a diabolical, devious antagonist? Oh, how he yearned for a true pharaoh—mighty and obvious in his cruelty. Pharaoh, honest and unrepentant, courageous and true in his evil, not hiding behind the skirts of kindness and health! Plague after plague, the mighty pharaoh spat in God's eye. Against him a Moses, half Yaakov Moshe's namesake, could stand steadfast and demand that he let the Jews go, but what could Yaakov Moshe do against a lovable old lady who saved the Children of Israel from Cossacks and women from miscarriages? The Krimsker Rebbe was at a loss.

Yaakov Moshe pictured the witch and himself locked in indecisive struggle, like Jacob and the angel. As months stretched into years, they remained tightly clutching one another, and Yaakov Moshe despaired of morning's arrival, when Esau's angel would have to flee and Jacob would be called "Israel," his reward for having successfully struggled with an angel of the Lord.

Yaakov Moshe had attempted to retreat from the struggle, but he could not. God seemed more abstract, and evil seemed more real. In the solitary depths of his study, he felt the witch's embrace. He smelled her breath, and at night she sent him Lilith, Samael's wife, the Queen of Zmargad. Lilith with her long hair entered when he was asleep and aroused him. She covered him with her caresses, and he responded. The nights when Lilith did not visit were the worst, for he longed for her with a bitter, burning bile, awakening in the night and tossing until morning. And after her visits, no polluted remnants remained. Clearly, Lilith was robbing him of his seed to create hordes of demons and spirits.

Yaakov Moshe realized that the struggle would not go on forever. He realized that, as with the patriarch Jacob, the other half of his namesake, he had to give himself totally to the contest. Had the patriarch failed, all the world of good would have been destroyed. Yaakov Moshe saw in that struggle the parallel for his own merciless encounter. The patriarch had to overcome Esau's angel at Esau's own forte, violence. Grannie Zara's weapon was deceit: death posed as life; impurity as purity; evil as good. So Yaakov Moshe had to risk his life in the world of impurity to overcome the witch. They were two deceitful creatures trying to suck the vital force from one another. Would Grannie Zara, saving Jews, choke on good before the Krimsker Rebbe, flaming with passion, would rot with evil?

The Krimsker Rebbe had lusted with such passion that his soul might have withered in shame. The Talmud taught the primacy of intention—a transgression in the name of Heaven is better than a good deed performed mindlessly. In a perverse universe of reversals, with truth in the ground, only the Jews who stood at Mount Sinai could have worshiped the golden calf, and only the pure Jacob could have stolen his brother's birthright and his father's blessing.

The Krimsker Rebbe plunged deeper and deeper into his supreme struggle. He concentrated upon the defeat of evil, swallowing it whole and rendering it harmless inside his very own body. One day his daughter Rachel Leah brought him his supper and innocently asked why he was doing this to himself, and he answered, "I am giving my life for God and his Torah." Rachel Leah's eyes brimmed with tears. "God bless you," she said. As she closed the door, the Krimsker Rebbe knew that through his foolish boast, the struggle was over. He had lost, and all his nights had been spent in sin. Perceiving the failure of his exile, he ended it on Tisha B'Av.

Tisha B'Av was the day the Krimsker Rebbe understood. The rebbe was most relaxed during the worst of times. He knew that it is easier to mourn than to serve through happiness. Yaakov Moshe was prepared to mourn, but he furtively harbored the hope that since he had admitted defeat, he might not be defeated.

As he entered the beis midrash, he was in search of honesty. Honesty brought him to the tabletop, to the floor, to his study, and to Boruch Levi, who had given him the incredible news that the witch of Krimichak had died. In victory the rebbe was exultant. He celebrated by sending his sexton, Reb Yechezkal, for Yechiel Katzman. It was time for Rachel Leah to stand under a wedding canopy, and the rebbe hurried to exploit the propitious hour.

According to the rebbe's calculations, precisely at the moment he had decided to return to the world, the witch had died. Just as the rebbe had suspected, they had been locked in a deadly duet, and at the eleventh hour he had triumphed when he was admitting defeat. Only he knew how weary that witch—may she burn in hell—must have been after all their years of struggle. Israel had struggled with Lilith and bested the Queen of Zmargard. Or so the Krimsker Rebbe had thought until his wife had enlightened him. Yaakov Moshe had not been struggling with the long-haired Lilith after all, but with his own petty, shrewish wife, Shayna Basya.

No man likes to be made a fool of. Least of all a rebbe, and least of all the Krimsker Rebbe. He had withdrawn from the foolish, frail, ephemeral world, risking, he had imagined, his very own soul, only to have his own foolish frail wife seduce him nightly in the guise of an ephemeral spirit. He would cry, "Lilith of a Thousand Desires, Samael's Queen, Unclean Beast," and a host of other names too foolish to be believed while Shayna Basya Grosbart from Bezin flipped around on top of him like a carp breathing its last in a fishmonger's stall! She had made a mockery of his life.

Yaakov Moshe had imagined that he was in the desert wandering along like Moses at the moment he saw the burning bush. Now he knew that he might as well have crawled into his wife's bed for five years. To think that he had accused Grannie Zara of hiding behind skirts! Where was he all those years? Hiding under his wife and screaming about the devil! At least there remained one giant in Krimsk—Grannie Zara.

He was overwhelmed by the desire to hurt Shayna Basya. He wanted to humiliate her in her nakedness the way she had humiliated him.

# CHAPTER THIRTEEN

SHAYNA BASYA WAS SITTING ON THE COUCH, AND THE Krimsker Rebbe was glowering over her. Blinded by rage, he struck an inexact blow. His openhanded slap glanced off her head, dislodging her matron's wig. The limp brown object gathered itself into a lump on the wall, where it seemed to hang for a moment like a spineless little hairy beast and then fell to the floor, revealing itself as a lifeless sham. The Krimsker Rebbe didn't follow its journey past the wall, and it came into Shayna Basya's field of vision only when it was on the floor. She made no move to retrieve it. Shayna Basya felt as if she were a hairy rag whose place was on the floor. Seeing herself there seemed to give her strength. She turned to face her irate husband.

"I beg the rebbe's forgiveness," she said.

He did not respond.

"I have betrayed the rebbe," she added.

"Betrayed the rebbe?" he repeated as if he were in another world.

"Yes," she said. "The rebbe did what he had to do, and

I carried on like a wagon driver's wife. It wasn't right. I ask your forgiveness. It was all my fault."

She continued to look at her husband, even though tears sprang into her eyes. His hand lay limply at his side, and he wore a distant expression.

The Krimsker Rebbe was indeed in another world. Yaakov Moshe had the sense of having been through this before. This was Boruch Levi accepting responsibility and asking forgiveness. Down to the detail of the wagon driver. And Yaakov Moshe had asked the wagon driver for forgiveness! Why in the world, the Krimsker Rebbe wondered, was he striking his own wife? He searched his mind for what he had told Boruch Levi.

"Enough," the rebbe said aloud, repeating his earlier conversation. "You are forgiven and I ask your forgiveness."

"My forgiveness?" Shayna Basya asked in quiet amazement, as Boruch Levi had.

"Yes, yours. If the shepherd does not remove the stone from the well, then the flock must drink where it can. Shayna Basya, I ask your forgiveness."

Shayna Basya looked at her husband, who still seemed to be in another world. But in all the years of their marriage they had never inhabited the same world.

"No, no, Yaakov Moshe, you must forgive me," she implored, and as she continued to cry, she quickly turned away, for she felt naked and ugly in his eyes. Now he was asking her forgiveness after she had so thoroughly humiliated him. She saw her matron's wig lying on the floor and wanted to put it back in place to hide her disheveled hair. As she moved toward the edge of the couch, her husband's hand intercepted her. His gentle, awkward touch on her naked hair seemed like a kiss, and she flamed crimson in shame. She tried to push past it to retrieve her wig, but the gentle contact proved insistent and guided her to look up into his face.

"Yes, it is you, my Shayna Basya of a Thousand Desires," he said softly, and he kissed her with a darting tongue. As he embraced her in his arms, she felt all the strength and enthusiasm that he had lavished on Lilith. She had already begun to respond in a rush of passion before his lips had even touched hers. When she heard him say, "My Shayna Basya," her face flushed even more—like that of a young bride on her wedding night.

Shayna Basya knew that she was competing against herself. She wanted to generate, at the very least, the passion with her husband, Yaakov Moshe, that the succubus Lilith had generated with the holy recluse, the Krimsker Rebbe. Maintaining contact with her lips, she ceased embracing Yaakov Moshe's neck. As she unbuttoned him, he began to unbutton her. In no time whatsoever, they stood clinging together like one body that had sprung full-grown from the pile of clothing encompassing their feet. Yaakov Moshe motioned to his wife to move onto the couch. Shayna Basya pulled away to blow out the kerosene lamp, but with the lightest touch, he restrained her.

"No, my angel-wife. We have done it in the dark for too long."

At those words, Shayna Basya spun back to him with a fervor and commitment that a "she-devil" could never generate. No sooner had Yaakov Moshe touched the couch than she was upon him with an assault upon his most private self that left him gasping. Shayna Basya hovered above him, and he swept upward to return the kisses. He continued to enact their love with Shayna Basya's name. He plunged into her, kissing with his penetrating tongue, and withdrew gasping for breath to call her by her rightful name—but the ritual name at this point was "Unclean Beast," and he hesitated for a second. She lowered her face to his ear and rasped, "Clean, my husband. Clean, always with you, clean."

With a sudden force, he flung her up and forward, calling hoarsely, "Clean Beast," as he returned to caress the source of her cleanliness and purity. Experiencing agonies of delight, she pulled away from his kisses and, reaching below, guided him into her. As they writhed in love, he called her Queen of Krimsk instead of Queen of Zmargard and Samael's Wife. Shayna Basya, resplendent in love, repeated only her husband's name—"Yaakov Moshe, Yaakov Moshe" and thought of nothing else.

Yaakov Moshe, too, was competing against himself, the false self of their earlier false performances. The Temple had been destroyed because of two wicks in one lamp, and the Krimsker Rebbe had been guilty of something similar; one wick in two lamps. It was even a sin to make love to one's own wife and to think of another woman. How much guiltier he had been in debasing his own wife by calling her the devil Lilith.

The Krimsker Rebbe was thinking of other things, too. From the day the Temple was destroyed, the spice of sex was taken from man and wife and given to transgressors. The Temple had effected the holy union between the divine and man's world upon which the holy union of marriage depended. With the Temple's destruction, only the complete union with sin remained. Rebbe and rebbetzin as man and wife were not transgressors. The rebbe intended this act of love to redeem their previous encounters as false transgressors. He continually called Shayna Basya "Clean Beast" as she tore at his lip and tongue. She easily surpassed her performance as Lilith. Yaakov Moshe felt that he was falling. He emphasized the word "beast" and thrust with a fury that would have done justice to any transgressor.

He hoped that his sexual union was to end all transgression. The Messiah was to be born on Tisha B'Av. No doubt this was metaphoric. The rebbe understood that conception and birth were equivalent. The Krimsker Rebbe had not fulfilled the commandment to be fruitful and multiply. He had fathered Rachel Leah, and he had fathered a son who died, but to fulfill the commandment properly, he needed both a living daughter and a living son. With the incredible progression from impure to pure in the events of this Tisha B'Av, culminating in Shayna Basya's pure movements upon him, he sensed that this was the most propitious of moments for Israel, for him, and for his family.

He had sent the sexton to bring the groom for Rachel Leah, but now he realized that the moment offered opportunities far beyond marrying his daughter to a local talmudist. The Krimsker Rebbe himself was to fulfill that most basic and first of all commandments, to be fruitful and multiply. What would be more appropriate than the messianic era beginning with the first of all the six hundred and thirteen commandments?

The Krimsker Rebbe closed his eyes and tried to attain his wife's impassioned rhythms. He knew that he should not think of the child's name, but precisely that thought kept coming to mind. It spurred him on to the inflamed ardor that rivaled his love with Lilith. He thought of their son's name, Emmanuel, and sought to accomplish in purity with his wife what no one had ever accomplished before. And he succeeded in bursting through into a world no less enchanting, no less passionate, no less exhilarating, no less exhausting, no less complete than that of the transgressors. And, certainly for Shayna Basya, more spicy than Lilith ever held upon her dark, moist, receptive tongue.

# CHAPTER FOURTEEN

Reb Yechezkal stood outside the beis midrash and observed Krimsk flowing by, but he did not see Yechiel Katzman. No one asked whom he was looking for, and he asked no one if he had seen Yechiel. Everything Reb Yechezkal had done for the Krimsker Rebbe, he had executed in the strictest confidence. Krimsk understood and appreciated that. As Reb Yechezkal stood reviewing the marching crowd, he felt a surge of pride that everyone knew that he represented the Krimsker Rebbe. Reb Yechezkal partially repented of this inflated feeling. Insofar as it represented the majesty of the Torah in the person of the rebbe himself, he felt perfectly justified in his pride. Insofar as it represented Reb Yechezkal's vanity, he felt that it was reprehensible and inappropriate, especially on a day of mourning. These concerns, however, were not paramount; locating Yechiel Katzman was. When he began to notice the same faces passing before him for the second time and he still had not seen Yechiel, he decided to try the Katzman home.

He joined the crowd as it circled away from the beis midrash in the direction of the forest. Everyone nodded to him with an almost conspiratorial glee that seemed to say, Yes, we know that the rebbe has returned, and you are doing his sacred bidding. Reb Yechezkal maintained a serious demeanor, but in his heart he shared their joy and their desire to savor it with the community, so he continued to nod seriously, almost ponderously, to almost every Jew who looked his way. His head moved up and down almost constantly, and as much as he enjoyed it, it tired him and he was relieved to turn off the main street into the lane where the Katzmans lived.

Reb Nachman Leib Katzman mended shoes, boots, bridles, and harnesses in a small front room of the low building. In the back lived the family—Nachman Leib, his wife, Hinda, and their four children. Yechiel, their oldest, had escaped the workshop through his considerable intellectual talents. Reb Yechezkal, as many other townspeople, took delight in Yechiel's success. Nachman Leib and Hinda were simple, hardworking people who were always courteous to all who entered their shop or home.

Yechiel was the apple of their eye. Every parent wanted a son to stand and say kaddish for him after "a hundred and twenty years," but the merits of such a great talmudist's kaddish must be incalculable. Nachman Leib was a very fortunate man, and if he were to become the Krimsker Rebbe's in-law and, presumably, the father of the next Krimsker Rebbe, well then, what could possibly be left for him in the World to Come after enjoying such rewards right here in Krimsk? There was no envy in Reb Yechezkal. Yechiel was a fine scholar, and although not as simple as his father—how could he be with his knowledge?—he was equally distant from vanity.

Reb Yechezkal should have been very happy about his mission, but he approached the leatherworker's low home with misgivings. He slowed his pace in the shadows that hid the uneven dirt path beneath his feet. Reb Yechezkal was afraid of other shadows. He was worried that Nachman Leib and his family might be severely embarrassed before the episode was over. After all, Rachel Leah was already engaged to Yitzhak Weinbach, a man not to Reb Yechezkal's tastes, but a man not easily given to graceful withdrawal. A man not given to learning either. The Katzmans would be humiliated because of their poverty, and this greatly distressed Reb Yechezkal. It upset him for the basic reason that it was just plain wrong, but it deeply disturbed him because of the Krimsker Rebbe's principles. The Krimsker Rebbe, almost alone among the important rebbes, had never let money influence him. The most famous case concerned the Angel of Death synagogue, but that was only the most famous. Anyone who came to pray in the Krimsker beis midrash knew that the rich would not be favored over the poor—or the poor over the rich. On the latter point, the rebbe had been very explicit with his sexton many years ago: it is as unjust to favor the poor, the unhappy, the lonely, as it is to discriminate against them.

If this policy had kept the Krimsker beis midrash poorer than those of the other rebbes, it had also kept it purer and more respected. The hasidim, though few in number, were loyal and had no illusions about why they came to the Krimsker Rebbe. He would not flatter them; he would not tell them what they wanted to hear; he often did not acknowledge them. One wag from a distant, glamorous hasidic court in Galicia spent a Sabbath in Krimsk and, as he was leaving, remarked that it was a good thing that the Jews of Krimsk took their petitions directly to the Holy One, otherwise they would never get any response. He added that what worried him most was the possibility that the Holy One might take his petitions to the Krimsker Rebbe, because there was no chance that the rebbe could be influenced, much less bribed.

As Reb Yechezkal approached the door, he hoped that the rebbetzin had kept her word and had gone to the rebbe's study as she had said she would. If the rebbetzin and the rebbe were in agreement, things would certainly reach a satisfactory conclusion.

When Nachman Leib told Reb Yechezkal that his son had gone out almost immediately after they had returned from the beis midrash, Reb Yechezkal was relieved. The more time the rebbetzin had to speak with the rebbe, the better it would be. Reb Yechezkal did not press the matter; he simply mentioned that the Krimsker Rebbe wished to see Yechiel. The urgency of the matter did not need to be impressed upon Nachman Leib, however. The fact that the holy rebbe wanted to see Yechiel was in itself a majestic summons. Yechiel's absence embarrassed Nachman Leib. He assured Reb Yechezkal that Yechiel would go to the rebbe as soon as he came home. Reb Yechezkal, disguising his own feelings, assured him that that would be fine. He said good evening and turned to leave.

Nachman Leib held the door open for him, throwing a weak, flickering beam of light onto the uneven surface of the lane. It did help, but Reb Yechezkal concentrated on his footing and did not look up until he had reached the street. He quickly composed himself for the veritable flood of greetings that he expected to encounter. When he did look up, expecting to find a sea of approving, almost worshipful faces, he could not understand what had happened. The street was deserted. For a brief second the thought flitted through his mind that without realizing it, he had spent the night at Nachman Leib's. There were many hasidic tales in which such things happened: a man closes his eyes for a moment and opens them to find the sun blazing down on the world.

But Reb Yechezkal had no memory of having closed his eyes. He could recall the entirety of their brief conversation. Not more than ten minutes had passed since he turned off the main street. In that time the flowing throng, nearly all of Krimsk, had disappeared. As curious as it all was, Reb Yechezkal was not overly concerned. Had anything catastrophic occurred, he and Nachman Leib surely would have heard the accompanying shouts. Standing near the door, they had heard nothing. On some vague level, he supposed there was justice in his not receiving admiring glances as he returned to the beis midrash. He had violated the spirit if not the letter of his mission. He had neither found nor wished to find Yechiel Katzman—at least not immediately. As he walked in solitude, he thought he detected that the air was slightly cooler than it had been, but he paid no heed to such frivolity.

He strode purposefully into the beis midrash and threaded his way down the rough aisle between the overturned benches until he reached his own bench. He sat and began to recite the compilation of penitential laments and prayers for the night of Tisha B'Av, but his mind was far from their anguished refrains. He positioned himself so that he could see the study door. If Yechiel did not arrive within a half hour, then he would knock on the door and explain that he could not locate the boy. As he glanced at the rebbe's door, he was curious as to how the rebbetzin was faring with the rebbe. No one had told him why the streets were empty, but as he stared at the rebbe's study door, the outside world held no interest for him at all.

# CHAPTER FIFTEEN

AFTER CALMLY WAITING UNTIL THE FRAMED SHAFT OF light ceased to illuminate Reb Yechezkal's path, Nachman Leib quietly closed the door and then hurried to the room immediately behind the shop, where he met his wife, Hinda, who wore an expression of grave concern.

"What are we going to do?" she asked shrilly.

"*Nu,* wake young Shraga," her husband said.

"How would he know where Yechiel is?" she asked in desperation.

"*Nu,* just wake him and bring him to me," her husband insisted.

She did as he asked, and soon Shraga stood before them, rubbing his sleep-filled eyes. He looked up at his father.

"Shraga, are you awake?"

Nachman Leib gently placed his hand on the boy's shoulder. Although thirteen, the boy had not yet matured physically and was short for his age.

"What?" Shraga said, but he had heard his father's voice, and although he continued to rub his eyes, he did so differently, more vigorously, as if trying to push sleep from them.

His father, noticing his efforts, said, "It's all right." Had it not been Tisha B'Av, Nachman Leib would have kissed him. Shraga was always willing to help, and so many burdens seemed to find their way to him. Tonight as usual his small, discolored, and calloused fingers eagerly executed his father's instructions.

Every day by his side in the workroom Shraga mended shoes, patched harnesses, replaced bridle straps. He put all his undersized body's weight behind the sharp gouging awl and the biting leather punch, and most difficult of all, he forced the large needles through the hard-baked, weather-beaten leather in regular stitches. Nachman Leib tried to reserve the more difficult tasks for himself, but there was so much to do.

For himself, Nachman Leib was satisfied with his share, but when he saw Shraga bruising his young fingers on a broken harness, the air seemed thick and stifling. He would rise from his bench and step outside to breathe the fresh air, but even that was not satisfactory. He would turn to see Shraga slaving inside, and the father would feel as if he had deserted his young, good-hearted son to his immutable, squinting, secondhand fate, stiff and unyielding as the used leather.

What was it the peasants said about their cracked and torn harnesses? "It's easy enough to kill them, but it's another matter to bury them." They couldn't afford to bury them, so they brought their ceremonially dead objects to the shop to be renewed. Until late in the night Nachman

Leib and Shraga cut, tore, twisted, glued, stitched, nailed, and wrestled them back into usefulness. Nachman Leib did it all resolutely, but he was haunted by the image of Shraga placing his own young son next to him on the workbench.

If the Messiah were to arrive in Krimsk, Nachman Leib would not waste time in welcoming him. But what if the Messiah decreed that the first order of business was to fix everyone's shoes? Nachman Leib smiled to himself: all the rebbes would suddenly present themselves as shoemakers, their pale, soft hands resting on their spotless, unsoiled aprons. Well, not quite all. The Krimsker Rebbe wouldn't. He would simply take off his shoes and humbly get into line.

In past years, Nachman Leib had noticed on many occasions that the rebbe's shoes always needed repair. Earlier in the evening he had instinctively looked at the rebbe's feet, but the rebbe had entered in stockings. In five years the rebbetzin had not sent him the rebbe's shoes once. The leather body was probably in bad shape, especially if the splashing everyone heard really was from Miriam's well. There is nothing harder on leather than water.

Nachman thought of the rebbe leaping in his stocking feet with Itzik Dribble, and he was overcome by desire to send Yechiel to see the rebbe as soon as possible. He felt his calm resignation deserting him as he pictured the rebbe pounding up and down on the table. Yechiel was thought to be his blessing, his joy, his assurance of post-earthly delights. The boy's grandmother, however, had been correct in pronouncing "Little children, little problems; big children, big problems."

"Shraga, are you listening?" The boy nodded. "Go to the watchman's house at the Soffer match factory and tell Barasch Limp Legs that Yechiel must come home immediately."

Shraga slid out of his father's grasp and slipped out the door. "Barasch Limp Legs?" Hinda mused in a puzzled whisper. She turned to her husband for an explanation.

"Yes." Nachman Leib nodded with a sad certainty that kept Hinda from pursuing the subject.

# CHAPTER SIXTEEN

NACHMAN LEIB HAD GUESSED CORRECTLY. YECHIEL HAD left for Barasch's home at the match factory as soon as the beis midrash services had finished. He was confused, and there he could feel most comfortable with his uncertainties. Barasch's home, however, had its limitations, too. Yechiel knew that he would be welcome only as long as the socialist revolutionaries who met there thought that he would become one of them. Everyone demanded belief—that one item that Yechiel did not have in abundance.

Barasch himself passionately espoused social revolutionary views. Yechiel was not very impressed with the social revolutionaries, if for no other reason than that Barasch himself was one. Although the cripple was a warm, generous host, he was not to be taken seriously. Not intellectually, at any rate. Yechiel appreciated him for what he was: the sexton of Krimsk's modern, heretical congregation of unbelievers. In his way, he was as conscientious as Reb Yechezkal in the Krimsker beis midrash or Reb Zelig in the Angel of Death. Barasch as heretic sexton suffered from a serious problem. He had no rebbe, and he himself, although not of rabbinic stature, was forced to lecture and teach. Yechiel was aware that technically Reb Zelig had no rebbe as well, but that situation was entirely different. Reb Zelig, Yechiel was willing to argue, did have the Krimsker Rebbe for his spiritual mentor. The Krimsker Rebbe, after all, had determined the fate of the Angel of Death, and Reb Zelig had accepted that decree willingly and without complaint.

The ameliorating aspect of Barasch's uncomfortable rabbinate was the small number of congregants. Counting both Yechiel and Barasch, there were only three altogether. Reb Yudel Zaks was the third.

Yudel had introduced Yechiel to Spinoza and the modern world, but Yudel was quite literally a fish out of water. He wasn't a hasid, which might have been understandable, but in addition he was from Lithuania, which was unforgivable. He was the only Litvak for miles around. He and his wife had come to Krimsk to inherit a small lumberyard his wife's cousin had left to them. No one in Krimsk ever understood how a hasidic girl could have married a Litvak, and before anyone became sufficiently friendly with her to find out, she died. Yudel, or as he was known, "the Litvak," stayed on. He made a respectable livelihood but suffered from boredom in the hasidic backwater. A talented intellectual with a gift for analysis, he had tutored Yechiel well. Yechiel knew him to be precise but weak conceptually—a man who could understand and explain systems but never create his own.

Their relationship never developed beyond the academic, and the highly rarefied academic at that. At one time Yechiel had hoped that it would. Yudel, too, after all, was very much alone in Krimsk. He made no close friends, and although he passed as religiously observant—Yechiel to this day was uncertain as to what Yudel did or did not observe—as a Litvak he did not participate in the religious life of the hasidim. The real problem with Yudel was that he was a cold fish. He had no need for other people and was altogether without passion. Whereas Barasch affectionately fancied Krimsk to be the Jewish proletariat, Yudel disdainfully scorned them as a primitive tribe of idolators. Yechiel was offended by this disdain for a community that supported him.

Yudel attended Barasch's radical gatherings out of boredom. He did enjoy the occasional discussion with some of Barasch's underground visitors, members of the various illegal organizations who stopped at the willing host's to rest. Some were simple fugitives, but others were intellectual leaders in the revolutionary ferment that was stirring all of Russia—except for Krimsk, of course. It seemed merely to pass through Krimsk without leaving any impression, much as Napoleon had.

The night of Tisha B'Av, Yechiel found himself walking toward the match factory the way Yudel did; there was nowhere else for him to go. Before attending the beis midrash with his father and young Shraga, he had sustained himself with the idea of escaping to Barasch's after suffering through the services.

Rabbi Eliezer and Rabbi Yehoshua weighed heavily on his mind. The idea of priestly tithes seemed nonsensical, and the idea of not saving the group of women by sacrificing one seemed immoral. And not just immoral insofar as the group of women was concerned; immoral in the greater sense that such stiff-necked inability to adapt to a social reality seemed to be the essence of the stifling, parochial vigilance that characterized the life of Krimsk.

Now that he found himself approaching his destination, however, he was in no great hurry because of the Krimsker Rebbe. Yechiel had been amazed and impressed by the rebbe's performance. The rebbe's humility and humanity overwhelmed Yechiel. He simply could not imagine a Rabbi Eliezer or a Rabbi Yehoshua showing such kindness and attention to an Itzik Dribble. Yechiel felt ashamed at having thought that the rebbe was the captain of the Ship of the Dead. Who could be more alive and loving than Yaakov Moshe Finebaum, who leaped on a tabletop in order to help a retarded child pray on Tisha B'Av? Who would have believed such a thing possible? Certainly not Yechiel, and as honest as Yechiel was, he knew that such an admission opened a floodgate of possibilities. Spinoza or not, priestly tithes or not, the tradition was alive and kicking—quite literally leaping on tables—right here in his own backward Krimsk.

No, he didn't want to be on the road to Barasch Limp Legs; he wanted to speak to the Krimsker Rebbe, but he had no idea such a thing was possible. Such a compassionate man would certainly understand Yechiel's agony and uncertainty. After all, the rebbe had interrupted the Tisha B'Av services with a wild, childish fairy tale to meet the needs of a troubled idiot. Yechiel had no doubts that the rebbe never believed such nonsense about a talking frog. He had read some of the rebbe's writings. They were first-rate intellectual achievements. Whatever else he was, the rebbe was as brilliant a creative mind as his hasidim believed him to be.

Yechiel entered the gate of the match factory, walked around the cavernous main building to the rebuilt shed that housed the live-in watchman, and lightly tapped the coded knock. Barasch responded, and Yechiel opened the door to the large, brightly lit room.

Barasch was seated in his usual easy chair at the head of a long plank table. On one side sat Yudel, already looking bored. Barasch waved his new guest to a place opposite Yudel. Yechiel noticed someone sleeping in the bed near the table but could not tell whether or not he knew him. Yechiel preferred to be able to see everyone in the room.

"No, I might wake him," Yechiel said as he sat down next to Yudel.

"Not the way they sleep," Barasch said. He pointed to the wine bottle and glasses in front of him. Yechiel noticed that Yudel was drinking on the fast day. Yechiel just shook his head.

He sat back and examined the sleeping figure to see whether he recognized him, but he could see no more than the man's back. Like all of Barasch's shadow visitors, he slept with his heavy boots on. This always struck Yechiel as absolutely uncivilized, revolution or not. Sleeping with filthy boots disabused Yechiel of whatever romantic notions of revolution he might have harbored. Why didn't they remove them when they slept in a bed? Aware that he was not paying attention to those who were awake, he turned to focus on his host.

From Yechiel's seat on a straight-backed rickety chair, Barasch's large, horsey head seemed to loll as if he were grazing on the table. From this curious oblique position, Barasch directed the discussion, an exercise that Yechiel suspected was staged for his benefit. Not that the positions argued were not sincere, but the entrance of Yechiel in his long black gabardine coat seemed to have abruptly switched the topic of conversation. They were now arguing the merits of various social ideologies. It was as if they were salesmen displaying the latest fashions before the customer, who wore an ancient ill-fitting garment that would certainly have to be replaced.

"No, Yechiel, Yudel is wrong," Barasch Limp Legs was saying. "Yudel doesn't understand the true nature of the Russian commune. It is the essence of the people. You don't go and ignore something like that. Labor should be meaningful. The commune must be transformed into a meaningful socialist form, both moral and democratic."

Yudel, a short, wiry, fifty-year-old man, chewed on the ragged edges of his gray beard. He did not disguise the fact that he considered their host a dull reflection of very distant lights that barely flickered even before Barasch added his own dimming distortions. Yechiel realized that Yudel, the man who had introduced him to Spinoza and Darwin, had abandoned the discussion out of boredom.

"Moral and democratic?" Yechiel politely queried.

"Yes." Barasch smiled and turned his head almost flat on the table as if offering himself in some sacrificial rite.

"Then how can you defend the Social Revolutionary Combat Group? Were the political assassinations of Bogolopov and Sipyagin moral and democratic?" Yechiel challenged.

"Yes, of course they were moral, or the Combat Group would never have permitted them. As for democratic, the central committee raised no objection, and they represent the people's interests."

"But then your commune in its meaningful moral and democratic transformation would be nothing but a gang of murderers," Yudel said sarcastically, the edges of his beard still floating in his mouth.

Barasch lifted his unsmiling head from the tabletop to an almost normal vertical position. His eyes blinked as if he had been stunned by an unfair blow.

"Yudel, surely you understand the necessity of revolutionary action?" Barasch asked, but he really could not defend his statement. Not to Yudel, who would twist his words around like a talmudist until everything stood on its head.

"Assassination may be the queen of the revolutionary arts, but that doesn't make it moral or democratic," Yudel answered with a weariness inspired by the knowledge that Barasch could appreciate neither his own nor Yudel's position.

The reclining figure on the bed stirred, stretched, and rolled over. Suddenly it sat up, revealing an unshaven young man in his early to mid-twenties whose rumpled clothes badly needed a wash. His face, however, was alert and without the least trace of the exhaustion that one would expect to see on someone who had been traveling hard with few resources. He swung his shabby boots across the bed onto the floor. Facing Yudel and Yechiel, he announced, "He's right, you know," in a confident and natural manner that Yechiel liked at once.

Yechiel warmly welcomed to the conversation someone

nearer to his own age. Someone who neither limped nor had a ragged beard; someone who radiated good health, energy, and enthusiasm.

"He is?" Yechiel asked in honest curiosity, which encouraged the stranger to continue.

"Of course he is. You can't make an omelette without breaking eggs. Look, God needed ten plagues to get the Jews out of Egypt, and when he killed the firstborn, he killed indiscriminately. Surely pharaoh was no more tyrannical than the tsar, but in several thousand years, it is we slaves who have advanced. We kill only our taskmasters. And we shall no more become a gang of murderers than the Jews did. If we execute proven murderers of the proletariat, then we are only protecting ourselves, and that is moral and democratic."

Yechiel warmed to this impassioned exhortation. Yudel, too, was taking notice; his beard no longer dangled from his mouth.

"Let us assume the rabbi's recipe for omelette is kosher," Yudel said in mild sarcasm as he warmed to invective. "The God of the Exodus exercised Divine Right, and he took the Jews out of Egypt to give them the Divine Law, the Torah. What is the name of your God, and where is he taking us?"

The young man accepted Yudel's chiding tone. He had a sense of dedication and an exuberance that gave him a tremendous amount of self-confidence. He moved over to the table and took a seat across from Yechiel and Yudel. He reached for the wine, and as he poured himself a full glass, he was already holding forth.

"Ah, yes. I know our people are afraid of blood except for circumcisions, of course. That useless snip is cheered and praised. A futile wound is blessed, but if the body is diseased, then the surgeon must cut and everyone shrieks 'murderer!' Never mind he must cut off an arm to save the entire body. And there is a social organism, too. Sometimes you may have to sacrifice a little to save a lot, but that is shocking when everything is static and sacrosanct. All you do is cry. You cannot resist evil. Who gives you the right, everyone screams, to take any life? All those I am saving give me the right. Society gives me the right. The party gives me the right."

He paused to sip his drink. Yechiel listened attentively. It was as if this stranger had attended Reb Gedaliah's class and knew Yechiel's most intimate thoughts about pharaoh's Ship of the Dead, Rabbi Eliezer, and Rabbi Yehoshua.

"I think I understand your concept of preventive destruction," Yechiel said slowly, "but who is to decide? Isn't there a question of ultimate authority?"

The stranger put down his glass. He, for his part, was taken with Yechiel. It was clear that this young talmudist did understand what he was talking about. The term "preventive destruction" was worth remembering.

"Let us be honest. You don't believe in your hearts for a moment that the Ten Commandments came from heaven. You despise the rabbis who teach them and pity the Jews who believe them. But just let someone come along who wants to change things, make the world a better place, and right away you demand that he present divine tablets from Sinai. The proletariat is in bondage to a Russian pharaoh. Surely it must be redeemed, and that can be only through revolution. Starting with the intelligentsia, we must build a strong, disciplined party that will represent workers' interests and educate the workers to their own interests. These things can be scientifically demonstrated if you have the time." Yechiel had the time and wanted to ask for a scientific demonstration, but the stranger waved his inquiring gesture aside. "But the reality is that the workers can throw off their chains. You must read his works for yourself. A bright fellow like you will grasp the truth at once and be able to make a real contribution. Just read him."

"Who?" Yechiel asked innocently.

"Vladimir Ilyich Lenin!!" the stranger proclaimed in a booming voice, an arm upraised in majestic self-accompaniment.

No sooner had he intoned the inspirational name than a loud knock exploded on the door. An unholy terror seized all present. Both Yechiel and the stranger instantly dived under the table. The penetrating knock insistently shook the room.

"C-c-coming," Barasch called in stuttering, fright-filled reply, as if his impediment had spread from his legs to his tongue.

Yechiel could see Barasch Limp Legs struggling across the floor. He felt someone touch his shoulder. He twisted backward to the stranger.

"Where are we?" the stranger asked in a sharp whisper that told Yechiel that his quick-witted companion had regained his composure and was already developing a plan of action.

"Krimsk," Yechiel whispered back, revealing the debilitating fear in his voice and the lack of any plan whatsoever. Yechiel felt like a crumb, incapable of initiative. Whatever broom pushed under the table would retrieve him. He pivoted slightly to see what his masterful companion was doing.

"Where?" the companion repeated too loudly for safety.

"Krimsk," Yechiel repeated as loud as he dared.

"My God!" the stranger mouthed as his face melted in fearful, amazed agony. In fact, Yechiel recognized that expression. He had seen it on his mother's face when she had heard the very personal, very tragic, and very threatening news that her sister had been killed. Before Yechiel had any chance to reflect on his companion's dramatic change of countenance, he heard a voice in the doorway.

"Reb Barasch, my father said Yechiel must come home at once."

It was his little brother's voice, thin but forthright and concerned. In reflex, Yechiel rose to greet Shraga and banged his head with a dull but conclusive thud into the table. Yechiel fell back, stunned, and the stranger's hand quickly steadied him, firmly cautioning him to remain silent.

From what sounded to be very far away, Yechiel heard Barasch say, "If I see him, I'll certainly tell him."

Barasch closed the door with a great gasp of relief and turned expectantly toward the table, but no one emerged.

"It's all right. You can come out now," he said, but no one appeared. He hobbled back to his chair and fell into it, lowering his horselike head beneath the level of the tabletop. He saw both young men sitting on their haunches as if stunned. Yechiel, his yarmulke off, was rubbing his head, and his young companion was staring back at Barasch with unseeing, bewildered eyes. The thought crossed Barasch's mind that they must have cracked heads together trying to escape, and that was the walloping sound he had heard from under the table. Some revolutionaries! At any rate, Barasch knew for sure that it was a very bad thing that Krimsk knew of their meeting. Barasch, too, had his instincts for survival.

"Hey," he said quietly but forcefully. The two looked over at him with desultory, almost drunken expressions. "You both have to get going," he ordered in an insistent tone that stimulated them to begin crawling from the shelter of their hapless refuge.

# CHAPTER SEVENTEEN

THE BOYS ARRIVED BACK IN KRIMSK EXHAUSTED FROM their frantic flight from the pond. When they came upon the throngs in the street, however, their excitement and desire to tell everyone overcame their enervation. Their story, spewing forth amid gasps and wheezes, focused on two elements: the near-murderous unprovoked attack and the miraculous rescue by the great frog.

The largest and most amazed group gathered around Alexander Bornstein himself. His narrative was the least coherent but the most inspirational. "Good Rabbi Chanina, save me!" he coughed. "And the frog attacked Casimir's eyes, blinding him." Soaking wet and looking half-drowned, Alexander sputtered and wheezed, "Rabbi Chanina, Good Rabbi Chanina," and his young eyes shined ecstatically in faithful testimony that he had called for deliverance and he had been delivered. To see him was to believe him, and Krimsk believed. All the great streaming swirl of Krimsk flowed toward the boys. Wave upon wave of new arrivals met the news of their miraculous escape. "The rebbe sent his magic frog, and it blinded the Polish boys!" "The talking frog!" "Look, he's still all wet; the frog dragged him out of the pond!"

As the outside of the circle pressed toward the boys, those in front milled in hesitation and let themselves be pushed to the side. With their thirst for the miraculous slaked so surprisingly fast, they stood around murmuring listlessly and uttering perfunctory thanks that the children were safe. They exhibited ambivalence and unease. It was, after all, Tisha B'Av, the day of calamities, and their Krimichak neighbors were trying to kill Jews for sport. On the one hand, not the adults of Krimichak but just some rowdy boys had attacked them; on the other hand, if troubles were brewing, how many frogs were there? Rabbi Chanina's frog at the pond was a wonder, but a small, distant wonder. It was an enchanting little miracle that would produce in time great legends, but Tisha B'Av was not a small, intimate, sheltered day. It was an exposed, gaping, timeless breach whose ragged edges continued to lacerate communities after millennia. Had not the Krimsker Rebbe himself said that the wondrous talking frog was crying today? To stop a Krimichak pogrom required a golem like the one from Prague, a veritable earthen monster, not a jumping frog, no matter how sophisticated its vocabulary.

A small figure pushed through the crowd's self-conscious, static center all the way up to the boys. He tugged on Yonkel Berman's hand until he got his attention.

"What were they doing on our side of the pond?" Matti Sternweiss asked.

"They tried to drown Alex to see if death was in the

water," Yonkel answered, expecting the crowd's continued approval, but the word "death" received a diffident response.

"Yes, but why were they on our side of the pond?" Matti insisted.

Yonkel paused a moment; this had not been part of the litany he and the others had been reciting. He took a deep breath as if to say, Where should I begin?

"Why on our side of the pond?" Matti Sternweiss demanded in unrelenting inquiry.

By now the crowd concentrated on Yonkel and Matti. People suddenly became attentive and jostled each other to draw closer.

Yonkel began pompously, "Well, Grannie Zara died and—" but before he could finish the sentence, people were already dispersing.

Some sighed, some emitted short cries of fright and foreboding. Many even spat to avoid the evil eye, but all turned to go. Clutching her son Froika's hand, Gittel Waksman spun around to spit three times—most of which inadvertently landed on Alexander Bornstein—and hurried down the street with Froika flying along under her arm as if he were a precious violin case. Shlomi Feldman's father kissed his sweaty head and started down the street, pausing only for a second to grab Alexander Bornstein, too, who lived next door. The streets of Krimsk emptied as fast as they had filled. Only Yonkel Berman and Matti Sternweiss remained.

Yonkel blinked in disbelief. Everyone was fleeing. He and his friends had been the darlings of all Krimsk. Why, their experience was even better than Itzik Dribble's. Itzik had only heard about the frog and had played at being a frog, whereas they had met the frog and had been saved by him! And now, after all that, Krimsk denied their chosenness.

Matti had more questions to ask, and since he was afraid that Yonkel, too, might run away, he held his arm, encouraging him to stay. Yonkel, of course, had no desire to run anywhere. He felt cheated and hurt, but he did feel very kindly toward his brilliant classmate Matti, who remained faithful when Itzik Dribble had bested them again.

"How do you know Grannie Zara is dead?" Matti asked.

Yonkel was not listening. "Why did everyone run away?" he asked.

"Because Grannie Zara died. They're afraid. How do you know she died?" Matti repeated.

"They told us they had to chase the cats off her with torches," Yonkel answered, but his mind was on fickle Krimsk. "What were we supposed to do? Jump on the table with the rebbe?"

"Yonkel, I don't understand," Matti began, but Yonkel, nodding in agreement, interrupted Matti.

"Neither do I. Why should they be afraid? Rabbi Chanina's frog saved us after Grannie Zara died."

"Yonkel, why did Casimir come to the Krimsk side of the pond after Grannie Zara's death?"

Yonkel blinked his eyes in silence.

"Were they running away from Krimichak?"

"I guess so; they all ran home, didn't they?" Yonkel said.

"No, I mean *to* Krimsk. Why did Casimir and Tadeusz come to our side after Grannie Zara's death?" Matti asked slowly although he was itching with frustration.

"Casimir thought Grannie Zara was the naked lady," Yonkel answered in frustration of a different sort.

"Naked lady?" Matti responded in unrestrained eagerness.

"Yes," Yonkel replied and then added, "You know you have to be an idiot to get anywhere in this place."

Matti agreed. On most days he would have told Yonkel Berman that indeed he was right, and therefore his future was assured. Tonight, however, Matti sensed that something profound was happening, and the introduction of a naked lady even exceeded his expectations. He thought that theft or mayhem might be involved; the naked lady came as a delightful surprise.

"Yes, Yonkel, you're right, but what naked lady are you talking about?"

"Oh, they said something about a naked lady," Yonkel said in disgust.

"What?" Matti pleaded.

"Every month at this time she enters the pond, mumbles something in Hebrew, and then dips under the water."

"Casimir thought she was really Grannie Zara muttering a spell, and he came to see if the naked lady would appear after Grannie Zara had died?" Matti suggested.

"Yes," Yonkel nodded, impressed at how quick and clever Matti was. No wonder he always had the answers at Reb Gedaliah's. Sometimes he seemed to understand the lessons better than Reb Gedaliah.

Matti turned to leave.

"Where are you going?" Yonkel asked, slightly hurt that the last of his audience was leaving.

"To the pond," Matti said. "Want to come?"

"Not me! I've had enough. I think I'll go home."

"Whatever you prefer," Matti said.

"Be careful, Matti," Yonkel said. His warning was sincere, but Matti was not interested in Yonkel Berman's advice.

"Say, Yonkel, when did Alex piss in his pants tonight?" Matti asked casually.

"Before they threw him into the water," Yonkel replied with a laugh, but there was no one with whom to share it. Matti was already down the road. What a strange thing to ask at a time like this, thought Yonkel. There was something very cruel and snotty about the question. Yonkel took comfort in the thought that earlier in the day they had confiscated Matti's candy. Alex had, too. It served Matti right.

# CHAPTER EIGHTEEN

MATTI'S INSTANT ANALYSIS TOLD HIM THAT THE NAKED lady was not Grannie Zara. First of all, Grannie Zara was too old to be swimming in any pond at night. Second, if the Polish boys came to the Krimsk side to get a closer look, then the naked lady must enter from the Krimsk side. And if she entered from the Krimsk side, then she must evidently be from Krimsk.

Since she was from Krimsk, it was obvious to Matti that she was ritually purifying herself after her menstrual period. What was not at all obvious was why she would choose to go alone through the woods at night to purify herself. According to the Torah, before any woman could have sexual relations after menstruating, she had to dip in a natural body of water or a man-made mikveh, but in practice only a bride or married woman would have any need to do so. Now, thought Matti, if the only reason for the naked lady to purify herself was to have sexual relations and the only reason for the naked lady to use the pond was that she didn't want anyone to know that she was purifying herself, it followed that she didn't want anyone to know that she was having sexual relations.

Matti's talmudic mind considered several possibilities. The most obvious was that the naked lady was an unmarried woman having an affair. In this category he included lonely widows. In fact, he considered a widow a more probable candidate. A young passionate girl would not bother with a mikveh. If she sinned, she would sin completely. A widow would have grown accustomed to the purification process during her marriage and might find it a necessary prelude. The trouble was that Krimsk did not seem to have any widows that Matti considered appropriate candidates. Still, who knows, someone is fooling someone. Well, if that were the most obvious possibility, there was a most ethical possibility. The naked lady had been secretly married against her parents' wishes and was purifying herself for her husband. The question arose as to where she could have gone to get married that Krimsk would not have heard about it. And frankly, such a possibility did not appeal to Matti because it was so ethical; it wouldn't even involve violation of a rabbinic proscription, much less a real Torah sin.

Another more complex possibility occurred to Matti. The naked lady was married, and indeed she did go to the mikveh in town, but she went to the mikveh in town later because she was also sleeping with someone else and she wanted to sleep with the lover first without being bothered by her husband. As long as her husband believed that she hadn't gone to the mikveh, he could not touch her. After several days of domestic quiet and adulterous profligacy, she would go to the mikveh in town and switch from her lover's bed to her husband's.

Such a duplicitous, degrading, and dishonest, not to mention sinful, possibility thoroughly appealed to Matti. It offered a cynical view of society and a rich, perverse view of the individual. And it was fundamentally sound, based on a violation of one of the Ten Commandments, adultery. Matti was very pleased with himself for having found such an altogether satisfying explanation. He particularly admired the perverse distortion of the mikveh: not one purification as the Torah required, but two in order to pursue the more stringent demands of sin.

Matti was aware that this premise of an adulteress going to a mikveh might be criticized as weak, but he sensed it was not all that weak. He was familiar with the talmudic concept of a "believer denying one principle only." Although quite young, he was incredibly precocious, and he understood the logic of illogic and the illogic of logic, or as he himself would have put it, "the torah of sin as opposed to the sin of Torah." Both appealed to him. Although too young for sexual appetites, he had insightful dreams. He dreamt that he was a Polish noble, and with his fair, blond lady at his side he sat at a great baronial table heaped high with rich delicacies and every manner of nonkosher trophy of the hunt, such as boar. One morning upon awakening, he reviewed the dream and was amused to discover that as a Polish prince he never had served milk and meat on the same cornucopic table. At a very early age he had developed a tolerance, even an appreciation, for the inconsistencies that were life.

All of Krimsk appeared inconsistent. Here were God's most beloved and chosen people living in the midst of and at the whim of an idolatrous empire. Life in Krimsk revolved around a hasidic rebbe although neither the Torah nor the Talmud knew of hasidim, not to mention their rebbes. Matti realized that most people were unaware of such inconsistencies, although others were aware and very disturbed by them. After Yechiel Katzman's agonized outbursts in class today, Matti strongly suspected him of belonging to the second category. No doubt Yechiel lost a lot of sleep over such things. Matti sensed that the trick was to enjoy the inconsistencies and not lose any sleep. Not to lose any candy either; Matti sincerely regretted that. He made one more mental note that he should not appear so dispassionate when someone acted a little meshuga. It was a general problem for Matti; people resent anyone who is untroubled.

He hurried toward the pond; he did not want to miss a performance of the naked lady. Any naked lady held great interest for Matti. In fact, he could not go to the mikveh Friday afternoons with his father without fantasizing about concealing himself inside until the weekday nights when the women came for their ritual immersions. Like most intellectuals, Matti indulgently considered that the world reflected his conception of it; consequently, he was enthusiastically anticipating the discovery of the naked woman's identity; he absolutely worshiped creative people.

At the pond, the crickets chirped and the frogs croaked —perhaps Rabbi Chanina's very own frog led the chorus— as if oblivious to the miracle that had occurred one short hour previously. The illuminating moon had moved closer to the horizon, and the silver-gray light above the lake had grown weaker. This delight was lost on Matti, too; he had not come in appreciation of nature but in appreciation of man.

Noting the moon's position, Matti glumly suspected that it was too late for the lady to come. She had probably come even before the Polish boys arrived; but then he grew hopeful and thought that since tonight was Tisha B'Av, her schedule might be different—and as he articulated that idea to himself, he realized what a fool he was. On Tisha B'Av no woman immersed herself. It was forbidden because of the fast, and it was unnecessary because sexual relations were forbidden. No wonder she had not appeared—and to think Casimir was convinced that the naked lady was Grannie Zara since she had not come tonight. Matti, the young cynic, shook his head; Krimsk faithfully believed the water in front of him swarmed with miraculous frogs, whereas Krimichak fearfully believed it was cool with death, and Matti, who believed neither, knew the sad truth: not magic frogs, not death, not a naked lady, was or would be in the water tonight. Such an ironic contrast amused but did not satisfy him. He had lusting appetites. He had lost those sweets earlier in the day. At this late hour he had come to observe something titillating, and he wanted to satisfy this desire. He thought of the cats being chased off Grannie Zara's dead body and wondered if the witch had been buried. Perhaps her body still lay in her hut; perhaps Krimichak was waking the body. That would be interesting.

# CHAPTER NINETEEN

FAIGIE SOFFER WAS APPROACHING THE STEPPING STONES when she heard frightened screams echoing across the pond. She could not tell whether they came from the Krimsk side or from Krimichak. Wherever their origin, they gripped her heart in fear, and she hesitated to cross the stream. As she stood barefoot, shoes in hand, she heard more yelling. She could make out that it was Polish and had something to do with an eye. She assumed it must be the evil eye and spat quickly into the stream. Bewildered, she stepped off the path into the surrounding wood, and as she did so, Casimir, Tadeusz, Stefan, and the other Krimichak boys came rushing madly up to the stepping stones and stopped.

The tallest one was clutching his eye in frightened, near-hysterical agony. He rocked his head and moaned, "I'm blind. I'm blind." The shortest one said, "Let's go. We're almost home." The injured boy cried, "There's death in the water!" in such terror that the others froze in fear. A pimply boy said, "Damn that Jewish witch," but two of the others quickly hissed in warning, "Sh, don't even mention the name." The short one, although fearful, said, "We can't stay here, can we? Give me your hand." He took the tall boy and led him across. The moaning grew louder like a strong wind as it crosses water. Then it dropped off, and Faigie heard them renew their mad dash toward Krimichak.

Faigie wondered what Jewish witch they were talking about. If she had a Jewish witch in Krimsk, then she had no need to go to Krimichak to see Grannie Zara. Having heard that death lay in the water, she did not want to tempt fate on a night like this; she had no one to help her across. As she peered out, the stepping stones seemed to be growing smaller and the dark stream seemed to be rushing faster and climbing higher.

The idea of a local Krimsker witch was very appealing. She wished they had mentioned the name. But surely she would have known about a local witch in Krimsk. It was the smallest of small towns. Who could it be? Everyone she knew in Krimsk who was capable of evil was an ordinary gossip. No one in Krimsk approached Grannie Zara's aloof dignity and bearing. With one exception—the rebbetzin, Shayna Basya. She had dignity and bearing, and she was aloof. But Faigie was unconvinced. The rebbetzin definitely was lacking something. Faigie could forgive her the lack of cats; no matter how enriching, they were only props. A purist, Faigie believed in the direct, immediate powers of the Other Side. Intermediaries—frogs or cats—were unnecessary. The problem with the rebbetzin was that she did not have much contact with people; Grannie Zara was approachable day and night. In addition, the rebbetzin did not have the cat lady's essential vigor. Of late, the rebbetzin looked faded and washed out.

Having rejected the rebbetzin as a candidate and with no others, Faigie stepped out of her hiding place to examine the stepping stones. She saw almost nothing in the increasing darkness. Tall trees stood on both banks and shaded the now-feeble light of the quarter moon, which itself had fallen helplessly toward the horizon. She wished her Itzik were with her. He never stumbled, even in pitch black darkness. Beryl was forever saying that he was part cat. Faigie never responded to that particular compliment, but she did have to admit that he had uncanny sight at night and remarkably graceful coordination.

Not knowing what to do, Faigie sat down. Although she could not cross the stream to Grannie Zara's, she could not turn back either. In spite of her dilemma, she remained convinced that fate demanded she visit both Grannie Zara and the Krimsker Rebbe tonight. Somehow she would cross the stream. At the moment, she had no idea just how she might do so, and it occurred to her that perhaps she might visit the Krimsker Rebbe first and Grannie Zara later. She quickly rejected this thought, for her deepest inner instincts were very clear to her—first the witch and then the rebbe. She must reverse the order of her visits before Itzik's birth.

As she sat, she wondered about the Krimsker Rebbe's jumping like a frog with her son. She was sure both things were connected, but she could not grasp what that connection might be. Would such things—had such things—set the earth rumbling toward her and her family?

She was sure that she heard something. Yes, the sound of someone on the path walking slowly and deliberately.

Certain that this must be the person to guide her across, she continued to sit with her shoes in her hand. Wondering who the Krimsker witch really was, she watched a short, pudgy figure come around the corner, moving calmly and carefully.

Faigie was afraid that he might not see her at all, that he might even bump into her, so she greeted him when he was still several steps from her.

"Good evening, Matti," she said with a trace of nervousness, even a twinge of disappointment. She was hoping for someone sturdier who might actually carry her across in his arms. There was, after all, death in the water.

"Ugh! Ugh!" Matti responded, his debilitating fright rendering him speechless. Cynical disparager of Torahs, rebbes, and witches that he was, it was still midnight on the path to Krimichak, home of Casimir, Tadeusz, and a host of other murderous hooligans. Paralyzed, he came to a halt as his heart careened madly on a journey of its own.

"Matti, don't be frightened. It's just me," Faigie said gently.

She was an expert at quieting a frightened boy. Through his fright, Matti heard the comforting assurance, and he started breathing again. His heart, still beating fiercely, seemed to have rejoined his body.

"Huh!!" he managed, and then "Huh?" to which Faigie replied,

"I'm sorry if I frightened you. I tried not to. Are you all right?"

"Uh-huh," Matti nodded. He came closer and said, "Hello," rather weakly.

"Come sit down and rest a minute." She patted the ground next to her.

Matti, whose eyes had not yet adjusted to the darkness as well as Faigie's, edged over until he felt her hand touching his. He self-consciously sat down with the clumsy, bulky grace of a small bear. Then he poked his head inquisitively toward her to see just who she was.

"I'm Faigie, Itzik's mother," she said.

"Oh, yes, good evening, Mrs. Dribble," Matti spontaneously greeted her, and as soon as he heard his own words, he realized what a horrible thing he had said.

"Yes, that's right. Itzik's mother, Mrs. Soffer. How are your parents?" she asked.

Matti heard that she was not really offended, and he was thankful for that. With the whole town thinking of Itzik as Itzik Dribble, it must happen to her all the time. Mentioning his parents was a gracious way to change the subject, although the inquiry sounded out of place. When Matti went out alone, his parents always seemed very distant from him, as if they were not related.

"You are Matti Sternweiss, the butcher's son, aren't you?" Faigie asked.

"Yes, I am. They're fine, thank you. How is Mr. Soffer?" Matti responded.

"Oh, he's all right," she said perfunctorily.

Hearing her speak of her husband in such a disinterested tone, Matti's heart began to beat quickly again. He looked at her quizzically. She must be the naked lady, he thought in triumph. What else would she be doing here in the middle of the night lounging by the water?

"What are you doing here?" Matti attempted to ask this in pleasant inquiry, and although the question wasn't unpleasant, it betrayed Matti's single-mindedness of pursuit.

"I was waiting for someone to take me across the stepping stones to Grannie Zara's."

Her voice, until now so calm and soothing, quavered on "the stepping stones" and positively shook with fear as she said the witch's name.

Not paying any attention to her tone, Matti blithely answered, "Oh, good, that's just where I was going."

"You were?" Faigie asked in distrusting astonishment.

"Yes," Matti said more somberly. He realized that he had repeated his old mistake of sounding unconcerned when someone was very troubled. And Mrs. Dribble was more than a little troubled. She could barely utter "Grannie Zara" without fainting. He had already offended her, and since he wanted to determine definitely whether she was the naked lady—in the back of his mind he had not given up hope of a performance this very night—and since he was, in fact, on his way to Grannie Zara's, he thought he had better make amends.

"Well, I wasn't really on my way to Grannie Zara's," Matti backtracked. "I'm really looking for the talking frog."

Faigie interrupted him, "The talking frog?"

"Oh, yes, you weren't in town tonight, were you? Well, you must know about Itzik and the rebbe, don't you?" Matti was fearful that she did not and that he would have to narrate the entire bizarre performance.

"Yes, but why do you think the magic frog is at Grannie Zara's?" Faigie asked.

"Well, some of Reb Gedaliah's students went to the pond this evening, and they were assaulted by Casimir and the Krimichak gang. They were trying to drown Alexander Bornstein, the cooper's son, when he called to Rabbi

Chanina's frog to save him and the magic frog attacked Casimir's eyes, blinding him and routing the Krimichakers. Our boys told everyone in town about it, and I wanted to talk to the magic frog. After all, he knows all of Torah, the Talmud, and absolutely everything."

Matti stopped. He had tried to sound possessed, inspired, and convincing, but he knew that he'd not done such a fine job pretending to believe such nonsense. He was hoping that she had enough faith in nonsense for both of them.

"Yes, but what makes you think the magic frog is at Grannie Zara's?" Faigie asked skeptically.

In his attempt to generate enthusiasm, he had forgotten to answer her question. No wonder all the enthusiastic people made so little sense; one can't babble and think at the same time.

"Oh, yes," Matti said. "Well, I called his name along the shore of the pond where he had saved Alexander, and I didn't get any answer, so I thought maybe he had chased the hooligans back to Krimichak. I assumed that once he crossed the stream, he would look in at the witch's, since they do have something in common."

"Oh," Faigie responded, unconvinced. "Aren't you afraid to go to Grannie Zara's?"

"Of course," Matti answered quietly, "but if the miraculous frog is there, I thought everything would be all right. He's on our side."

Faigie did not believe the part about his fearing Grannie Zara. Earlier, he had answered quickly and naturally. Faigie had seen Casimir holding his eye, and she had heard the shouting, and she didn't think Matti would make up the frog story that he claimed to have heard in town. That could be easily checked. The rebbe had told the Rabbi Chanina story to her Itzik. That part was true, but Matti's search was an invented afterthought. And how—on a night like this—could a young boy not be afraid of Grannie Zara? Unless, Faigie wondered—she had heard the Polish boys talking about a Jewish witch. Who wouldn't be afraid of a witch, she reasoned, except for another witch?

Now it was Faigie's turn to examine Matti. Could this strange little child be the Jewish witch? Faigie had not seen or heard any frog hopping after the Polish boys. She wouldn't be at all surprised if Matti had that very frog in his pocket right now. But it was too dark, and he was sitting down. Faigie was indignant that this child thought she could be so easily fooled. If, however, he was the witch, then he most certainly could get her safely across the death-churning waters. And he might be of help at Grannie Zara's. She had better not offend him.

"I guess he's at Grannie Zara's. Where else would he be?" she asked rhetorically.

Matti thought she lacked enthusiasm, but who could get excited over such nonsense anyway? Maybe she did have *some* sense. Then he realized that this should not surprise him; the naked lady with a mikveh here and a mikveh there, a lover here and a husband there, was a very creative person.

"I suppose we might as well get started," Faigie said.

"Yes."

They both stood up.

"Aren't you going to get your towel?" Matti asked.

She seemed not to know what he was talking about. Her husband must not suspect a thing. Matti was impressed.

"Don't you have a towel in the bushes?"

"No, why should I have a towel in the bushes?" He didn't sound so much like a witch as a fool.

"In case you want to take a little dip in the water," Matti said. She was not admitting a thing.

"I wouldn't put a finger in that water. There's death in that water tonight," she said fearfully.

Matti assumed that she was coyly hiding her true interests. The ethical onus of adultery as well as the biblical punishment was death. Through a literary reference, she was saying that anything connected with adultery is death. Very clever. Well, two could play the same game.

"Death? How silly. Why, this is a natural mikveh filled with life. How else could it purify you?"

Oh, thought Faigie, that's what the little devil was getting at. A sly one, isn't he? Bragging that he need not fear the water.

"You aren't afraid of the water?" she asked.

"No, of course not. Nothing could be more attractive or convenient," he answered, hoping that his praise might encourage her to avail herself of its purifying properties.

Faigie was never one to play games, and this arrogant little devil was getting under her skin.

"If you're so concerned about convenience, then you might have said something," Faigie said rather waspishly.

"What are you talking about?" Matti asked. Now that he was on the defensive, he was not so assertive.

"The women don't have enough to do? You couldn't save them a trip to Krimichak in the middle of the night?" Faigie accused him fiercely.

"What trip?" Matti asked in amazement.

"To Grannie Zara, where else?" she said.

Matti thought that Beryl Soffer might be the luckier of Faigie's two men. What lover would welcome a madwoman? Had Matti believed in witches, he would have thought Faigie bewitched. She wasn't making any sense at all. Maybe the rabbis did know what they were talking about when they taught that no one sins unless the spirit of foolishness possesses him. Faigie's foolishness rivaled the magnitude of her sin. Matti wondered if she had been so disturbed before she became an adulteress. He considered fleeing back to Krimsk, and he well might have done so had she not commanded him to cross the stream.

"Go first and hold my hand."

Matti squinted down into the dark water where he knew the stones must be. After a moment, he could see a massive amorphous shape sitting darker than the water. Since the water was no more than three feet deep and he had no great fear of falling in, he was not overly anxious. He was more concerned about falling onto the stones themselves; that would be dangerous. The five stones were large, flat, and close to one another. Matti stepped onto the first one and edged toward the center until he was sure that he had left enough space behind him for Faigie. He pulled on her hand and drew her onto the rock.

She tightened her grip until his hand ached, and when she stood next to him, she put her arm around his waist. He felt the tension coursing through her thin arm until it was taut like a wire.

"Fine, now let me find the edge." Using his foot as

a cane, he tapped forward. She followed so silently that Matti could not hear her. He wondered if she were holding her breath.

"I'm stepping onto the next one."

Holding her hand, he stepped across.

On the fourth stone, he paused. Her anxiety must be contagious, he thought, for he felt his legs tightening. He forced himself to concentrate and held his breath as he stepped onto the next stone. When he reached the Krimichak bank, he did not say a word.

When she felt the earth underfoot, she breathed a sigh of relief and hugged Matti in a quick, steely embrace that left him gasping. Still holding his hand, but more relaxed, she stepped past him and led the way along the path. They creeped along slowly for several minutes until they saw the break in the foliage that permitted them to view the stars. After the suffocating blackness of the leaves, the sparkling heavens seemed light and airy. Straight ahead lay Krimichak, off to the right was Grannie Zara's cottage. Faigie hesitated, and Matti led the way.

In a few moments they could see the dark shape of the cabin sitting like a large shadow. It was totally dark and so quiet that Matti realized that Grannie Zara must have already been buried. He was curious to see what Faigie wanted in Grannie Zara's empty home. He suspected that she wanted to retrieve something. A magical incantation? Sometimes such amulets contained personal names. Matti suspected that one might have the name of her lover.

"Are you going around the back?" she asked in a hoarse whisper.

"No."

To Faigie's amazed horror, Matti opened the door without hesitating. Acting as if he were a member of the household, he walked right in. Perhaps he was a blood relative. Either that, or—Faigie tightened her grip on his sweaty hand to feel his smooth human skin and to make sure that he had not transformed himself into a furry cat as he entered the witch's den. The last time someone had taken her hand at Grannie Zara's, she had paid dearly for it.

# CHAPTER TWENTY

EVEN WITH THE DOOR OPEN, MATTI COULD NOT SEE a thing as he entered Grannie Zara's cottage. He stepped forward and felt sharp flashes of pain bite into his shin. "Ugh," he moaned as what sounded like a small stool crashed across the floor. In reflex, Faigie squeezed his hand even harder. He knew that if he could not light a candle quickly, he would scream from the pain. She was crushing him in an iron vise; he sensed that it would be futile to ask her to release him. In the midst of his agony, his ironic mind was active; the only thing superhuman about all this was Faigie Soffer's strength. Her last name gave him an idea.

"Do you have any matches?" he whispered.

There was no reply. If she weren't breaking his hand, he would never have believed that she was with him.

"Faigie, do you have any matches?" he hissed.

What if she were paralyzed with fear? He doubted that he had enough strength to break her grip.

"Faigie Soffer, put your hand in your pocket and give

me the matches right now," he commanded in a desperate but insistent tone. "The matches, Faigie, right now!"

She was tugging and manipulating something awkwardly with his hand. He assumed these were the phantom parallel movements of her free hand in her pocket. Then he felt her pressing something against his arm.

"I can't light them; let go of my hand and hold my arm," he said as he took the box of matches.

He felt her loosen her crushing hold and slide her hand up his arm. She held him above the elbow. Matti seized the opportunity and dragged a match over the roughened edge of the box. It screeched into a blinding explosion of light and then descended into a small yellow flame. Faigie, fearful of what she would see, gripped his arm as tightly as she had held his hand. Ignoring this as best he could, he stepped over to light the candle on the table and then sat down. He tried to remove Faigie's grip, but she seemed oblivious to his attempts to peel back her fingers.

"You're hurting me."

She removed her hand.

"Have a seat," he suggested, but Faigie continued to stand. She turned around in a complete circle to make sure nothing was behind her.

Seeing how naturally Matti made himself at home—sitting right down like that at Grannie Zara's table—left no doubt that Faigie was with the Jewish witch.

She looked down at Matti, who was massaging the area where she had held his arm. The imprint of her fingers stood out clearly. Well, she thought, just like they say, even a witch gets burned by the pot. She wondered when Grannie Zara would return.

As Matti methodically rubbed his arm, he flexed his all-but-numb fingers and looked around at what had been Grannie Zara's home. It looked like any well-to-do widow's, except that it was so remarkably neat. Not so much clean as orderly. Everything seemed to have a preordained position, and all the insignificant objects together exuded a harmony like a symphony but played much too loud. Matti had never experienced anything like it. He kept looking around —at the andirons, at the broom, at the few books, at the crucifix on the wall—to discover what caused the strange effect. Matti would not realize until years later that the secret lay in their relationship to one another.

"Why did you come here?" he asked.

"Why aren't you looking for the frog?" she retorted.

Matti wondered how she could be so hostile. She certainly never could have made it here without him, but she was right about the frog. Matti had forgotten; Faigie had not.

"Oh, he might show up. I can wait."

As Matti spoke, they heard the low, grinding whine of the door hinges; they turned to see the partially open door slowly opening itself even farther. They could see no one pushing it, and there was not the slightest hint of wind. Faigie's eyes popped open wide, her mouth tensed, and she emitted a low, trembling note. Even Matti, who did not admit the existence of witches, sat up in fright. Undeniably, the door was moving. He felt Faigie's torturous grip on his other arm and then he saw the large calico cat padding around the corner of the cabinet. With supreme feline certainty and self-assurance, it leaped onto Matti's lap, nuzzling against him. Faigie removed her hand from Matti and stepped back. Matti felt a similar rubbing sensation on his legs and looked down to find four or five normal-sized calicos at his feet. Two left him and mewed in the direction of a large double cupboard.

"They must be hungry," Matti said. "See if there is anything in the cupboard," he suggested, but Faigie did not move.

He turned to look at Faigie, who stood in the shadows behind him. The large calico with the outsize paw looked in the same direction.

"Stay away from me, Zloty," she warned.

The cat returned to rubbing Matti's chest with its head.

"You know her?" Matti asked, turning back to scratch the cat behind the ears. She purred with delight.

"Yes," Faigie answered.

"They must have seen the light and thought that Grannie Zara had returned," he speculated.

"I wish she would," Faigie said.

"Why did you come here?" Matti asked her. She was so frightened and yet so insistent on staying.

"You're waiting for Rabbi Chanina's frog?"

Matti nodded.

"Well, I'm waiting for Grannie Zara!"

Matti burst into laughter.

"What's so funny? I think there's more chance of her arriving than a talking frog!" she said petulantly.

"Grannie Zara is dead," he said, but before he could tell her that the witch had already been buried, he heard a piercing, ghastly scream the likes of which he had never heard and was never to hear again during his entire life. His hair stood on end, and he felt the frightened cat's claws dig into his thighs as Zloty sprang off his lap. The great cat flew out the door, followed by the others. At that second Matti felt no pain, just the sensation that claws were digging into him. His only awareness was of that awful wrenching scream, as if Faigie's chest had been torn wide open. The deafening cry did not last long, but it echoed in his ears for five times as long as it rent the night.

When he was certain that it had ended and that he was still in one piece, Matti stood up and turned around to Faigie. He thought that she had disappeared until he saw her feet. She lay face down. He ran over and began to roll her onto her back as he called, "Faigie, Faigie, are you all right?" Blood trickled from a bruise above her eye where her head had hit the sandy floor. He wiped it away with his finger and began to pat her cheeks the way he had seen the women reviving one another on Yom Kippur when the fasting had overcome them. He was not succeeding.

Matti wanted to leave Grannie Zara's as quickly as possible. That scream frightened him as he had never been frightened before, and he was sure all of Krimichak had heard it, too. He looked around the cabin for something that might help. A white earthenware jug stood on a shelf next to the bed. He ran and shook it, but heard no water inside. To be sure, he turned it over on his hand, but to his disappointment, no liquid came forth. His leg, however, felt damp. He looked down to see that his pants were wet. It must have happened when she screamed. He knew that this must be Bornstein's revenge, but he dismissed the thought; he had to get out of that cottage before all of

Krimichak arrived, and he couldn't leave Faigie there. He had to revive her immediately.

Kneeling, Matti made one last frantic effort to pat her back to consciousness. When that failed, he graduated to sharp slaps, and when that did not succeed, he leaned over her and brought his soaking wet pants front down onto her forehead. He gently rubbed against her, then moved away and massaged the urine into her temples. Faigie groaned, and Matti patted his wet fingers onto her cheeks and chin. Finally, Faigie's eyes opened. They were alarmingly wild with fright. She moved nothing but her eyes.

"Are you all right?"

She did not answer.

"You screamed and fainted, Faigie. Do you hear me?"

She nodded slightly.

"We have to get out of here before anyone comes. All of Krimichak must have heard you. If we can get you back to the stream, a little water will refresh you."

Faigie's eyes rolled in horror at the suggestion. Matti suddenly remembered her obsession that death lay in the water. He clenched his fist in frustration.

"Faigie," Matti begged, "we have to get out of here."

He dragged her into a reclining position with her head resting against the base of the wall. "Say something!" he pleaded.

"You killed Grannie Zara," she said in a voice lacking all strength.

"What are you talking about? She died. I don't even know how she died. She died."

"You're the Jewish witch," she said.

"You're crazy. You're mad. Faigie, there are no such

things, but there are goyim, Faigie. If they find us here, they'll kill us."

"You're a witch," she repeated.

"We have to get out of here!" he screamed.

"I can't leave," Faigie said in despair.

"Try and stand. I'll help you."

He moved closer.

"No, I can't leave without Grannie Zara."

"Why not?"

"You know," she said matter-of-factly. Now that she had nothing to lose, she had nothing to fear.

"Tell me, Faigie! I'll help you," Matti said.

Faigie looked at him with interest.

"The broom," she said. "The broom and the cat."

"What about the broom and the cat, Faigie?"

"Itzik Dribble's father," she explained.

My God, thought Matti. She's gone mad.

"The broom and Zloty the cat," she repeated.

"Forget the broom and the cat!" he said.

"No, they are alive," she insisted.

Matti did not understand whether she thought Grannie Zara was still alive, but he was not about to tell her again that she was dead. Perhaps she thought Zloty and the broom were Itzik Dribble's father and she wanted to reunite the family.

"Faigie, you want the family together? We'll take the broom and the cat with us. Just let's go."

Without waiting for an answer, he jumped and plucked the large yellow broom from its resting place by the hearth. He ran back to her.

"Here it is. Come on, we can get the cat outside. And if

we can't find her, we can come back with a bowl of milk when there's more light. Now please get up and we'll go."

As he finished speaking, he noticed that the cats had returned.

"Faigie, here's Zloty!"

She closed her eyes and moaned.

"Let's go!" he begged.

Faigie opened her eyes, took one glance at Zloty, who had walked over to her, closed them again, shook her head, and moaned, "No, not that!"

Matti was thoroughly perplexed.

"Grannie Zara is dead," she said.

Matti stood tongue-tied. Faigie opened her eyes and looked at Matti. She was certainly mad, but at least she was no longer hysterical and she was speaking directly to him.

"Grannie Zara is dead," she repeated. "They must die, too. Both of them," she commanded.

Matti listened to Faigie, but he also heard a distant shouting in the woods. He could barely distinguish the faint "hulloos," but the sound pierced his heart with fear the way stranded travelers on a winter's night hear the first faint echo of the wolves' howl. He swallowed, and his dry throat ached.

Having no awareness of the enmity the woman harbored for her, Zloty had stepped closer to examine Faigie. She looked straight at the curious cat.

"Kill them both or I can't leave."

Kill them or we shall be killed, Matti thought. Death was in the forest, and it was stalking the cottage. He looked at the fireplace. The heavy straw-brush broom would burn easily, but how was he to kill the cat? He glanced at Faigie, lying against the wall. She would be of no help at all. Matti had seen his father slaughter chickens by slitting their throats, but his father had held them tightly so they couldn't jump away. How could Matti hold that large, clawing cat long enough to slit its throat?

"Faigie, we'll do it!" he said with a determination that caused her to sit up. A "hulloo" softly reached them. Matti was certain that he was not imagining it; Faigie had heard it, too, and cocked her head slightly.

"We need a sharp knife and something for Zloty to eat," Matti said quickly, as if naming the things he needed made them more accessible.

He placed the broom on the table and turned toward the large wooden double cupboard. Matti slid open the metal bolt fasteners on the bottom cabinet. Inside he found pieces of crockery, pots, pans, and various utensils, including the sharp knife for which he was looking. As he removed the knife, he had to push the purring, mewing cats away. Zloty stood closest and, purring all the while, rubbed her majestic leonine head against Matti's elbow.

"Yes, Zloty, it won't be long now," Matti muttered quietly. He closed the lower cabinet without bothering to fasten the doors and stood up. He was praying that he would find something edible in the upper cabinet. In his anxiety he fumbled with the small bolts and had to steady his trembling hands before trying again. The cats had begun a frenzied chorus of meows and simpering cries that further agitated Matti. Finally he succeeded in opening the cabinet, to be greeted by a sour smell of cheese or milk that had been left too long in the infernal summer heat. Matti received the rancid odor with a rush of delight and a touch of fear now that he was getting so very close to slicing Zloty's neck with the smooth, shiny metal blade.

Considerably higher than the candleholder on the table, the upper cabinet remained in shadow. Matti turned to get the candle and illuminate the cabinet. Once he knew exactly what was inside, he would take the appropriate bowl and serve it to Zloty on the table so the other cats would not get in his way. As Matti reached for the candle, he heard a heavy thumping sound in the top cabinet. This was soon followed by two softer thumps. With the candle in hand, he turned back to discover that Zloty and two of the smaller calicos had been unable to resist the tempting odor and had leaped into the cabinet. He brought the taper close enough to be certain that Zloty was inside. The cats had knocked over a milk pitcher and were ravenously lapping the spilled milk off the bottom of the cabinet.

Quivering with excited delight, he slammed the cupboard door, imprisoning the cats. Inside, the gluttonous slurps continued. Leaning on the door, Matti held the candle in his left hand and fumbled with the fastener. He finally managed to slide the small metal bolt into the lock position and put down the candle before reaching up to lock the higher one.

Quickly stooping to the open lower cabinet, he began to shovel the crockery and all but two pots onto the floor. As the platters and cups clattered and broke in ragged pieces and the frying pans clanged against each other in a medley of metallic madness, two small cats leaped aside. Matti positioned the two remaining pots about half a meter apart in the cabinet. He ran to the fireplace, dragged the kindling basket over to the cupboard, and placed a substantial pile of kindling between the two pots. Using the pots as andirons, he balanced two small logs on them. For good measure, he spread kindling into the corners and over the exposed areas of the cupboard floor. He reached for the broom and was already placing the straw end into the cabinet when he realized that it would not fit. He withdrew it and tried to break it over his knee, but the haft would not give. Matti dashed to the fireplace, placed the end of the handle under one andiron, and laid the rest of the broom over the other. He fell on it with all his weight, and it snapped with a wicked crackling into two pieces. He placed both on top of the two logs and snatched the candle from the table.

Faigie was standing on the other side of the table with a frenzied, almost exultant gleam in her eyes.

"Get out! I'm going to light it!" Matti yelled at her.

She fairly skipped to the doorway, where she turned on the threshold to observe her tormentors' doom.

Candleholder in hand, Matti approached the cupboard. Hearing the meowing and scratching of the cats behind the upper door, he hesitated and glanced at the plain wooden slab. The bolts were securely in place. He stooped to the lower cabinet and lit the straw brush. The broom caught at once; the sprigs shriveled and then burst into flame. Then he touched the candle to the kindling under the logs. The shavings and small sticks were so dry that they caught fire in a cacophony of crackles. The flame itself encompassed the entire cabinet so quickly that Matti leaped back from the withering heat. He left the candlestick on the table and raced to leave.

Faigie, her face glowing in accompaniment to the swelling flames, blocked the exit.

"Come on," he said, pushing her, "we have to get out of here!"

When he closed the door behind him, he could barely hear the flames crackling because of the tortured screams of the immolating cats.

# CHAPTER TWENTY-ONE

Reb Yechezkal was struggling to his feet—sitting on an overturned bench was every bit as uncomfortable for a man his age as the most stringent rabbi desired it to be—to tell the rebbe that he had not succeeded in finding Yechiel Katzman when the young scholar walked into the beis midrash. Reb Yechezkal stretched his neck in an unsuccessful attempt to remove a crick, then threaded his way through the scattered furniture to the center aisle to receive him. Reb Yechezkal appreciatively noticed the young man's very serious, almost troubled mien. That, thought the sexton, is the proper Tisha B'Av deportment, and Yechiel knew enough not to extend a greeting on this day of mourning.

"I shall see if the rebbe will receive you," Reb Yechezkal said.

Yechiel nodded, and the sexton knocked on the door to the rebbe's study. To his surprise, he received no reply. He knocked again and called, "Rebbe."

"Wait a minute," he heard the rebbe call back.

As he waited, Reb Yechezkal imagined that all eyes in the beis midrash were on him. In fact, everyone had his eyes on Yechiel and wondered what he was doing visiting the rebbe on the night of Tisha B'Av. Yechiel himself wondered the same thing. He knew why *he* wanted to see the rebbe, but he had not been able to imagine any reason why the rebbe wanted to see him. He hoped that he would have an opportunity to discuss the things that were bothering him, but he didn't quite see how he could manage that since it was forbidden to study Torah on Tisha B'Av except for material relevant to the day itself.

Reb Yechezkal thought that he had heard the scurry of people running around inside the rebbe's study, but he attributed this absurd notion to his own overactive imagination. After everything that had been happening tonight, how could his imagination not be overactive? His reverie was interrupted by the rebbe's saying, "Yes," and Reb Yechezkal entered, closing the door behind him. Not surprisingly, no one else was in the room. Just the rebbe, and far from running around, he was sitting on the floor, leaning against the couch as a backrest. He was sweating profusely and breathing deeply. On the floor to the side of the couch the chenille tablecloth was spread over something low and lumpy like cushions. Reb Yechezkal noticed that the table was bare, and although he didn't remember the cloth covering it, he assumed that was where the cloth had come from.

"Yechiel Katzman is here," the sexton said.

Still breathing deeply, the Krimsker Rebbe lowered his head slightly, dipping his brushy eyebrows in what Reb Yechezkal knew from years gone by to be a nod of assent.

He returned to the beis midrash and told Yechiel that the rebbe would see him. Reb Yechezkal had no doubt that Yechiel would leap at the opportunity to become the rebbe's son-in-law and successor. As he returned to reading the supplementary lamentations, he wondered about the bedspread on the floor. He was getting older, and he could not remember whether the rebbe had bedded down on the floor in previous Tisha B'Av nights or not. It had been six years since he was in the rebbe's study on this day, and he just could not remember. Of course, he must tell his own wife to prepare a bedspread and cushions for himself. If the rebbe did it, it certainly was worth emulating.

Yechiel knocked and received what he assumed to be an assenting grunt. He felt overwhelmed to be in the private presence of the Krimsker Rebbe. Knowing that he could not greet him this night and feeling at a loss as to what he should do, Yechiel just stood there, continuing to hold the door open for support.

"Close the door and sit down," the rebbe said.

Yechiel closed the door and wondered where he should sit. The rebbe pointed to where Yechiel was standing in front of the door and waved his finger up and down, commanding him to be seated. Yechiel seated himself with his back against the door and looked at the Krimsker Rebbe, who sat as if he were alone in the room. His great hazel eyes focused on some deep inward rumination. Yechiel nervously looked around the study and noticed the lumpy bedspread. Assuming that the rebbe slept there on Tisha B'Av, Yechiel deduced that although there was no prohibition against lying in a normal bed, there must be a stricter concept to which the rebbe adhered.

"How are your studies, Yechiel?" the rebbe asked.

Yechiel hesitated. For a brief moment he considered opening his heart to the rebbe, but he could not. He could not lie either and utter the expected, "Thank God."

"They are not what they should be, rebbe," he answered truthfully, if somewhat disingenuously.

The rebbe nodded. "They never are. It is a wise and modest man who knows this, but nonetheless, Yechiel, I hear very fine things about your studies."

Yechiel felt like a fraud and did not know how to respond.

"How old are you, my boy?" the rebbe asked wearily.

"Eighteen, Rebbe," Yechiel answered.

"The time has come. Yes, the time has come," the rebbe said and nodded.

Yaakov Moshe saw that the modest young man was perplexed. Ah, well, he thought, so I must have been, also.

"Do you understand me?"

"No, Rebbe," Yechiel answered truthfully. Does he mean that the time has come for me to leave? Did he call me in just to tell me he has heard good things about me? After all, the rebbe had been so loving and kind to Itzik Dribble, perhaps he sensed that I, too, need guidance and support.

"Eighteen is the appropriate age to stand under the wedding canopy," the rebbe said.

Yechiel was absolutely stunned.

"The holy rebbetzin and I would like to welcome you into the family under the wedding canopy as the groom of our pure and radiant Rachel Leah," the rebbe said in a most casual manner, as if the conversation bored him, which it most certainly did. This tone made it especially difficult for

Yechiel, who was not expecting such a dramatic proposal, to believe what he was hearing. He just smiled weakly.

"We want you as our son-in-law," the rebbe said forthrightly.

Yechiel leaned back in amazement and knocked his head against the door. A throbbing pain shot through the bump that he had received from Barasch Limp Legs' table.

"Rebbe," he said, rubbing his painful souvenir of revolutionary involvement. "I am unworthy. Thank you and the rebbetzin, but I am absolutely unworthy."

"Yes, I thought the same thing when the sainted rebbe of Bezin offered me his holy Shayna Basya. I, too, was right, but I still married her."

"But Rebbe, *I* am unworthy," Yechiel insisted. "I may be a heretic and a sinner," he added, shamefaced at his confession.

"Don't bother about such things. Soon you will be married and have other things to worry about."

Yechiel didn't understand what was happening. Nothing he said dissuaded the saintly rebbe. He couldn't let this go on.

"May I speak freely with the rebbe?" he found himself saying.

The Krimsker Rebbe nodded.

"I cannot marry the rebbe's daughter," he stated flatly.

Yaakov Moshe looked at Yechiel. The young man had said that he could not marry "the rebbe's daughter." Yechiel was afraid of becoming the next Krimsker Rebbe. Yaakov Moshe glanced over at the bedspread. Now that the holy rebbetzin was pregnant with—well, with a son who certainly, at the very least, would preclude any dynastic demands on Yechiel, there was nothing to worry about.

"You have nothing to worry about. I understand you. You will not marry the rebbe's daughter; you will only marry Yaakov Moshe and Shayna Basya Finebaum's daughter."

This should set the boy's mind at rest. How could he make it any plainer? Yechiel was bright and should understand.

Yechiel did understand that he was being offered the daughter without the position of rebbe. Since the position was strictly hereditary and Rachel Leah was an only child, he assumed they would permit him to think whatever he wanted to think now and then ease him into the inevitable. If by some chance they could not succeed in gaining his acquiescence, at the fateful moment the hasidim would thrust the hasidic crown upon him. Yes, but the problem was not Yechiel's becoming rebbe; the problem was that he really was unfit to marry Rachel Leah Finebaum.

Why was the rebbe suggesting a match on Tisha B'Av? Why couldn't it wait? If he can discuss such things, Yechiel thought, perhaps I can talk about the things that are bothering me.

"Rebbe, Tisha B'Av is a day of great pain and suffering for the Jews," Yechiel began in awkward introduction.

"No one suffers the way I do," the rebbe snapped.

He was staring right at Yechiel; he no longer seemed so kind and loving.

"Of course, Rebbe, forgive. I didn't mean . . . I just wanted to ask . . ." His voice trailed off in despair that his attempt at a graceful transition had failed so miserably.

"What?" the rebbe demanded.

"This morning I taught Reb Gedaliah's students the eighth chapter of the Tractate Terumah. In the dispute between Rabbi Eliezer and Rabbi Yehoshua as to what one is permitted to do in order to save either the impure wine or in the later cases, the Jewish women . . ." He paused.

"So?" the rebbe asked impatiently.

"Rebbe, haven't we suffered enough? Why can't we face the modern reality? Isn't it better to sacrifice one so the others survive? Goyim are drowning Reb Gedaliah's students, and they are studying the laws of a Temple that was destroyed two thousand years ago. Why, Rebbe?" Yechiel finished in a plaintive cry.

Even the rebbe heard the pain in the boy's outburst.

"Yechiel, you think that Rabbi Yehoshua does not go far enough. He goes too far. It is Rabbi Eliezer who makes sense. There is no 'modern' reality. There is an eternal reality that has not changed since God gave us his holy Torah. We are a holy nation commanded to sanctify his holy name. Do you think we are a nation of numbers? The goyim have numbers; we have a holy spark. Without that spark, we have no meaning. We fan that spark by sanctifying his holy name."

"But don't our lives have any meaning?" Yechiel asked.

"Do not underestimate evil," the rebbe intoned.

Yechiel was confused by the rebbe's answer.

"Study, do not question!"

"Maybe Rabbi Eliezer and Rabbi Yehoshua are wrong," Yechiel said quietly.

"Heretic and sinner!" the rebbe spat at Yechiel.

"Yes, well, I shall be leaving Krimsk," Yechiel said by way of apology.

The rebbe laughed a raucous, cynical laugh at Yechiel's announcement.

"Unfortunately for me, you will never leave Krimsk. Others might, but not you. You can walk in Warsaw, you can sing in Paris, you can dance in America, but you, Yechiel Katzman, will never succeed in leaving Krimsk."

Although he did not know exactly what the rebbe was saying, Yechiel feared that he was telling the truth, or at least something that would haunt him for the rest of his life.

"Why?" he asked simply.

"For them it is too small, but for you it is just right. We always have enough room for sinners and heretics. Vermin take up very little space!" he blazed, and then he looked pained, almost regretful. "Where is pharaoh?" the rebbe cried in despair. "Even Napoleon would do," he added as an afterthought. "But this?" and he dismissed Yechiel with a flip of the wrist that suggested Yechiel's total insignificance.

Shaken by the rebbe's onslaught and peremptory dismissal, Yechiel held his throbbing head and staggered to his feet.

"I'm sorry," he stuttered.

"Get out and close the door behind you. Close it well!" the rebbe shouted.

Yechiel left quietly and closed the door tightly behind him.

The rebbe, breathing heavily, stared at the door as if his gaze could destroy the Torah's enemies. He took several breaths, crawled over to the chenille cloth, and energetically yanked it away to expose holy Shayna Basya. His rebbetzin lay huddled nude, her knees drawn up, and in her arms she clutched her clothing. Under the suffocating cloth, she could not escape the heat. Her entire body dripped with glistening sweat.

"Oh, my pure one," he whispered, kissing her instep. This, he thought, is how the Krimsker Queen must look emerging from the mikveh covered with holy dew.

Shayna Basya had been smiling rapturously even under the heavy cloth, for her husband had twice referred to her as his "holy" Shayna Basya.

He pointed to the buttons on his shirt, and she began unbuttoning them at once, falling on his neck with kisses.

He drew her to him with the ardor of messianic expectations. Each act of love now would strengthen the embryo. That is what the Talmud teaches—and the Krimsker Rebbe believed.

# CHAPTER TWENTY-TWO

YECHIEL WALKED STRAIGHT OUT OF THE BEIS MIDRASH without looking at anyone. He reached the empty street and wondered where he could go. After what had happened, he could not go home. The mere thought of his family flooded him with a sense of sadness and shame. His father, mother, and little Shraga had struggled to support his studies. What was worse, they lived through him; his achievements were their achievements, his rewards were their rewards. And how did he thank them? When the rebbe offered him his daughter—which would make them the in-laws of the present Krimsker Rebbe and the family of the future rebbe!—he confessed that he was a heretic and a sinner.

It saddened him that he loved them so and seemed capable only of hurting them. With their lack of education, he could not even explain to them why he believed—or, more properly, why he did not believe—what he did. They could only view him as the rebbe had, as a vermin—something alien, repulsive, and corruptive. They would never yell at him although he wished they would. No, they would look at him with sad, loving eyes that asked why. Why leave your family and your people? They could never understand his rejection, and he could not explain it to them.

In spite of the rebbe's prediction, Yechiel would have to take his chances and leave Krimsk. He had no choice. He knew that he was neither a Yudel who could live alone within a community nor a Barasch who could live alone outside of one. Yechiel loved and needed people, but he had no idea where to go. He did not even know where he could go right now. He considered going back into the beis midrash to read the dirges composed for the fast day. At least he would have a place to sit, but after what had happened in the rebbe's study, he could not avail himself of the rebbe's beis midrash. And after the attack on Reb Gedaliah's students, he did not want to wander outside Krimsk. Barasch's home was no longer a possibility; since Shraga had knocked on the door, Barasch was expecting arrest. Yechiel had no success in explaining that little Shraga was not a colonel in the tsarist police. He hadn't been very successful in convincing anyone of anything this evening. Even though he had no idea where to go, he could not regret what had just happened. Things just couldn't go on the way they were; that was intolerable. Conscience was always more important than comfort. At least he did have that belief in common with the Krimsker Rebbe. He smiled ruefully; Yechiel had had no idea how difficult it was for a vermin to find comfort. Apparently much harder than for a frog.

He took a step backward and sat down on the wide step leading up to the beis midrash. Forever the talmudist, Yechiel decided that sitting on the outside step did not contravene the rebbe's order to get out. He was certain of that. Indeed, he probably could sit on the threshold itself since that also was not "in" the beis midrash; it must, perforce, be "out" and therefore permissible to him in his status as vermin. The more he thought of himself as vermin, the greater the desire he had to scratch. And he was casually scratching his side when someone spoke to him.

"I see that you have returned to the beis midrash," a warm, lively voice said with a hint of humor.

Yechiel looked up to see the enthusiastic stranger. He wore a rough twill jacket and had a faded knapsack slung over his shoulder. On his head was a small-beaked leather cap that he pushed back when he talked. Yechiel felt an affinity for him and smiled in delighted surprise at his unexpected appearance.

"I'm still on the floor," Yechiel said.

"At least Barasch can't throw you out of here," the stranger said.

"He doesn't have to. The Krimsker Rebbe already has," Yechiel answered truthfully.

"Yes, but if you jump up now, at least you won't bump your head," he joked.

"That's already happened again, too," Yechiel rubbed his twice-bumped head.

"It sounds interesting."

"Join me on the scholar's bench," Yechiel said sarcastically, pointing to the step on which he sat.

The stranger glanced up and down the street. Although he seemed reluctant to accept, he acquiesced. "I suppose a few minutes wouldn't hurt." He sat down and put his knapsack next to him.

"My name is Yechiel Katzman," Yechiel said.

"I'm Hershel Shwartzman, but my friends call me Grisha," the stranger responded.

He extended his hand. Yechiel glanced around, saw that no one was watching, and shook it.

"One isn't supposed to shake hands on Tisha B'Av," he explained, embarrassed at having hesitated to take Grisha's hand.

"I thought you were on the way out," Grisha said.

Yechiel nodded and shrugged his shoulders like the oldest of hasidim. "Yes, but not everyone travels so fast, especially when he doesn't know where to go."

"Do you *mind* if I sit here?" Grisha asked.

"No, I'm very pleased that you came."

A shadow appeared where the light from the beis midrash doorway played upon the street near them. They both stopped speaking and sat silently until the shadow disappeared. When it did, they listened to the steps fade back into the beis midrash.

"We must go somewhere. If we are noticed together, it will ruin both our reputations," Grisha said very seriously.

"Don't worry about mine," Yechiel said blithely, but with an earnestness that always seemed to be his lot.

"If you say so, I won't, but I'm concerned about being seen here with you."

He was referring to the beis midrash, and Yechiel, to his surprise, saw that he was not joking. All humor had disappeared from his voice and person. He betrayed a fearful tenseness, as if some personal monster could come leaping out of the darkness.

"Are there so many Marxists in Krimsk that you will be seen?"

"No, but we are a pure party. We must be disciplined and work at protecting our purity," Grisha said dogmatically.

Yechiel was struck by the similarity to what the rebbe had told him. It seemed that Grisha sided with Rabbi Eliezer as well.

"Don't you know someplace where we could talk?" Grisha asked.

Yechiel did not, but he didn't want to lose Grisha's company.

"Where were you going?" Yechiel asked him.

"If I don't find a shed or a porch with a dark corner, I shall walk into the countryside to look for a haystack or a carriage shed or even a wagon. In this hot weather, the nights are no problem. They're easier than the days."

Yechiel realized that he had spent his entire life in Krimsk but had no idea what was in it. There must be sheds and such places where they could talk, but he didn't remember seeing any. He never looked for those sorts of things. Yechiel had a sense of having searched for very little, if anything, outside of books. Grisha came walking out of nowhere and probably had seen more in the middle of the night in Krimsk than Yechiel ever had. He felt helpless, even foolish. How was he going to strike out on his own when he couldn't even escape from the step of the beis midrash? No doubt the hasidim would attribute his failure to the rebbe's prophetic curse.

"It doesn't have to be outside or in a partially exposed place," Grisha said. "It might be an abandoned building or one that no one will use at night. Many times I have slept in small synagogues, but I don't imagine there are any empty synagogues on the night of Tisha B'Av."

"Follow me," Yechiel said quietly. He stood up and walked into the darkness. Grisha's echoing steps gave Yechiel courage; he was not alone. Yechiel led him down the street and to the right toward the marketplace. He would never have thought of it had it not been for Grisha's remark. They walked alongside the dark, open expanse of the empty market to a large handsome shadow of a building, then rounded the corner of the Angel of Death synagogue.

Yechiel stood very still to make sure no one was nearby. Satisfied that they were alone, he turned around and leaned across the sill to push open the window. He had noticed one thing in Krimsk: Reb Zelig the sexton opened only this window daily to air out the Angel of Death. It gave, and he continued pushing with all his strength. The large window began to move with an awful caterwauling noise. With Grisha's help, they soon had enough space to climb through. Yechiel hoisted himself onto the sill in a kneeling position, but when he went to swing his feet inside, he discovered that his knees were pinning down the skirt of his long coat and he could not move forward. He jumped back down to where he had started and began gathering the lower part of his coat above his waist.

"Take it off," Grisha whispered.

Why hadn't he thought of that? Handing his coat to Grisha, Yechiel hoisted himself onto the windowsill a second time. Now he easily swung his feet inside and explored the area under the window to make sure there was no furniture beneath. He had never been inside the Angel of Death, but he assumed that if this was the window that Reb Zelig chose to open every day, it must have unimpeded access. Feeling nothing, he eased himself carefully onto the floor.

"Here, take these," Grisha whispered.

Grisha handed his pack, both their jackets, and his leather cap through the window. The cap surprised Yechiel. How could a nonreligious Jew, even a revolutionary, enter a synagogue without a hat? Then he remembered that he had not told Grisha it was a synagogue; but he suspected that it would not have made very much difference anyway. Grisha climbed inside, and Yechiel immediately handed him back his hat.

"Should we close the window?" Grisha whispered.

"No, I don't think so. No one comes this way, and if they do, they would never notice it."

"God, it's warm in here. We can use the air. Where are we?"

"It's a synagogue."

"Why don't they use it?"

Yechiel hesitated. No doubt followers of scientific socialism were not supposed to be superstitious, but Yechiel had noticed the strange, terrified expression on Grisha's face at Barasch's after he had been told that they were in Krimsk. Yechiel had a presentiment that telling him the story of the Angel of Death would be a grave error. Yechiel did not usually have such premonitions; indeed, he did not believe they existed. Anyway, he didn't care about the Angel of Death. He wanted to talk about more interesting and relevant things.

"They don't need it; the beis midrash is big enough," he answered.

"Will they pray here tomorrow?"

"They use the beis midrash. No one will come in until the day after tomorrow," Yechiel said, confident that Reb Zelig would be at the beis midrash praying most of the day.

"Good," Grisha said. "By then I'll be far away from here. Can we light a match to see where we are?"

"We'd better not," Yechiel said, although he really didn't think it would make any difference. Who would believe that they saw light in the Angel of Death on Tisha B'Av?

"Might as well get comfortable. Are there benches here?"

Yechiel wasn't sure.

"Here they are. They feel like good ones, too. More comfortable than that step you were on, aren't they?"

Yechiel reached over and found them. "Yes," he agreed, sitting down. The Angel of Death was surprisingly comfortable.

"You said the rebbe threw you out?" Grisha inquired.

"Yes, he did," Yechiel admitted.

"Why?"

"Are you familiar with the Talmud? The Mishnah really?" Yechiel asked.

"Not very. My father died when I was very young, and my religious education stopped. I picked up a few things here and there."

"Well, I had a problem with a Mishnah—" Yechiel paused.

"You didn't believe it?" Grisha suggested.

"Something like that. I suggested that the rabbis might be wrong, or at least, their advice inappropriate for our days."

"What were they saying?" Grisha asked.

"It's somewhat complex. The most troubling situation was the one in which a group of Jewish women are walking along and a band of goyim tell them to give them one woman or they will rape them all. In that situation, both rabbis agree that you cannot give them even one soul of Israel. In other words, all the women will be raped."

"What do you expect with that kind of class consciousness?" Grisha replied.

"How does that work?" Yechiel asked.

"In a fair and just classless society, all people will act fairly and justly. People's material environment determines how they will act. If man's environment is perfected through socialist equality, then man will be perfected. You won't have the goyim attacking the Jews, and you won't have the Jews responding with absurd bourgeois notions of martyrdom. The only way the Jews will ever be safe is in an egalitarian, classless society."

"Oh," said Yechiel.

"How did the rebbe react to your criticism?"

"He said that evil should not be underestimated."

"Yes, he's right. Oh, how he's right," Grisha declared so enthusiastically that Yechiel had to quiet him down. "He's right. It must be torn out root and branch before it can inflict more evil. The system cannot reform itself; reform is nonsense. It must be totally destroyed and a new system built to take its place. He's no fool, your rebbe."

"I don't think that's what the rebbe meant. I think he meant that evil is totally corrupting and must be absolutely avoided. It is an incurable contagion that is best quarantined. It is like vermin. They enter easily and inconspicuously, but they do not leave without great suffering and sorrow," Yechiel said.

"But if all the women get raped, isn't that suffering and sorrow?" Grisha asked.

"I think so, but the rebbe would answer that surrendering someone to them would be far worse because the Jews themselves would be actively committing evil."

Since Yechiel did not seem to believe that, Grisha did not feel compelled to argue against it.

"Grisha, at Barasch's you said that if we had the time, you would prove scientifically that the proletariat is in bondage to a Russian pharaoh and that it could be redeemed only through a revolution created by a strong disciplined party. I would be interested in hearing the proof."

"It's very complex and involves many steps. You are a talmudist who would want to analyze every one of them. Yechiel, you should go to the sources. Read Lenin, Marx, too, of course, and there you will have it all laid out for you. You will be convinced, I promise you, and then you will join our noble revolutionary struggle." The last, Grisha expounded with considerable fervor.

"You really believe in the revolution, don't you?" Yechiel asked.

"Yechiel, it is a historical necessity. That is what the dialectic is all about. The Russian pharaoh must fall."

"The Krimsker Rebbe is always talking wistfully about the pharaoh," Yechiel mused.

"Well, there are parallels. Marx explains that each epoch contains the seeds of its own economic destruction. The system destroys itself through its very success. Pharaoh's slave system demanded more and more production from the workers, and finally they revolted. Of course that is a simplification, but it is not so different from capitalism today. The success of the capitalist factory system will create a workers' revolution. Comrade Lenin in his brilliance explains that even agrarian workers can be of use in the revolution. Yechiel, we need good minds like yours; there's a lot to be done, and we can do it. There may be suffering in the process, and that is unfortunate, but we must not lose sight of our goals."

"Grisha, have you ever killed a man?"

Grisha hesitated. "No, I haven't." He sounded disappointed that he had not. "But it is difficult to imagine a revolution without blood. When I said that you cannot make an omelette without breaking eggs, I meant it. I will do whatever is necessary as a member of the party to create the conditions for a revolution and to create a classless society afterward. We must do more than say psalms, we must remove the suffering that motivates people to say psalms."

Yechiel's silence suggested that he was not convinced.

"Yechiel, what *do* you believe?"

"It is easier to criticize than create; I admit that. I suppose I believe in God, but not the God who tells Jews how to tie knots on the fringes of their garments. I think Spinoza was right. There is some force that controls the way the stars move in the heavens and the way the waves flow in the sea. Those things are not random. Whatever that force is, that determination, I call God. As for specific remedies to our problems—personal, national—I'm not so sure," Yechiel answered.

"Read Lenin and Marx," Grisha urged.

"Maybe," Yechiel said noncommittally.

"They will answer all your questions. Why don't you want to read them?"

"You may be right, Grisha. Don't be offended, but if you cannot explain them—or you are unwilling to—then I cannot have too much confidence in them. Admittedly, without having read them, I cannot be sure, but I suspect that they will not answer my questions. I feel like a man who has a suit that no longer fits. Once it was very beautiful, but now either it is worn out or I have outgrown it. That is literally the suit I am wearing now, the Krimsker Rebbe's suit. And you are promising me a new, beautiful suit that will fit perfectly, but that suit, unfortunately, has not yet been made. Someday you might manufacture it, but it does not exist now. The cloth does not exist, nor do the tailors. So what am I to do? If I take off the ill-fitting suit and you do not produce the new one, I am left naked. It is not an easy decision."

Grisha laughed.

"Is that so funny?" Yechiel asked, offended at Grisha's lighthearted reaction to his dilemma.

"No, Yechiel, it is not funny. Forgive my laughing. You are a serious, gifted person. I wish that I had your abilities. I was laughing at myself. I think of myself as the midwife of history, ushering in the new era for all mankind, and you turn me into the ghetto tailor that my grandfather was, forever taking orders that he could not fill."

Grisha's voice trailed off into chuckling. Yechiel smiled, too, but given the night's events, he could not laugh. "Yes, it is funny. The sages say that there is nothing new under the sun."

"For the sages maybe there wasn't, but for us . . ."

"You are already taking measurements?" Yechiel interrupted.

"Of course, the trick is in the means of production," Grisha said in utmost seriousness.

Yechiel was still smiling in the dark. Revolutionaries and rebbes have very little sense of humor when they are talking shop, he reflected. He felt very tired, and although he did not want to go home, he knew that they were waiting for him while he talked of revolution. Forever talking.

"Grisha, I must be going. My parents must be wondering what happened to me. Will you be all right?"

"Yes."

"Do you need any food?"

"On a fast day?" Grisha asked in mock horror.

They both laughed.

"I forgot," Yechiel said.

"No, you forget nothing. You remember too much," Grisha said seriously, but not unkindly. "Thank you, Yechiel, I have enough. I played on Barasch's guilt over driving me away. But you were like Abraham, who welcomed strangers and gave them hospitality."

Yechiel did not know whether he was joking or not. "And you are like one of the angels who visited Abraham on his way to destroy Sodom."

"Yes, and you cannot look back. Yechiel, come with me. And if you cannot come now, contact us through our newspaper, *Iskra.*"

Grisha felt Yechiel's hand on his shoulder. He stood up and turned around to shake it.

"Good-bye," Yechiel said.

"Good-bye."

Grisha walked to the window and held the scholar's long coat while Yechiel climbed out; then he handed it to him.

"You had better close the window before you go to sleep. Do you want me to help you close it now?" Yechiel offered.

"No, I won't forget. Those things I remember. Thank you."

"Good night," Yechiel whispered and slipped into the dark night.

# CHAPTER TWENTY-THREE

No sooner had Yechiel entered than his parents called his name and came into the workroom where he was arranging several large cushions into a straight line.

"Yechiel, what are you doing?" his mother asked.

"The rebbe sleeps like this on Tisha B'Av, so I thought I would, too."

"Sleeping on the floor on Tisha B'Av?" his mother said quizzically.

Nachman Leib placed his hand on his wife's arm to still her. "Yechiel, you went to the rebbe?"

Yechiel busied himself aligning the cushions.

"They're dirty," his mother said.

"It's Tisha B'Av, Mother."

"I never heard about sleeping on the floor, and your grandfather, may he rest in peace, was a very religious man," she huffed.

"*Nu,* Hinda, if the rebbe does it, Yechiel can do it."

"Yechiel isn't the rebbe," Hinda said.

Yechiel felt his neck flushing in response to his mother's

words. He turned around and sat facing them on one of the cushions.

"Yes, father, I went to the rebbe."

"You were there this late?" his father asked.

"No, the rebbe spoke to me almost immediately. We talked for fifteen or twenty minutes, then I wandered around the rest of the night. I sat and I thought and I walked."

"What did the rebbe want?" his mother asked.

"He told me that he had heard good things about my studies."

"Do you hear, Nachman Leib. Good things about his studies!" she exclaimed.

"Shh! Hinda, let the boy talk."

"Then he asked me how old I was, and when I told him that I was eighteen, he said that an eighteen-year-old should stand under the marriage canopy."

"He talked to you about a match?" his mother asked in astonishment.

Yechiel nodded.

"So who was she? A mother has a right to know!"

Yechiel looked at his excited mother and his concerned father. Then he looked down at the floor and said, "His own daughter, Rachel Leah."

His mother gasped audibly, then recovered to exclaim, "Rachel Leah?"

"Yes, Mother."

"God in heaven!" she murmured. "Do you hear, Nachman Leib! The rebbe's only child and our own Yechiel!" Overcome, she began to cry. "*Mazel tov,* Yechiel, our groom!" She turned to share her ecstasy with her husband, but he looked very grave, almost morose.

"When?" she asked her son.

"Shh! Hinda. What did you answer the rebbe, Yechiel?" Nachman Leib asked.

Looking at his father, Yechiel said calmly, "I told him that I could not marry her."

His response did not surprise Nachman Leib, but Hinda's eyes fluttered and her mouth opened into a small circle. She panted in short breaths. "No, no," she said quietly to herself as if what she had heard could not possibly be true. "No, she's a lovely girl. A little quiet, but a good girl. A fine girl, a very religious girl. No!"

"I told him I was unworthy," Yechiel added.

"What did the rebbe say?" his father asked.

"At first, he wouldn't accept it. He said he felt that way, too, when the Beziner Rebbe offered him his holy Shayna Basya."

Suddenly Hinda returned to the conversation, exploding forcefully, "It may not be too late!" And then she continued in frantic optimism, "Yechiel can run back to him right now and beg his pardon. Come, Yechiel! The rebbe will understand. Nachman Leib, tell him to go at once. The holy rebbe will understand!"

"Mother, it's too late! Other things happened!" Yechiel stated definitively.

"No, Yechiel, he's a rebbe, a holy man. He'll forgive you. You're a young, poor boy. You were overwhelmed. Surely he can understand that. Nachman Leib, go in to the rebbe with him. Beg his forgiveness! It's not fair," she continued, "a young boy makes a tragic mistake because of his modesty. He's from a poor home. In the house of Israel that is no sin. So was the rebbe himself.—Go, go, it's getting late. Avoid the rebbetzin. With her Minsker nose in the air, she won't have any pity, but the rebbe is different. Look what he did this evening with Itzik Dribble, and it wasn't just because he's a rich man's son. All right, it didn't hurt that his father has the match factory, but the Krimsker Rebbe isn't like the other rebbes. The Krimsker Rebbe chose our Yechiel to be his son-in-law!" Her hysterical prattling gave way to a great burst of bawling as she said, "Our Yechiel," and heaved with sobs.

Nachman Leib put his arm around her, and when that didn't comfort her, he took her in both his arms and embraced her, rocking her gently. He told her that it wasn't always so easy to know what was for the best. Sometimes, he said, you can't even tell a blessing from a curse. Hinda was so distressed that she could not understand her husband's words. She looked up from Nachman Leib's chest and sobbed, "Why, Yechiel? Why can't anything good happen to us?"

"Hinda, Hinda, don't talk that way. So much good happens. Everything is good," he said.

Yechiel, who was sitting quietly and feeling miserable, suddenly realized how much he was his mother's son. He refused to accept things the way they were, nor could he see the good in situations. He was his mother's son, and Shraga, with his deep faith and loving nature, was his father's son. Yechiel was her son, but he couldn't comfort her. He began crying, too, but even that was based on *his* understanding of her pain.

"Hinda, Hindale, it's all right. Come, lie down in your room. Let me talk to the boy."

Nachman Leib led Hinda out of the room. Yechiel heard her weeping and his father's soft voice trying to comfort her. And it had to be Tisha B'Av, when she would not sip a drop of water. In tomorrow's heat, she would suffer terribly if she continued crying like that.

His father returned and sat down next to him. "Are you all right?"

"Yes, Father, why?"

"You're crying, too, you know."

"Yes, but not like Mother. I'm sorry," Yechiel said.

Nachman Leib put a comforting hand on his son's knee. "Yechiel?"

"Yes."

"What were the 'other things' that happened at the rebbe's?"

In his retelling Yechiel omitted that the rebbe had called him a "vermin" because he thought that would be too painful, and he neglected to tell his father that he was planning to leave Krimsk because he thought that could be left for later. He had enough unpleasant news without his impending departure.

"It just cannot be. I hope Mother understands."

"No, it cannot be. With what you feel, you did the right thing. You could not marry the girl; that would be unfair."

Yechiel was moved by his father's sense of decency. He wanted to tell him that Shraga was worth ten of himself, but Shraga would never be offered the rebbe's only daughter. Undoubtedly, his father was worried about him not only because he had turned down such a spectacular match but also because he was a heretic and a sinner. Yechiel wished that his father would cry like his mother, but he simply turned to Yechiel with the question, "Why?"

Yechiel answered, "Father, why does any man believe what he does? He looks into his heart and it's there."

"Maybe you didn't look long enough. Sometimes the heart is a very confusing place. We think we believe something, but when we search more carefully with the help of our Torah and teachers, we find something altogether different."

"I don't know, Father. It's something that has been bothering me for a long time. I wouldn't say something like that to the rebbe unless I had thought about it very carefully."

"Yechiel, I know that. You are a very good and honest son. Your ability made us proud and brought us happiness, but that wasn't what we treasured most about you," his father said.

"Earlier, I wanted to go see the rebbe," Yechiel said, "but then I had no idea that he was seeing hasidim. I was very moved by his kindness to Itzik Dribble. I was even jealous of Itzik because I wanted to talk to the rebbe and tell him the things that were bothering me. I wanted him to help me, to guide me, to show me something I had overlooked. Instead, he got angry and called me a heretic and a sinner."

"Yechiel, you know the rebbe expected more from you because of your scholarship. He even expected you to be the next rebbe. And he offered you his daughter and his kingdom. The rebbe is still a father. He must have been hurt that you rejected his only daughter. After all, a father can accept insults to himself, but not to his children. Those are so much more painful. I know."

"I suppose so, but I was hoping that he would understand. I didn't want to hurt him."

"But don't you understand, Yechiel? You are hurting him because you are hurting God—and because you are hurting God, you are hurting yourself, too."

"And I'm hurting you, too. Forgive me."

"Raising children involves pain. If one can't accept that, he had better not be a father. Yechiel, maybe you have been spending your time in the wrong places with the wrong people."

"You mean Barasch and Yudel?" Yechiel asked.

"Yes, I do. They might not be so bad themselves, but you might see things differently if you weren't around them so much."

"Father, I went to Barasch's tonight because I felt uncomfortable in the beis midrash and I felt uncomfortable about coming home."

"It's not just tonight."

"I don't think they corrupted me, even though they tried. I have not been seduced by foreign gods. I don't see that the foreign gods are any better than the one we have in Krimsk. I wish that I had discovered some truth to guide me, but I haven't. I feel as if I have lost the truth I had and I don't have anything in its place."

"You shouldn't be afraid to admit that you made a mistake if you have made one. I know you are a fine scholar and a brilliant young man; with some problems, however, time is more important than intellect. It's difficult to see the beauty in a poor, persecuted town like Krimsk when you are young and expect the sun to shine on the world as if it were the Garden of Eden. But, Yechiel, there is beauty in

Krimsk. A quiet and holy beauty. The rebbe is right that we are a holy nation. I'm not talking about the beis midrash with the rebbe and the Torahs and all the other books. They certainly are very holy, but I cannot appreciate those the way I should. I see the beauty in our holy nation when the poor, tired Jews wish each other a good Sabbath on Friday nights as they enter and leave the beis midrash. We are a holy nation, and we have a holy day. The Shabbos is our bride, and no matter how difficult, dreary, and even desperate our world can be, there is always a corner of the week that is pure and holy and good, when God is very close to us. That is the corner we live for during the week that is our true home.

"Yechiel, I did not appreciate these things when I was younger. I still see the hunger in Krimsk. I see Shraga slaving away on filthy leather. I know that Alexander Bornstein was almost killed tonight by those bloodthirsty goyim. I don't know if we shall have enough money to buy everyone shoes. I cannot always sleep at night. I lie awake worrying about you, too, and I don't know why we have to have these difficulties, but we do or God wouldn't give them to us the same way he gave us his holy corner, the Sabbath."

"Tatta, I love you," Yechiel said, calling his father the name he had used when he was very small and his father carried him through the muddy streets to his first religious classes.

"And I love you," his father replied. "There is a lot in Krimsk, don't think there isn't. Yechiel, have you thought about what you are going to do now?"

"I don't know."

"I suppose you cannot stay in the beis midrash," his father said sadly, knowing that Yechiel could not, but wishing as only a father can that he could.

Yechiel just shook his head. His father placed his hand on his son's shoulders and leaned over to embrace him delicately. Yechiel turned to hug him with all his might, the way he had when he was a child and knew that whatever strength he could give his father, he would receive more in return. His father held him gently.

"Now you must rest, my son. That can help, too." Nachman Leib stood up. "Just rest."

"Good night, Father."

"Yes, good night," he said and left the room.

Yechiel lay back on his cushions, which were surprisingly comfortable, and thought that he did have something in common with the rebbe. He closed his eyes and opened them again. Somewhere—probably in the kitchen—a candle was burning. Around him he could make out various forms. All kinds of objects, large and small, crowded the workroom. In the faint shadow of light they assumed the most monstrous and fantastic shapes, but their chaotic turbulence was nothing compared to the thoughts and ideas that swam inside his head. When he closed his eyes, things were even more monstrous and fantastic. Krimsk, the rebbe, Grisha, his father, Spinoza, Shraga, his mother, Rabbi Yehoshua, Rabbi Eliezer, Rachel Leah, Lenin, even Matti Sternweiss guzzling candies, danced before him.

This confusion lasted for the longest time. It was so overwhelming that Yechiel could not respond. He had no hope of sorting things out.

When the parade of images finally began to slow down, however, Yechiel tried to calm himself further with his tool for relaxation, intellectual analysis. He focused on the fascinating similarities between the Krimsker Rebbe and his newfound friend Grisha, who preached such antithetical doctrines. These comparisons had impressed him very strongly earlier in the Angel of Death, and he began to formulate them.

Both men were fanatical, fiery in their exposition. Each believed not only that the world depended entirely on himself but also that the world was literally in his hands to shape as he would. Grisha and the rebbe both agreed that the present situation was intolerable and subscribed to messianic redemption that would drastically change both the individual and society. Of course the rebbe believed that absolute truth resided in the Torah, whereas Grisha had his holy writings in Marx and Lenin. For them, Yechiel reflected, all these works are so convincing that both the rebbe and Grisha tell you not to question, just study. And both are willing to sacrifice the individual to a greater good, all the while maintaining that through some extension of identity—either the sanctity of God's name or the revolutionary struggle—such sacrifice is in the individual's self-interest. And of course, Yechiel thought somewhat humorously, they both hate each other with a passion.

Yechiel was not one of them. He admitted to not having the truth, and he could not believe that the world depended on him—which, he confessed, was very fortunate for the world. He believed that the individual was sacrosanct, not some theological or ideological abstraction.

And Yechiel was not a mass of energy; he wanted to relax. His father's concept of a holy corner in time was very relaxing, and he would like to enter that sacred corner with him. But that took more than time; it took love, too. Although he dearly loved his father and family, Yechiel knew that he did not have the kind of love his father had. Yechiel could not envision his future any more than he could identify the strange shapes in the darkness, but he knew that his future led out of Krimsk.

# CHAPTER TWENTY-FOUR

HUFFING AND PANTING, BARASCH LIMP LEGS CORK-screwed down the road to Krimsk, pursued by a nightmare, but not his usual one related to his physical appearance.

Barasch Limp Legs had a long, horsey face, as if a barrel had rolled over it, leaving it flat and long with a brutish texture. This was ironic, for a barrel had injured his legs, not his face. Barasch Limp Legs still had nightmares in which black barrels fell off a wagon and bounced toward him. As they hit his legs, he would awaken with such excruciating pains tearing through his shins and knees that he fully expected to find the barrels larger than the house, their bulky obtuse tops poking among the fuzzy clouds as their dark, filthy, rotting bottoms crushed his legs. The crippling accident had occurred when Barasch was a child of eight. Now the twisted legs reached different lengths. He poled along on his short left leg, while the long, powerless right leg trailed, making a negligible contribution, a broken paddle floundering uselessly above the water's surface. This skewed, trailing leg, which caught everyone's eye, was responsible for his nickname of Barasch Limp Legs.

This leg now flailed uselessly about in the direction from which he had come as if frantically waving goodbye to someone on the disappearing horizon. In addition, his back curled and uncurled, which, joined with the skewed leg, created the unbalanced spinning appearance of a corkscrew.

His spine was straight, but in order to balance himself as he reeled about, Barasch had to double himself over. Strangers watching him walk often mistook him for a humpback. When one of them asked to rub his hump for luck, Barasch liked to effect a sweet revenge. By balancing on his long, weak leg, he straightened himself up to his full, considerable height and stared down at his tormentor. That ploy, too, had its tottering dangers; Barasch never attempted it on windy or wet days. Before he had joined Beryl Soffer at the match factory, there had even been a strange compensation for his pretzel-bent gait. Barasch had worked in a local inn as a kitchen assistant and waiter; during the fair, gypsy women entered for refreshment and were always pestering to rub his nonexistent hump. He invited them to do so in his dark cubbyhole of a room. These nocturnal visits bred the legend that Barasch was a great lover who could satisfy the most lust-crazed gypsies.

Barasch preferred to sit behind tables or other objects that masked his painful embarrassment. In his room at the Soffer and Company factory, he relaxed in a moth-eaten, overstuffed easy chair behind a long plank table. All the pieces of furniture were relics from Soffer and Company;

indeed, direct bequests from Beryl himself. The chair had lost its pile under Beryl's presidential itch. While the chair had grown smooth, the table had become rough as myriad matchsticks slid across its surface, each causing the most minute abrasions until the table itself was as pitted as a ploughed field.

Beryl enjoyed the idea of getting further use from the table, but the sight of Barasch Limp Legs sprawled in maimed majesty upon the easy-chair throne in which Beryl's magisterial presence had previously resided did strike Beryl as decidedly inappropriate. At such moments Beryl confessed to himself that he had created a monster and swore that he would have Barasch fired at the end of the month. But no sooner would Beryl return to his office than he would be sending another gift to Barasch Limp Legs—his table, his stool, his shirts, his pants, his cufflinks, even Beryl's own underwear.

Beryl knew that he needed Barasch in the worst way. Beryl feared fire: self-destruction by his own creation. If his former assistant Yitzhak Weinbach represented a commercial expression of such anxiety, and Itzik the filial variety, the matches themselves constituted the great, haunting daily terror itself. When Beryl was in his office, he felt that his presence assured the factory's safety. It was in his absence that the great flammable empire became so tragically vulnerable. Beryl knew no peace until he had forged his understanding with Barasch Limp Legs.

Barasch understood that he was never to leave the factory grounds when Beryl was absent. One of them, dressed in Beryl's clothes, had to be there at all times. The bachelor had no skills, lacked mobility, was trustworthy, and had ceased to attend prayers and to observe the Shabbos long before Beryl had hired him. Beryl did have pangs of conscience on that point. He was forever encouraging his other employees to observe the commandments and be good Jews. Generous in providing time for afternoon and evening prayers, he even closed the factory at noon on short winter Fridays so that everyone would have time to prepare for the Sabbath. All except Barasch. Instead, Beryl showered upon him his old suspenders, his old socks, his old shoes, until even Beryl, seeing Barasch dressed in all the gifts, realized that in some crazy way Barasch had become a part of him and he had become a part of Barasch. Beryl did not explore this thought, but, practical man that he was, when choosing cloth for a new garment, he considered how the material would look on Barasch as well.

Barasch, for his part, accepted this suffocating nurture. He suffered the cripple's tragedy: he believed what others believed about him—that he was a well-meaning, useless freak. In the great march of history, he was condemned to hobble slowly and out of step, whereas on Beryl's coattails he was freed from the harsh, demanding pace.

The town wits were forever taunting, "Hey, Barasch, does your ass itch yet?" Barasch knew that he and Beryl had more in common than their clothing. Barasch was not the atheist everyone believed him to be. True, he did not attend services and he did not observe the Sabbath, but he was not as "anti" as he made himself out to be. Furthermore, he knew that Beryl was not as pious—at least not as committed a believer—as he appeared to be. Both men led ideological lives that were as much designed to convince themselves as they were to serve God and his Torah, as was the case with Beryl, or to encourage radical social change, as was the case with Barasch. Both appeared to be leaders, but in reality both were followers who took great satisfaction from the preaching of believers.

When the town wits shouted their barbed taunts, asking Barasch whether his ass had begun to itch yet, he was hurt, but he thought them fools. Didn't they know that a capitalist spits on all members of the proletariat? While he was waiting for the revolution, why not wear the boss's clothing? It was better made, more comfortable, and free. In simple truth, Barasch genuinely both liked and disliked Beryl. After all, he was entitled to the original wearer's most intimate feelings toward himself, and these were decidedly ambivalent. So Barasch appropriated them, too, along with the clothing, food, and shelter.

Theoretically, he was willing to appropriate Beryl's entire factory and fortune, too. Not for himself, of course; for the people. But as in the case of so many theories, a slight encounter with reality destroyed it. Young Shraga's harness-needle-toughened knuckles rapping on Barasch's door, which sent Grisha and Yechiel sprawling headlong under the table, had a telling effect on Barasch himself. He was jarred by the realization that he loved Beryl, his provider, and not those ne'er-do-wells who were camping out at his and Beryl's table.

This outburst of love was stimulated by the cripple's new nightmare: the tsarist police, he was certain, were about to end his secure, easy, comfortable life forever. The authorities would surely send him to the Arctic forests or the Siberian mines. How long could a cripple survive in regions that mutilated and crushed the strongest of men into lifeless pulp? Why send him so far for burial? They might as well dig a trench in the factory yard and fling him in. They would be saving themselves trouble and Barasch agony.

And what had Barasch done to deserve this? To occupy his time he indulged in idle gossip against the tsar. And with whom? Yudel the Litvak, that charismatic firebrand, and Yechiel the talmudist, dynamic man of action. The tsar should pay Barasch to form such ineffectual revolutionary cells as Yudel, Yechiel, and himself. The investigators would release the asocial Litvak and the incompetent scholar in an hour with the warning to avoid bad company, but Barasch had hosted revolutionaries, social revolutionaries, Bolsheviks, Marxists, and anarchists! Would the tsarist police believe that he knew nothing more than Grisha's name? Would they believe that Barasch could have hosted scores of dissidents without playing a key role in the revolutionary underground? As he had heard the knock, the terrible fluids rose in his throat until Barasch could taste their acidic burning and he recognized them for the corrosive harbinger of his fate.

The secret police would torture him. The investigators would believe the usual foolishness that a spine-bent, leg-smashed excuse of a man must be inured to incredible pain and would exercise all their ingenuity and cruelty to make such a long-suffering stoic talk. Barasch sadly knew better. He had never adjusted to pain. Quite the contrary, his tolerance lessened as he grew older. Twinges that he could have ignored in his youth now wracked his entire frame, leaving him dizzy and enervated.

His only refuge against pain was his ample shelter at

Soffer and Company, and now all of this was to be taken from him. Why? Because he had shown hospitality to those foolish young vagabonds like the cowardly Grisha under the table. Did he think that the tsarist police wouldn't have enough sense to look under a table? Barasch could not stand the thought of Grisha, for he seemed to be pushing Barasch into a Siberian mine. He wouldn't last a week north of the Arctic Circle, but all those healthy young troublemakers who had nothing better to do than to troop around the countryside enmeshing innocent men in their diabolical schemes, they were young and strong and could live through anything. They would return after five, ten, twenty years and rear a family without even recalling the face, much less the name, of the poor suffering wretch they had buried beneath the brutal police truncheons. He should only live so long as to reach Siberia. When they discovered he would not give them any information, would they believe he didn't have any? They would flay him alive!

When Barasch had opened the door and discovered Yechiel's little brother, he realized that he had been granted a temporary reprieve. But only temporary, for if Nachman Leib knew where Yechiel was and how to find him, too many people knew. Every political fugitive who came near knew of Barasch Limp Legs and his legendary hospitality. Only one had to betray him and he was finished. It need not even be a purposeful betrayal. Some young trusting zealot and would-be-revolutionary fool discloses to a friend where he is going or where he has been, and the information continues circulating until it reaches an informer or someone who wants to curry favor with the police. What could be easier than to accuse an anonymous man who is no more than an impersonal, far-flung name, like Alaska or Siam on a map of distant lands?

When he had seen little Shraga, he had tried to swallow the taste of choking putrefaction, but he could not. Barasch had been foolish for too long with too many. Yudel and Yechiel left at once, but Grisha, shrewd manipulator, played upon Barasch's fears. Grisha suggested that if he got caught foraging near Krimsk, it would go very badly for everyone. Barasch bought him off by giving him so much food that such an obnoxiously healthy creature could walk to Paris without stopping for provisions. In return, Grisha had promised not to sleep anywhere near Krimsk and to walk for miles before even stopping to rest.

Once Grisha was gone, Barasch could not be apprehended with revolutionaries in his house, but he still needed an alibi. He had to be seen somewhere so that people could testify that he had been with them this evening. Staying alone at the Soffer factory tonight as his job demanded was simply inviting his own execution. Barasch decided to do something that he had never done before—abandon his beloved patron's factory when neither Beryl nor anyone else was there.

As Barasch came zigzagging down the road pursued by his new nightmare of Siberian hardships, he did not even know whether he had closed the yard gate. What was more, he didn't care. Now that he knew the revolutionary cat was out of the bag, he had to prove that he was nowhere nearby when the special police came to investigate the hut that had sheltered such dangerous antisocial predators as that confessed Marxist-Leninist-Bolshevik Hershel Shwartzman. "My friends call me Grisha," he had said so warmly. Barasch made a note to refer to him in all his police interrogations as "Shwartzman," or at the very worst as "Hershel Shwartzman." Perhaps he could claim that he never even knew Grisha's name at all. No, that would sound as if he were hiding something. He must appear to be simple, open, and honest, with nothing to hide. With a lonely job, in the biblical tradition he welcomed strangers, but when he had heard that Shwartzman was speaking against "our little father" the tsar, he threw him out of his house at once. They weren't even with him very long. And if they didn't believe him, he had spent time with his dear friends the . . .

Sweating like a horse, Barasch arrived at the outskirts of Krimsk. The first ramshackle house with junkyard belonged to his dear old friend, Boruch Levi. Yes, Boruch Levi, ruffian and boor, was indeed a generous friend. Whenever Boruch Levi was riding by in his swaybacked wagon pulled by that miserable nag—Piffle Fart, he called him—he would always ask Barasch if he needed some help. Boruch Levi's two hands could lift the weight that demanded four others. He would do a man a favor and neither ask for nor expect immediate reward. Of course, when something had to be junked from the factory, Boruch Levi received first call, and Barasch never quarreled over his price. What could be more natural on a dull, warm, exceptionally lonely night like this than Barasch strolling into town to spend some time with his dear old friend and business associate, Boruch Levi?

A faint flicker of candlelight appeared to be dancing within. Barasch slowed down, hobbled into the junk-filled yard, and knocked on the door more quietly than Shraga Katzman had pounded on his.

Malka, Boruch Levi's sister, opened the door and greeted Barasch with an effusive, gap-toothed smile wholly inappropriate to Tisha B'Av. Amidst his heavy breathing, which shook his long head up and down, Barasch managed a warm smile in return.

"Barasch, is anything wrong?" she asked in great concern.

Barasch coughed and shook his head.

"You're all hot and excited. Have you been running?"

Barasch managed to control his breathing for a moment. "It's hot! Terribly hot!"

"Yes, just awful. I suffer from it myself. Just something terrible. Why don't you come in and rest a moment?"

"Thank you," Barasch said with a smile.

As he entered, he heard her take a deep sucking breath. The forceful and rapacious current of air in the gap between her two front teeth sounded like a rising spring stream. It made him nervous.

"Who's there, Malka?" a tired, older woman's voice called.

Barasch knew that it was Sarah, their mother. Barasch wanted to announce his presence, but before he could, Malka spoke.

"No one, Mama, just me. It's so hot inside, I thought I would step out to the yard for a moment to get some air."

She took Barasch's arm and led him outside. He was not inclined to follow, but before he knew it she had led him into the shed in the junk-filled yard where she graded the rags that Boruch Levi collected.

"How is everything at the factory, Barasch?" she asked.

"Fine, everything's all right. I just came by to be

sociable. To see how the neighbors are doing," Barasch said matter-of-factly.

"Oh, I can imagine how lonely you must be out there, Barasch. I often think how much you need a companion to cook for you and to take care of you."

As Barasch's breathing calmed, Malka's was quickening. She made no effort to hide her growing excitement.

It was dark, but Barasch knew what she looked like. He had seen her often enough as he passed by on his way to and from town. She had met his glances with a frank, welcoming gaze of her own that said, Yes, that's right. If you're interested, come right in. He would turn away and hurry on. He would have liked to come in.

Malka was a large, powerful woman. She had dull brick-red hair and a large square face with a pug nose and a fleshy, lascivious mouth. The eyes were clear and crafty but too small for her large face. They laughed easily and communicated bold, unlicensed desires. They might have appeared weasel-like were the face any narrower, but in such a full face they appeared porcine, especially when Malka stood by the fence munching a loaf of bread. Even then, the craftiness never left her eyes. Although it was too dark to see them, he knew they were focused on him the way a cat stalks a bird with a broken wing.

Yes, Barasch found Malka attractive. For all her strength and bestial coarseness, she was a woman. Stronger than most men—Barasch had seen her flinging pieces of metal from one pile to another that would make a teamster grunt—and yet for all her bovine bulk and power, there was something deeply and provocatively feminine about her. A lame, broken creature, Barasch was enticed by her well-knit, gross, beefy excess. Others were, too. When negotiating over bottles, rags, or some metal, a peasant might be tempted to paw at her abundant, unrestrained breasts or touch her large, boxy hips, only to be sent sprawling into the dirt with a swipe of her clublike arms.

Malka would stand above him with laughter in her small eyes as if to say, Yes, you're right, but it's not for you and you're not man enough to take it. And she could bargain, too. The peasants said she drove a harder bargain than her brother, but she lacked Boruch Levi's fierce concentration. Her commercial instincts seemed to share a common source with her womanly passions: it was either feast or famine. Barasch understood that she had invited him into the yard to feast.

Malka's brother, Boruch Levi, however, unlike his sister, was very straitlaced and abstemious. When he chanced upon Malka and a customer involved in unorthodox negotiations, Boruch Levi would send the poor devil flying over the fence into the road. The one who incautiously remained conscious soon regretted his error. Boruch Levi wasn't above giving his sister a good smack either. Although Malka must have weighed as much as he did, he was not beefy but muscular. She dared not raise a clublike arm to his steely sinews. What if Boruch Levi were to emerge and find Barasch with his sister?

But Barasch had come for a reason. He needed witnesses for his alibi. Malka was just one, and a problematic one at that. Would she be willing to testify that Barasch had been with her all night? If she did compromise her honor, the police would think that she was doing so to protect her lover, whereas Boruch Levi would certainly believe her, and

Barasch might be better off facing trial as a revolutionary. Boruch Levi had a temper, and his wrath was ferocious.

"I came to see Boruch Levi," Barasch said.

"You should have come earlier. The dear boy is asleep now. They're all asleep except for me. Why don't you sit down here next to me? The rags make a very comfortable couch."

Barasch should have stepped back, but he hesitated, thinking that if he did live to be exiled, he would regret forever not having accepted Malka's invitation to share the soft rag pile with her. In the still heat, her steamy female odors assaulted him; they were every bit as overpowering as her punch. If he did establish an alibi and save his freedom, he would come to get her.

"Malka, it's late," he said rather weakly.

"Not for us gypsies, Barasch dear," she said.

Malka correctly interpreted his hesitation. She reached up and yanked down on his belt. Barasch felt himself falling and grabbed the shed pole for dear life as she tugged on his pants. He tried to work away from her grip, and his long limp leg uselessly kicked into some empty bottles. They tinkled like a bell before one shattered in a hearty explosion of broken glass. Malka stopped pulling, and they both listened for a moment. To Barasch's disappointment and Malka's delight, they heard nothing in the house.

Malka's mother, Sarah, however, had not gone back to sleep. Instead, she had peeked out the window to discover Malka entertaining Soffer's gimpy watchman. She was debating whether or not to awaken her hardworking son, Boruch Levi, who so richly deserved to rest. Having heard stories of Barasch's associating with the gypsies, she did not believe that any good could come of this night's romance. The bottle breaking seemed to symbolize the best she could expect.

Although she firmly shook her son's shoulder, Boruch Levi was very slow in getting up. He was having a strange, troubling dream in which cats were burning.

"Check the yard, son."

"You heard something, Ma? Did Thunder neigh?" he asked. He respectfully never referred to his horse by any other name in front of his mother.

"She's out there with someone."

"On Tisha B'Av? . . . The slut," he said, putting on his pants.

"Take a candle," she said.

"Ma, I had a dream of burning cats."

"Pooh, pooh, pooh," she spat. He did, too.

"That's not good. Throw some salt on your way out and don't say anything else till you do."

He threw the salt and went into the yard with the candle, to find Barasch clinging naked to the pole and Malka sitting on the rag pile with his pants in her hand. The cripple's naked legs were quivering like leaves in a storm, but the knees couldn't knock since one was so much higher than the other. He could see from Malka's sullen disappointment that nothing had happened.

"Ma wants you in the house, quick," he ordered his sister.

She let go of Barasch's pants and stood up. She knew better than to say anything when Boruch Levi acted on their mother's authority. Pouting with no sense of shame, she went into the house.

Barasch let go of the pole to pull up his pants and fell over onto the rag pile. He floundered around trying to hitch up his trousers until Boruch Levi lifted him to his feet.

"Barasch, if I catch you here again, I'm going to straighten out your legs," Boruch Levi said quietly.

"Boruch Levi, it's not the way it looks," Barasch whined, twisting his long face into a simpering smile.

Had Barasch not been a cripple, Boruch Levi would have wiped that smile off with his left hand, breaking the jaw in the process.

"Get going, Barasch!"

"I came to be sociable. I just wanted to say hello to you," Barasch pleaded.

"You said hello, and if you want to be sociable, try the Waksmans next door. They're very sociable. Froika will even play the violin for you."

"Yes, that's a good idea. I think I'll do that." Buttoning Beryl's old pants, Barasch hobbled out as fast as he could.

Boruch Levi stood alone in the yard, contemplating his dream of burning cats. What could it possibly mean? He remembered that the holy rebbe had told him that the Evil Inclination would try anything.

# CHAPTER TWENTY-FIVE

GITTEL WAKSMAN HAD TAKEN HER SON FROIKA HOME AT once when she heard that Grannie Zara had died. The witch had been one of the polestars by which Krimsk had charted its course, and it was as if the heavens had changed. Good or bad, no such fundamental change could be anything but frightening. Gittel, like most of Krimsk, believed in the witch's powers and had always felt it wise to consult the cat lady before beginning any serious undertakings.

When she decided that Froika should study the violin, Gittel took the instrument in its felt-lined carrying case to Krimichak. She opened the case, explaining that she desired her son to become a great violinist who would play for the tsar. The witch plucked feebly at the strings and asked, "What is it?" Gittel replied that it was a violin. The witch repeated her question, and Gittel replied that it was her son's future. The witch cryptically responded, "For heaven's sakes, make up your mind!" and then added, "Whatever it is, keep it shiny. Such things look better when you can see your face in them."

Since then Gittel had polished the violin until it gleamed. Had she discovered a way for Froika to play it without touching it, she would have been ecstatic. So would Froika. Had he ceased playing altogether, all of Krimsk's living creatures with the exception of Gittel and the deaf cemetery attendant would have said psalms of thanksgiving. Froika was tone-deaf. Putting a violin, even a shiny one, into his hands was as sensible as putting a Talmud into Itzik Dribble's. That boor Boruch Levi once approached the house and shouted that he didn't care about himself, his sister, or his aged mother, but his poor horse Piffle Fart couldn't sleep and the Waksmans should take pity on a dumb beast at least. His foulmouthed sister Malka was heard to remark in the marketplace that Gittel should not have been so cheap: she should have taken the violin to Grannie Zara herself and not settled for the caterwauling cats.

Froika hated the violin more passionately than any Jew hates Haman on Purim, but he played it, and he practiced on it. His father, Menachem the shoemaker, considered piercing his ears with an awl. Menachem said that he envied the dumb shoes around him that had tongues but no ears. He confided his little joke to Froika, who laughed heartily. Froika's tone deafness spared him part of the misery, but he stood closer than anyone else, and as they say, you don't have to be a hen to tell a rotten egg.

Gittel made all the decisions. Menachem considered himself fortunate that Gittel focused her attention on the children. Before their arrival, Gittel had been toying with the idea that she and Menachem should open an inn. This idea expired graciously with the birth of their first child. This was Menachem's great reward in fathering them. To his dismay, Froika, their fifth, was also their last. If they could not produce number six soon, Gittel might turn the force of her unbridled ambition back onto Menachem himself. His specific fear was that Froika would run away and that he himself would be forced to play the violin for Gittel and Nicholas II. Since this melodic specter dwelt with Menachem on his workbench, he did not intervene in Froika's musical education. Although Menachem did not expect Froika to blossom into a musical prodigy overnight, he prayed sincerely that the gradual process would begin. He had a similar attitude toward the messianic redemption. At any rate, the shoemaker feared the shiny violin and did not intercede on his son's behalf.

Surprisingly, Froika tolerated his violin lessons. A clever, headstrong boy in addition to being youngest and really quite spoiled, he rarely did things that he did not enjoy. He realized very early, however, that in certain matters he was no match for his mother. Few were. Gittel, a small, well-proportioned woman, appeared calm, reasonable, and affable. Froika knew that she had a remarkable power to gather all the chaos and confusion in her life—the very stuff that drove others to distraction—compress it into a single thread, and follow it with maniacal dedication wherever it led. In his case, to the throne room of the tsar. He understood that her mad projects were designed to improve his and his family's lot. He appreciated that, but ultimately the generosity of her motivation was irrelevant. With his perceptive maturity and common sense, he knew that the path of least resistance was his only option.

He had no choice, but he did learn a valuable lesson—that every simple human being contains the potential for madness, strength, and purpose that his mother had. The only other person he knew who seemed to realize some of his potential power was the Krimsker Rebbe. As Froika sawed on the shiny violin, he wondered what great things he might be capable of some day. If he could unlock the power that he possessed, he might reach anywhere—even into the tsar's court, although that held no attraction for him. Especially tonight.

Froika had been pleased to return home. He had grown weary of repeating the pond story. Next time they might not be so lucky. The more he thought about what had happened, the more he became depressed. He sat by himself and thought. His mother came over to hug him periodically. His father said "Thank God" every time Froika caught his eye.

The incident at the pond was over and had ended very satisfactorily, but Froika was frightened about the future. The Krimichak boys might easily have drowned Alexander Bornstein and gone unpunished; killing a Jew was no crime. Froika had heard how Grannie Zara had saved Krimsk from a pogrom with her upraised broom, but now she was dead, and her protection had been incomplete anyway. The goyim were known to beat, maim, rape, even kill Jews, and the Jews accepted this as if it were in the nature of things—"our unfortunate but fated perils." The Jew could run away, but there was nowhere to run. Nothing changed: in Krimichak the goyim were still goyim, and in Krimsk the Jews were still Jews, and sooner or later there was sure to be another murderous assault.

Froika had read a newspaper account of the Kishinever pogrom, which had occurred in the spring. Thousands and thousands of Jews had been murdered. He was sure that nothing had changed in Kishinev either. The goyim would go unpunished, the Jews would not learn to protect themselves, and it would all happen again. There would be the usual blood libel, and it would be Jewish blood that would flow. Froika had read in the same article that the goyim believed that the Jews needed the blood of a Christian child to make the Passover unleavened bread. Initially he was incredulous at such an obscene absurdity; every schoolboy knew that the Torah called the blood the soul of the creature and forbade it. Even the blood of a kosher cow or chicken was not permitted. The only person he had ever seen drink blood was a Krimichak farmer who had slaughtered a pig and poked his cup into the dark red stream pouring forth from the creature's neck. The goy saw the Jewish boys and laughingly offered them some; Froika was revolted. As they ran off to the woods, he thought to himself, the goyim will eat anything. How could the Jews refute such foolishness if the goyim willingly believed it? Facts and reason were simply irrelevant, so there was no possible way to educate anyone to the truth. That murderous fool Casimir believed that Grannie Zara was a Jew. Froika found that laughable, too, but he had an uneasy feeling in his stomach that no good would come of that nonsense. Yesterday Kishinev, tomorrow Krimsk?

Froika could no longer sit still. He jumped up and began pacing.

"You are safe at home. Relax," his father said.

But Froika could not relax. He was at home, all right, but he was not safe. Jews were never safe.

"We have to leave Krimsk," he said with certainty.

"You had a fright this evening. It will pass," his father answered.

"We have to leave Krimsk. There's no other way. We have to leave Krimsk," he repeated.

His mother came to him and took his hand. "Yes, we must leave Krimsk," she agreed with even greater passion.

Froika was delighted that someone had understood.

"Do you know how to leave Krimsk?" she asked her son.

"No," he answered. That was the problem.

She led him to the crude sideboard and pointed.

"Do you know what that is, Froika?"

Froika stared in disappointment at the bumpy, grainy black case. "A violin," he said.

"No, make up your mind, Froika. It is a means of conveyance," she said with deep satisfaction that she had finally answered Grannie Zara's riddle. "It must become your vehicle, Froika. You must see your face in it, traveling to St. Petersburg."

"It's a violin," Froika repeated.

"No, it is a magic chariot if you wish," she said excitedly.

Froika stared at her in frustration.

"Look, I'll show you something no one else has."

She opened the case and reverently removed two small stones from beneath the felt lining.

"Grannie Zara gave me these just last week. I went and told her that you were not progressing as rapidly as you should. She told me to put them inside the violin case. Now that she is no more, we have the last of such magic. You must practice harder than ever, Froika. With these in the case, we cannot fail. Look at them."

His mother carefully placed the stones in his open hand.

Froika examined the small, ordinary, smoothly rounded objects that had come from the streambed. He returned them to his excited mother.

"These are plain rocks, and that's a violin," Froika said.

Before Gittel could answer, they heard a knock at the door. Menachem opened it, and Barasch Limp Legs hobbled into the room.

"Good evening, I was strolling around and thought I would be sociable," he said. He saw that the Waksmans were surprised and not very pleased by his entrance. "Actually, I was visiting my dear friend and business associate, Boruch Levi, next door, but he's exhausted after a long day. He suggested that I drop in on all of you. I saw the light and heard voices. Here I am, a good neighbor."

His equine, obsequious smile was no more successful on the Waksmans than it had been on Boruch Levi. Menachem wondered whether Barasch had been drinking. One couldn't tell from the way he walked; he was perpetually off-balance and staggering. He did not know Barasch to be a drinker, but he had no other explanation for his oddly affected behavior, and all that nonsense about Boruch Levi was tipsy talk.

"It's late," Gittel said curtly. She wanted Barasch to leave so she could deal with Froika's heresies. The boy must understand what was at stake—everyone's future.

"Oh, no, we're just talking. Please come in and sit down," Froika said effusively.

Seizing the invitation, Barasch awkwardly lowered his ungainly frame to the floor to join the Tisha B'Av mourners. He tried various positions, but he could not find a comfortable one. Taking pity, Menachem handed him his own cushion. Somewhat apologetically, Barasch accepted it and thanked him.

Froika started to speak, but Gittel directed an ominous look at him that told him he dare not discuss sacred familial subjects with a stranger. In fact, Froika had no desire even to think about the instrument of torture on the sideboard; he was searching for information. While prowling around Yudel the Litvak's lumberyard, he had fished a Yiddish newspaper out of a trash barrel. A grisly picture of corpses from the Kishinever pogrom caught his attention. Froika furtively read the article. Captivated by the journal, he snuck it home where he hid it under his mattress and subsequently read it all. He discovered another article about a subject rarely discussed in Krimsk, the return of Jews to the Holy Land of Israel. This whetted his young appetite, but he had no way of satisfying it. Repeated forays to the trash barrel proved disappointingly futile. Preparing for bed on the long summer evenings, Froika had often noticed Yudel on his way to Barasch's and had conjectured that the two good friends might be planning their return to the land of Israel. The hasidim talked of both Barasch and the Zionist settlers on communal farms in the Holy Land as heretics. Perhaps Barasch could answer some of his questions.

"After what happened at the pond tonight, Froika can't sleep from fright, so we are keeping him company," Gittel explained.

"From fright?" Barasch asked. "What happened at the pond tonight?"

Since Gittel did not trust Froika to speak, she told the complete story herself. Barasch, who wanted to stay at the Waksmans' for as long as possible, listened avidly, affecting amazement, sympathy, remorse, horror, joy, and thanksgiving as the narration demanded. In addition to hanging on every word, he evinced further interest and concern through his numerous and specific questions, for many of which Gittel had to rely for an answer on Froika, who succinctly supplied the desired information in a dull monotone. Gittel excused Froika's rude brevity by explaining that the boy didn't want to talk about it since it was so terrifying. Barasch assured everyone that he understood Froika's reaction perfectly and couldn't be any more sympathetic had it been his own child.

The only time the communal felicity faltered was at the mention of Rabbi Chanina's magic frog. Barasch admitted his ignorance of this wonderful creature, thereby calling attention to his continual absence from the beis midrash. This occasioned an embarrassed pause before Gittel related the events between the Krimsker Rebbe and Itzik Dribble. "How marvelous!" exclaimed Barasch, and Menachem concluded definitely that Barasch was drunk.

When Gittel finished the story, Barasch said, "Froika, you have a lot to be thankful for. Thank God you and your friends returned safely. Yes, there's no doubt in my mind that you were saved by a miracle."

"It is late," Menachem said, inviting the drunk Barasch to leave.

"I'm still frightened, and I can't sleep. Since my family is tired, perhaps Barasch will keep me company," Froika appealed to the visitor.

"Of course I will. I know what it is to be a boy and be frightened," Barasch responded magnanimously. "Of course, after such a miracle, you should have faith, Froika."

And now talking of faith! Drink alone could not have done this to poor Barasch. Someone must have hit him on the head, thought Menachem. He's speaking as if his head, and not the Bornstein boy's, had been held under water. Froika couldn't possibly be left alone with him.

"We must leave Krimsk," Froika said and looked at Barasch to see his reaction.

The cripple looked nervous, and Froika interpreted this as evidence that Barasch and Yudel the Litvak must be planning their imminent exodus.

"Froika, stop talking foolishness," his father said.

"He doesn't show it, but he's very frightened," Gittel explained.

"Of course," Barasch agreed, thinking that any road out of Krimsk would lead to a penal colony.

"Thousands of Jews were murdered in Kishinev," Froika remarked.

"This is Krimsk, thank God," his father said.

"Thank God," Barasch said dutifully. Thank God this is Krimsk and not some Arctic forest.

"It can happen here, too, and sooner or later it will," Froika declared.

"God forbid!" his father said.

"God forbid," Barasch echoed.

"Froika, bite your tongue!" his mother barked.

"No, I won't bite my tongue, Mother. The goyim can do what they please with us. Had Casimir drowned Alex, what would have happened to him? Nothing, except he would have gotten better service and lower prices in the Krimsk market. The goyim believe blood libels—they will go on killing us. Do you know what those crazy Krimichak boys are saying now? They believe Grannie Zara was Jewish. Whatever they didn't like about her will be blamed on us. Have you ever heard of anything so crazy?"

"What? Grannie Zara was Jewish?" exclaimed Gittel, believing it immediately and wholeheartedly.

"Yes, the goyim are crazy," Froika said, slightly pleased with himself for saying something that amazed his mother.

"She didn't speak Yiddish," said Barasch.

"How do you know so much about what happened in Kishinev? Did Reb Gedaliah talk to you about it?" Menachem asked his son.

"No, I found a newspaper in a trash barrel in town," Froika explained, ever so slightly relocating the trash barrel. "Father, why don't we go to America?"

"What would we do there, Froika? We are Jews, and the rebbe, all the great rabbis, say that even the stones in America are trayf," Menachem said quietly. Obviously, the thought had occurred to him, too.

"Of course," Barasch said.

"There must be somewhere to go," Froika suggested, looking directly at Barasch, but Barasch hoped that he could remain where he was for a good long time.

Menachem asked, "Where, Froika, where?"

"Are the stones in the Land of Israel trayf, too?" he asked provocatively.

Again Barasch seemed indifferent.

"No, son, they're not," his father answered.

"Then why don't we go there?" Froika asked bluntly.

Nothing from Barasch, but Menachem answered, "The

Jews who are going to Israel do not believe in God and his Torah. The rabbis call them wicked. It doesn't make sense that unholy men should rebuild the Holy Land, does it?"

"I guess not, but it doesn't make sense to stay in Krimsk," Froika repeated.

"Krimsk is our home," Menachem said.

"Yes," agreed Barasch sincerely. "Thank God. Krimsk is our home."

"Don't you understand that? Man must have a home. We aren't gypsies who can wander about the countryside," Menachem said.

"I don't understand. In America the stones are trayf, in the Land of Israel the Jews are trayf—only in Krimsk and Kishinev are both the stones and the Jews kosher, which would be fine except for the fact that the goyim keep flinging those kosher stones at the kosher Jews," Froika said bitterly.

Menachem thought Froika was exaggerating. America and Israel had their share of problems, too, but he chose not to answer. His son was speaking in his mother's uncompromising tone, and Menachem had learned long ago never to argue with that.

"What do you think, Barasch? What would you do about the pogroms?" Froika asked.

Barasch coughed, then stretched his long leg over his short leg, and then his short leg over his long leg, and then he suddenly stopped as if he had run out of combinations of long and short. He looked at Froika as if he were a police investigator. He wondered how far Grisha had gone. He sensed a trap. His forehead burst into sweat when he thought that Grisha might have been apprehended and revealed their discussions and where they had taken place. Froika's question could put him in the bottom of a coal mine. His tongue felt limper than his leg.

"Your father is right, Froika. Krimsk is our home. It's not so bad," he said simply.

Froika looked at Barasch and his simpering smile. True, the man could not talk openly in front of his parents, but he seemed sincere.

"What should we do about the pogroms?" Froika asked.

Barasch looked around to see if a police stenographer crouched in the corner or hovered behind one of the chairs. Even Barasch could not hypocritically suggest prayer or study or evoke divine protection.

"I am maimed, Froika. One can get crippled anywhere. Even in America or the Holy Land," Barasch said, suddenly believing his own words.

"We just sit here waiting for it to happen?" Froika said aloud.

Barasch was sympathetic to the boy. Froika was too young to work, and when he did, he would probably become a shoemaker like his father. It was one thing to own a match factory or to live comfortably inside one, it was another to be a poor shoemaker whose son gets drowned by the goyim. Barasch coughed and recrossed the legs he was so fortunate as to have mangled without crossing any oceans.

"Practice," Barasch said with certainty. "You should practice your violin."

Froika looked at Barasch as though he were Itzik Dribble. "I'm going to bed," he stated.

"Good," his father said.

"Of course," added Barasch.

"Good night," his mother said, although she was interested in hearing more about the discovery that Grannie Zara was a Jew. This helped confirm her theory that all the great people were Jews. It added to her sneaking suspicion that Tsar Nicholas II was one as well. How could anyone but a Jew love a whiny violin? Hadn't someone once mentioned something about the tsar and Reb Zelig being switched as infants? But it was too late for the boy. He had been through enough for one day. She turned to Barasch and said, "Good night."

Barasch had wanted to stay longer, but he himself seemed to have terminated the evening by his remarks.

"Good night," he found himself saying.

As he reached the road, he decided that it was too late for any more social calls, so he headed back toward his wonderful room in the fortresslike factory. Boruch Levi's home was now dark. He wondered whether Malka, wonderful, sensual Malka, was asleep. Barasch felt a deep-rooted urge for a companion and offspring. Tonight he felt different, better than he had felt in a long time. In spite of having been caught with his pants down and having spoken like Reb Yechezkal the sexton to Froika, he felt a satisfaction that had long eluded him—the joy of belonging. He was a part of Krimsk. Some desired him, some tolerated him, some supported him, some ridiculed him. Plain, homey Krimsk. No more revolutionary foolishness for him. As he marched along with a sense of well-being, he thought he saw a single figure moving in front of him. His heart fell. Could Grisha be returning? If so, he would surrender him to the police. No one was going to be a better citizen in Krimsk than Barasch!

# CHAPTER TWENTY-SIX

CLUTCHING MATTI TIGHTLY, FAIGIE HAD RETURNED over the stepping stones to the Krimsk side. No sooner had she set her foot down than she released him and reverted back to the pleasant, relaxed, confident woman whom Matti had met earlier in the evening at that exact spot. Had she not casually asked him, "Do you think the cat and broom are destroyed by now?" Matti would have believed that their journey across the stream to Grannie Zara's had been simply a nightmare of his dark imagination. "Good," she had responded to his assurances, and they paused to rest a minute.

For a moment, Matti thought that Faigie had stopped to retrieve her towel or even to dip, but he soon realized that he didn't much care anymore. Drained both physically and mentally, he had had enough for one night. Upon their return, an energy exchange had occurred. Faigie had become loquacious, alert, and animated, whereas he had become dull, quiet, and depressed. She seemed perfectly pleased with his company, but Matti wanted to get rid of her. He was reminded of Jacob's crossing the stream, wrestling with an angel all night and then, lamed, returning home.

Grannie Zara was nothing but old grandmothers' foolishness to him. His frightening and momentous struggle in her cottage had been with Faigie, and he thought he had won, but now he was not so sure who had bested whom. Exhausted, his own urine and blood soaking his thigh, he was lamed, all right, but Faigie seemed whole, even vivacious.

Matti just wanted to go home, wash, and rest. He walked away from Faigie and started along the Krimsk path. She quickly rejoined him and chatted amiably about the weather and a hundred other nonsenses. Saying nothing and ignoring her, Matti slowly felt his way through the leaf-enshrouded darkness, but Faigie walked along with a natural, easy gait, just as if she could see in the dark like a cat. Matti had no idea what the night's events might mean to him, to her, or to anyone. He was too tired to care. When they emerged from the forest, Matti wordlessly turned away onto a path that skirted Krimsk and would take him directly to his house.

"Matti, wait a minute, please," Faigie called.

She followed a few steps after him and called his name again. He turned around, expecting a thank you, but Faigie reached out and lightly touched the damp front of his pants pocket. Although not his primary concern at the moment, he was embarrassed at having wet himself when she had screamed.

"It happens," he said.

"Please show it to me," she requested with a conspiratorial charm—even a flush of pride at having guessed Rabbi Chanina's magic frog's hiding place.

Amazed at her obscene interest in his boyish anatomy, Matti said, "You crazy whore," and marched away.

Faigie couldn't comprehend his vulgar hostility. After everything he had done for her, she didn't understand why he should treat her as among the uninitiated. Even with his proficiency in the black arts, he remained a child. Faigie understood that growing up is difficult for everyone, even for witches, and she regretted offending him. Turning down the road toward the Krimsker Rebbe, she soon regained her good spirits. Everything had gone so well.

Everything did not go so well at the rebbe's. Faigie came to the beis midrash doorway, but decided that was inappropriate. She went around to the family's private apartment and awakened Rachel Leah, who greeted her kindly and asked her to wait a few moments. The girl went to consult her mother. Although she had recently gone to bed, poor Shayna Basya seemed half dead. Rachel Leah had to poke her into wakefulness. When the rebbetzin awakened sufficiently, she told her daughter to escort Faigie to the rebbe's study and announce her. Shayna Basya dismissed her daughter's fears of disturbing the rebbe so late, saying impatiently, "He awakens with the night," but when Rachel Leah knocked on the study door, she received no response other than steady snoring. She knocked louder and was ready to quit when Faigie pushed her aside and started a banging that Rachel Leah expected to splinter the door. The rebbe mumbled a "Yes," and Faigie rushed into the room unannounced. Rachel Leah quietly closed the door and returned to her own room.

Faigie found the dozing rebbe seated on the floor with his back against the couch.

"Rebbe," she began. "I am here to ask for your blessing."

"You have it," he said, and promptly closed his eyes.

When she repeatedly addressed him to no avail—the loud snoring sounded like a motor in need of oil—Faigie sat down next to him and pinched his arm. The rebbe awakened with a start and began to rub his arm, although he did not associate Faigie with the pain. Faigie plunged into the story of her evening. Much to her surprise, the rebbe did not respond at the mention of Grannie Zara. Yawning, he asked Faigie to come back in the morning, but she refused to leave, saying that she had to have his blessing this very night. She related her visit to the witch's but could detect no response in his obtuse, hazel stare. He listened passively to her tale of Matti's escorting her to Grannie Zara's and destroying the broom and the cats.

"You killed her cats and burned her broom?" he asked sleepily.

"No, I didn't. I wanted to, but I couldn't. Matti Sternweiss did. He's a witch, I know," she said, somewhat embarrassed to be gossiping, but it seemed to her that the rebbe should know about it.

"He's a tzaddik, I know," the rebbe corrected her.

Faigie did not argue the point; she suspected that the two might not be so very different from one another. She explained to the rebbe that one Itzik Dribble was enough, and now that things had concluded satisfactorily at Grannie Zara's tonight, she was certain that with the rebbe's blessing everything would be all right.

"What makes you think we are partners? Either you go there or you come here. You went there; you are her customer. Good night," the rebbe said and flicked his wrist.

But Faigie didn't leave. "Of course you are partners. For me and all the simple Jews. Yes, you are partners and I demand your blessing," Faigie said.

"Madness," the rebbe replied calmly. He yawned. This foolish woman was not a very serious person.

"But true, rebbe. You sent your magic frog to the witch's this very night. If you did that, you can give me your blessing. Everyone says an old woman came to you, and nine months later she gave birth to a healthy set of twins."

The rebbe shrugged.

"It's not true?" Faigie demanded.

"I had nothing to do with it. God must have! Stop desecrating His name through witchcraft and pray to Him the same as I do," he said and then added, "In the morning."

"You think everybody sits around thinking about holy things like you do? Well you're wrong; they don't. You once said visiting Grannie Zara was like building the golden calf. Yes, it is, and I'll tell you why the Jews built the golden calf—because they had to."

"I wouldn't know," the rebbe answered, with a glance at the door intended to encourage his visitor's departure.

"I do. Who would take his own gold and build a golden calf if they didn't have to? They had to, and so did we. We didn't create the world, God did," she said. Then she continued, "My child looks like a golden calf—"

The rebbe interrupted, "Itzik has a wonderful soul."

"Rebbe, I want a healthy child. Give me a healthy child!" Faigie cried.

"I can't," the rebbe said wearily.

"I won't leave here without your blessing!" she said fiercely.

The rebbe raised his voice in harsh protest. "What are you wrestling with me for? You're not Jacob, and I'm not an angel. What are you doing here? You want a healthy child? Go to your husband's bed. God knows what will happen in your husband's bed. I don't!"

# CHAPTER TWENTY-SEVEN

BARASCH LIMP LEGS COULD NOT RUN FAST ENOUGH TO catch up with the figure in front of him. When he arrived at the gate, he found a slight woman staring through the bars into the factory yard. Expecting to find Grisha, he thought for a moment that the woman must be a friend of that troublemaker. He had never seen a girl hanging around the gate at this hour. As he approached, he called officiously, "Hey, what are you doing here?"

The figure turned around to reveal herself as Faigie Soffer, the wife of his employer, to whom Barasch had sworn eternal fealty only a few minutes previously. And here he was caught derelict in his duties on the night of Tisha B'Av. Since he had spent much of the last several hours feeling sorry for himself, he had no trouble now wallowing in self-pity over getting caught one of the few times he had deserted his and Beryl's post.

"This rarely happens," Barasch said, fumbling in his pockets for the keys.

"Yes," said Faigie, assuming that the watchman was

referring to her presence at the factory in the middle of the night.

Barasch managed to open the gate and said, "Come in."

Faigie had not come with the intention of entering the factory. At least no conscious desire. After she had failed to receive the rebbe's blessing, she had departed in great distress. The only person who she thought might influence the rebbe to change his mind was the little witch, Matti Sternweiss. The Krimsker Rebbe had even called him a tzaddik, which would give Matti all the more suasion. Faigie desperately wanted the blessing no less than Jacob had desired the angel's, and like Jacob, she was willing to struggle all night. She had the patriarch's objective: the establishment of a genetic line. If Matti hadn't made such a vicious parting remark, she would not have hesitated to go to the Sternweiss home to enlist his aid again.

Faigie had no desire to return home to Beryl. In her present state, she would break down in front of him and reveal her desire for a healthy child. Beryl was no more at fault than she. Bringing the problem into the open would only make them miserable, each mutual glance a bitter reminder and subtle recrimination. And the way the rebbe had screamed that God only knew what would happen in her husband's bed filled her with fearful misgivings. Perhaps she herself had "opened her mouth to Satan" by stating that one Itzik Dribble was enough. Might she not give birth to something even less desirable than Itzik?

Feeling defeated, she had wandered aimlessly away from the rebbe. Not realizing where she was headed, she was surprised to find herself leaning on the Soffer and Company factory gate. As she felt the cool metal of the protective bars on the warm night, she had two insights as to why she had wandered there.

Soffer and Company was the full, rich bank account that paid for Itzik's empty head. She might remedy that by burning the factory to the ground; it wouldn't be her first arson of the evening. Although the night had made her desperate, she knew that the crippled watchman lay inside, and his innocent presence prevented any serious consideration of the idea. Nevertheless, she had reached into her pocket, only to discover that her matches were not there. Matti had returned them to her—she was almost certain of that—so she must have lost them herself. Not that she couldn't burn down a match factory with its own products. There must be myriads of finished matches crowded inside, each capable of destroying its own industrial creator and all his fellows. The thought of the matchsticks, however, determined that she could never burn down the building. Even if they were her unwitting opponents, each match was a beloved particle of Beryl's hard-won world.

If the factory represented the fateful riches that impoverished her child, it also provided her a place where she could commune with Beryl's mad ambition and mourn her own. In the offices of Soffer and Company, Beryl acted with a courage and passion that Faigie could muster only on her way to Krimichak. If husband and wife could neither share nor appreciate each other's goals, they could at least recognize the ferocity with which each pursued his own. Far from soft Beryl, she could lean on his rigid fence and feel close to parts of him that she could never possess.

Faigie entered the factory yard like a calico cat visiting the neighbor's garden, looking about with curious detachment and stepping carefully and quietly. Barasch, lantern in hand, led the way. Faigie followed along, staring curiously at the piles of neatly stacked lumber, pulleys, winches, wagons, and soaring chimneys as if she were touring her husband's sleeping mind. Barasch went to check the office door and asked her if she wanted to go inside.

"Everything is so quiet," she responded.

"Yes, I was gone for just a few minutes," Barasch said, unlocking the door.

She entered after him and walked silently through the entire complex. Faigie said nothing, looking about and breathing deeply as if trying to capture an aura, a presence, a sense of someone who was not physically present. They toured the yards behind the factory all the way to the fence.

"That's it. Everything is just fine, thank God. Reb Beryl can sleep tonight. You've seen everything except my room."

Faigie said nothing, sniffing the warm air noncommittally. Barasch was sure that no damage to Soffer and Company lurked in his room, but, burdened as he was by various guilts—his guest Grisha the revolutionary, Barasch's own desertion of his post, his awkward lust for Malka—he imagined that Faigie had been sent to spy on him. Beryl probably couldn't sleep, and Faigie as a loyal wife had offered to examine things. Above all, Barasch wanted to appear forthright and open. If the authorities arrived tomorrow and had questions about who was at the factory during the night, it would be very valuable to have his employers testify that they had thoroughly inspected the entire premises and found nothing amiss, certainly that no strange persons were present. Faigie Soffer's testimony about the factory visit, Boruch Levi's about Barasch and Malka (with discretion, of course), and the Waksmans' about his neighborly visit would provide him with several witnesses at three different places during the evening. Really very impressive. Barasch hobbled purposefully toward his room; Faigie followed in a quiet trance.

Tired from all the walking during the last several hours, Barasch quickly sat down in his easy chair. He wanted to apologize for leaving the factory, but he did not know how much Faigie knew. If she had been waiting only a few minutes, then his tardy arrival meant very little.

"Now you have seen everything," he said.

Not listening, Faigie looked around like a visitor to a foreign land who finds everything very familiar. Here in this strange hut were Beryl's stool, table, chair, and mirror.

Barasch cleared his throat quietly. "How long were you waiting at the gate?" he asked. His throat felt drier than the caked, dusty yard.

"Give me your shirt," she said.

"My shirt?" he asked.

"Yes, the one you're wearing. The seam in the sleeve is tearing. I've already mended it twice," she said.

"You have?"

"Yes, it's Beryl's, isn't it?" she asked.

"Oh, yes, it is," he said, finally comprehending what she was talking about. "Of course, it's Beryl's. Everything here is Beryl's. Your husband is very kind. He's given me everything in the room. I'm wearing his shirt, his pants, and this is your husband's chair, but it was in the office here so you might not recognize it. But you must remember your husband's bed."

"Your husband's bed," Faigie slowly repeated the rebbe's words.

"Yes," said Barasch, pointing to it. "Your husband's bed."

Faigie walked around the table and sat down possessively on the bed. She looked down at the familiar sheets and blanket, delicately fingering them.

"It's all your husband's. The bed, the blankets, the sheets, everything. He's never far from my thoughts. I can't tell you how generous he is with me." Barasch delivered this encomium with his attempt at an ingratiating smile.

"Close the door, please," Faigie said.

"It's cooler this way," he protested.

"Close the door," she repeated firmly.

"Yes'm," Barasch said, hoisting himself to his feet.

When he turned back from the door, Faigie had taken off her shoes and was pushing back the sheets on the bed.

"Come over here," she said.

Confused, Barasch hobbled over to the bed.

"What are you doing?" he asked.

"Is this my husband's bed?" she asked.

"Yes," he answered.

"Then I belong in it," she explained.

"Oh," he said, not understanding.

"Take your shirt off," she ordered.

"But I don't have a needle or thread. Beryl never gave me any."

"Take it off and sit down right here." She patted the sheet.

Barasch took off his shirt and sat down. He handed her the shirt and she flung it onto the table.

"Reb Beryl didn't send you?" he asked, watching her disrobe.

"No, the Krimsker Rebbe did," she answered. She didn't think it necessary to mention Matti the witch, too. Barasch wouldn't have heard anyway; he was breathing as heavily as a horse.

# CHAPTER TWENTY-EIGHT

WHEN THE HASIDIM APPEARED AT SIX-THIRTY FOR morning prayers, the hazy streets and shaded alleyways had a refreshing cool quality suggesting that after the night's respite from the sun, the coming day would be more comfortable. Sparrows and starlings swiftly darted through the long shadows with energetic staccato calls. Butterflies—pale ivory, cadmium yellow, and regal orange mosaic limned in black—floated and leaped on delicate unseen wisps of air. The earthbound, hungry Jews plodded to the beis midrash to offer heaven their prayers and praise. Tired or rested, alert or befogged, all moved toward the overturned benches and disarray that meant Tisha B'Av morning.

When a number of hasidim had arrived, Reb Yechezkal signaled for Reb Muni to begin the preliminary service describing the morning sacrifice in the ancient Temple. The hasidim joined him in an undercurrent of droning and murmuring like the subtle diurnal rhythm of bees and other swarming creatures. Some latecomers conscientiously rushed to catch up; others simply joined the prayer in progress. With varying degrees of concentration, the congregation forged ahead in an active, concerted effort that left no time for personal reflections or private speculations.

The crescendo of praise should have reached its zenith with the cantor's call to "Bless God Who Is Blessed," the beginning of the service proper, but the Krimsker Rebbe had not appeared. Reb Yechezkal cautioned the cantor to wait. The rhythmic refrain of softly uttered praise came to an abrupt halt, and a sudden quiet burst upon those few who were still catching up; they immediately adopted hushed tones or with fervent lips articulated silently.

At this point the rebbe used to enter punctually. Now that the wondrous rebbe had returned so dramatically and so forcefully—receiving supplicants until all hours of the night—Reb Yechezkal was certain that the old regimen was to be observed.

Initially, the congregation sat expectantly awaiting the entrance of their beloved rebbe, the sun of Krimsk's firmament. As minutes passed, hasidim rose and stretched to alleviate their acute physical discomfort on the overturned benches. With nothing to do but wait, they soon discovered that their attention began to wander.

Alexander Bornstein's father reminded himself that he had to intone publicly a special blessing occasioned by his son's fortunate escape. The mere thought of last night's murderous attack at the pond moved him to put a reassuring hand on the boy's shoulder. Alex looked up quizzically, and even though it was Tisha B'Av, the father smiled furtively. Alex shyly returned the smile. Comforted, his father considered whether or not to remind Reb Yechezkal to call him to the Torah to recite the special blessing. Deciding not to, he kept his hand on his son and looked up toward the rebbe's study door, wondering whether the magic frog might be inside. When he made the blessing for Alex, he must utter it loudly enough so that anyone inside the study could hear it clearly. Overwhelmed with gratitude and on the verge of tears, he wished the miracle-working rebbe would enter.

Although Menachem Waksman shared the feelings of gratitude and relief, he remained concerned about Froika's obsessive fears. The grisly premonitions were bad enough, but even worse, they might push the boy toward some imagined paradise in the Holy Land. If they did not fade in time, Menachem would insist that Froika speak to the rebbe. But Menachem didn't want to be caught in the middle of any struggle between the Krimsker Rebbe and his own wife, Gittel. He hoped that after a few days the fright would disappear and Froika would return to the routine of Reb Gedaliah and the violin. Just let things get back to normal, and everything would be all right. And normal meant no more visits from that neighborhood drunk, Barasch Limp Legs. He had acted as if he planned to visit them regularly. Menachem had enough problems without that.

Boruch Levi was similarly reflecting that he could do very well without the company, much less the family membership, of Barasch Limp Legs. He was also considering Barasch's midnight playmate, Malka. Now that Boruch Levi was certain to be staying in Krimsk and equally certain of financial security—promised by the holy rebbe himself—he had better marry off his slut of a sister before she started producing any little bastards. If Malka broke his mother's heart, Boruch Levi would certainly break his sister's head. His sainted mother hadn't seemed very thrilled with the prospect of the cripple as a son-in-law. It was just as well; Barasch wouldn't last very long. Malka needed some pious teamster who would keep her pregnant and make sure she behaved. The only thing Malka respected was a sound blow. Boruch Levi wondered how much a brother-in-law like that would cost.

Beryl was wondering about his beloved sylph, Faigie. He had been sick with worry when she had returned in the middle of the night. Exhausted, his wife had collapsed into bed. In response to his frantic inquiries, she told him that she had been to see the rebbe. She had assured Beryl that, indeed, he had been right all along. The Krimsker Rebbe was a very great man, and from now on she was following only his advice. But what was that advice, Beryl had asked. It was too late to discuss it, she had answered, and to Beryl's surprise and dismay, she had leaned over into his bed on Tisha B'Av night and kissed him smack on the lips, telling him that she loved him. How could she do such a thing on Tisha B'Av after having visited the rebbe? he had demanded. "I'm only following the rebbe's advice," she had answered simply, and dropped off immediately to sleep.

Beryl spent the rest of the night wondering what the advice could possibly have been and why when she had kissed him he smelled smoke in her hair. In the morning as he was dressing, she rolled over and told him to leave Itzik at home so he could eat a good breakfast. Then she went back to sleep without explaining anything. She probably never would. Faigie was like that. How could he ask the rebbe? Beryl sat in the beis midrash wondering what the rebbe had advised her.

To Nachman Leib's surprise, his son Yechiel had accompanied him to the beis midrash. Although Nachman Leib had cautioned Shraga to tiptoe quietly, Yechiel awoke nevertheless and asked them to wait for him. Nachman Leib sat between his sons, but he knew that the situation was temporary and even sensed that this was Yechiel's farewell to the beis midrash. Nachman Leib was in no hurry for the rebbe to appear. He wondered where his older son would be sitting next year.

The Krimsker Rebbe was sitting on his study floor, wondering whether a frog could swim the ocean. He was at a loss to explain why he was considering a matter that did not hold any great fascination for him, but which, nonetheless, he could not get out of his mind. Floating amidst enormous, billowing gray waves, a large green frog steadfastly kicked its dark green legs in powerful jerking thrusts. As far as the eye could see in all directions stretched the undulating sea. The rebbe was watching the frog's minute progress when Reb Yechezkal knocked.

"Yes?" the rebbe said.

Reb Yechezkal entered and closed the door.

"Oh, it's you," the rebbe said, slightly surprised to see anyone other than a wet green frog.

Reb Yechezkal was taken aback. Had he forgotten some appointment of the rebbe? Who was the rebbe expecting?

"Well, what is it?" the rebbe asked.

"We have arrived at the morning service proper. Shall we wait for the rebbe?"

"Aha," the rebbe said, "that's it." The sudden silence must have awakened him. He had been dozing and had abruptly opened his eyes to see the frog in the ocean. "I'll be right in."

For the second time in twelve hours and for only the second time in five years, the study door opened and the Krimsker Rebbe stepped across the threshold into the beis midrash. As he entered, everyone stood up, but this morning they were expecting him and greeted him much more quietly and soberly than they had the previous evening.

The hasidim watched the rebbe with affection and delight, but with little amazement. As expected, the rebbe sat low and still on his overturned table, and the cantor quietly concluded the preliminary praise service with kaddish, then chanted in a strong, clear, measured voice, "Bless the Lord Who is blessed." The congregation answered, "Blessed is the Lord Who is eternally blessed," and the cantor repeated it. Everyone then continued individually, "Blessed are You our Lord, King of the Universe, Creator of Light, Creator of Darkness, Creator of Peace, and Creator of Everything."

The prayers continued in the most ordinary and routine manner. Reb Yechezkal called Alex Bornstein's father to the Torah in order to make the thanksgiving blessing on Alex's behalf, but even that hardly caused a stir as the congregation responded, "May He Who has treated you kindly, continue to treat you kindly in the future." They sat languorously doing their duty, waiting for the day to end. The morning sun had brought a return of the enervating heat, and on a day without food or drink the increased temperature easily induced an indifferent lethargy. And, too, in the morning light the previous evening seemed far away.

Everyone focused on the long, difficult, broiling fast day in front of them. To dwell on the past would only draw out the afflicting of one's soul.

Except for Froika Waksman, no one felt serious concern over the events at the pond. Certainly the rebbe didn't this morning; he was not suffering in tears. He seemed not to be suffering at all. He was sitting in a near stupor, expressionless and unresponsive to the services. The rebbe's momentous return had been discussed for hours. Such miraculous ecstasy could not be maintained in active consciousness for very long. It could continue to loom large, miraculous, and majestic only as a part of the past, to which it had already been consigned. The one thing that might have occasioned comment, and indeed still did so in various homes, was the death of Grannie Zara, but she was thought to be the absolute antithesis of the pure, holy rebbe. How could any discussion of the impure witch pollute the domain of the holy miracle worker?

Yechiel's attendance was indeed a farewell. He had decided that his presence in the beis midrash was no insult to the rebbe. Quite the contrary, the rebbe could take pride in it as an affirmation of his prediction, but Yechiel suspected that this morning the Krimsker Rebbe did not even know who was in the beis midrash. Yechiel's presence was an insult only to himself, but he chose to accept that and appreciated the lack of enthusiasm and fervor that gave him a respite from his difficult dilemmas. He wondered where Grisha was and what he was doing.

Matti Sternweiss also appreciated the dull, unemotional atmosphere. Last night he had stealthily washed in the yard and then sneaked into the house. His father had awakened him all too early for prayers. In the quiet, soporific, subdued mood of the beis midrash he could slump forward and doze. His father had nudged him awake several times, but not very vigorously. How could he? Matti exhibited the same sluggish behavior as the holy rebbe.

The day grew brighter, and the heat increased. Birds returned to their nests or roosts, and dogs sought the shade. Inside the Krimsk beis midrash the droning murmurs continued. The service wound on its way for hours as slowly, inexorably, and almost as impersonally as the River Nedd twisting through the forests and fields under an impossibly bright sun, beseeched by the myriad creatures that came to siphon life from the edges of its sustaining flow. Indoors and chanting to itself, the Krimsk Tisha B'Av service progressed, isolated and insulated from external events. The hasidim felt the heat, but they did not see the sun.

The River Nedd lay exposed. When the denizens of Krimichak and the residents of the outlying hamlets and farms crossed the bridge toward Krimsk, their shadows stained the river's bright, reflecting surface. Their slender scythes, pronged pitchforks, curved picks, and thick clubs that coursed ominously through the air danced innocently and lightly as reedlike shadows in the brilliant waters below. The mob's harsh, bloodthirsty grumbling, however, echoed loudly across the placid river.

The hasidim in the beis midrash saw neither the goyim nor the steely glint of the sun off their blades. They did not hear them enter Krimsk, and they did not smell the smoke when Wotek the herdsman set fire to the largest and most handsome building in Krimsk, the Angel of Death synagogue.

# CHAPTER TWENTY-NINE

Casimir and Tadeusz's arrival back in Krimichak had created a great stir. Within minutes, everyone had heard how several score of Jewish ruffians lay in wait by the dark pond for innocent Polish children. The diabolical Yids had attacked Casimir with a poisonous frog named Rabbi Chananiak. Soon after, Grannie Zara's cottage burned to the ground, and Yiddish voices had been heard in the vicinity at the time of the blaze.

Different theories quickly developed. Some people maintained that Grannie Zara was a Jew. How else could one explain her dipping at the Krimsk side of the pond and muttering Hebrew prayers? Although she did not keep her monthly appointment in human form, appearing as a frog she had attacked the Polish boys. Why were the Jews forever visiting her? And why had Grannie Zara saved *them* from a Cossack pogrom? Pretending to be one of them, Grannie Zara had tricked Krimichak. Hadn't the Jews prospered while Krimichak languished? Because of Grannie Zara the Jews had built a synagogue in Krimsk larger and grander than any church in the district. Additional proofs of her Jewish identity were adduced. She was so very neat, once she had lit a candle on Friday nights, and Zloty, that miserable, rapacious Jewish beast, had disappeared with her foxy, deceitful Jewish mug.

Others remained convinced that Grannie Zara had been a good Christian witch all her life, and that she had saved Krimichak from the satanic Jewish plague of Krimsk. No Jew, no matter how vicious and deceitful, had dared attack a Krimichak child while she lived. The Jews had flocked to her and begged for her blessings, but now that Grannie Zara lay dead—her body not even cold in the grave—they attacked her flock and burnt her Christian home. How that neat, angelic cottage must have stuck in their filthy, lice-ridden Jewish craw! And where was that noble, loyal, leonine creature, Zloty? Grannie Zara's beloved companion had to be driven off her mistress's body with torches. Zloty would never have disappeared on her own; the Jews must have trapped and killed her. They must be stopped before they put all of Krimichak to the torch.

Krimichak debated some minor points. The "Jewish" school wondered why a Christian witch would be uttering Jewish prayers. That was easy: the only way to fight fire was with fire. And the "Christian" school wondered why the Jews would bother to burn down the home of a Jewish witch. But nothing could be simpler: they did it to destroy Hebrew amulets, prayer books, family bibles, and other evidence of her Jewishness. These discussions were very much halfhearted, because they were irrelevant.

Jewish thugs had attempted to murder young Polish children, and everyone knew why Jews wanted innocent blood. How clever to do it so much in advance of Passover that no one would suspect their true motive! Equally undeniable was the arson that had destroyed Grannie Zara's cottage. Early in the morning all of Krimichak had visited the scene of the skullduggery. In the still morning air the smoke huddled like a poisonous mushroom in a dome-shaped mass where her home had been.

Both schools agreed that the poisonous mushroom must also be sown in Krimsk, and both agreed that the target should be the synagogue grander than any church. With allies easily recruited from the countryside, and undeterred by their differing yells of "Death to the Yid witch!" and "Death to the Yid witch-killers!" the mob crossed the bridge to Krimsk. They were indeed wise in ignoring their vocal variorum, for as they approached the synagogue, they were chanting only one slogan, "Death to the Yids!"

The goyim noticed immediately that the streets of Krimsk were absolutely empty. It was as if they had come to destroy a ghost town or to slaughter a beast that had already died. They had expected some form of opposition, no matter how feeble. Something that at least would prove entertaining: a cripple to be chased, a child to be maimed, a cow to be stuck with an unclean knife so the stinking holy Jew could not even gorge himself on its nonkosher carcass. The absence of life unnerved them, and they fell strangely quiet. It was as if the want of focus had undermined their resolve, which lacked steel because Grannie Zara's death, the very thing that had motivated them, also left them vulnerable. If a Yid, as some suspected, Grannie Zara might still champion the Jews even after her death as she had at the pond. If a Christian, as others thought, she was no longer alive to protect her holy flock.

In that moment of hesitation, the fears that had fueled them turned to debilitate them. Perhaps they had walked into a trap? In this mire of indecision, Wotek stepped forth to save the day.

He commandeered a torch and, eyes bright with brutal lust, bellowed in his deep, forceful voice, "We've come this far. Let's see some flames!"

"Yes, yes, flames!" the crowd echoed instantly.

"The windows!" someone screamed, and a group of men dashed around to both sides of the building and with their pitchforks and scythes quickly smashed both panes and frames in the huge mullioned windows. Wotek flung in the first torch. All the others quickly followed.

Moving back to enjoy the flames, the crowd leaned on their pitchforks and other instruments of mayhem to view more comfortably the conflagration that they had come to understand as their just portion.

# CHAPTER THIRTY

THE HASIDIM AT THE BACK OF THE BEIS MIDRASH WERE desultorily following the reading of the lengthy laments, whose archaic, poetic language was beyond their appreciation. Idly glancing about for any minor distraction, they were unexpectedly treated to a major one when Yudel the Litvak burst through the doors into the beis midrash. Looking in astonishment at the intruder, who had never before so much as peeked inside, they exclaimed to each other, "It's the Litvak!" Without acknowledging their greeting, Yudel, breathless and red as a beet, ran into the center of the hall and shouted, "Jews! A catastrophe! The goyim are burning the Angel of Death!"

Punctuated by oys and gevalts, and even short screams, a shudder of horror swept through the beis midrash. Some hasidim leaped to their feet; others sat glued to their seats. All eyes turned to the Krimsker Rebbe, but the rebbe, lower than everyone, fingering a book of lamentations, rocked with his head collapsed onto his chest in the most abject, depressed mourning. The Krimsker Rebbe continued to doze through Yudel's stentorian announcement and the congregation's frightened response. Sweating with fear, Reb Yechezkal bent over and touched his shoulder. The rebbe snorted and tried to ignore the intrusion. Reb Yechezkal lightly shook his shoulder. The rebbe's eyes opened into his most obtuse hazel stare.

"Rebbe! Rebbe! The goyim are burning the Angel of Death!" Reb Yechezkal called out.

His eyes open, the rebbe continued to rock slowly without registering any comprehension.

"Rebbe," Reb Yechezkal cried, tears streaming down his cheeks, "the goyim are in Krimsk and they are burning the Angel of Death!"

"Eieeee!" A piercing shriek burst quickly and powerfully from the rebbe, as if it were an instant involuntary reflex to a burning hot metal hook raking his flesh. In one swift leap he stood on his feet, with his arms outstretched above his head both in supplication to heaven and in exhortation to his holy hasidim. His eyes blazing in righteous fury and impassioned indignation, he demanded and importuned, "We must save the sacred Torah scrolls!" and in his stocking feet he burst for the door. Rushing down the aisle, he sidestepped seated hasidim and leaped over benches. Those in his path remembered the burning eyes and the long coat, beard, and side curls all swinging behind in a desperate effort to hang onto the flying rebbe.

The hasidim who were already on their feet immediately began running after him. Those seated jumped up in hot pursuit. Even Yudel the Litvak found himself sprinting after the Krimsker Rebbe. Within seconds the beis midrash was totally empty and all of the hasidim, led by the rebbe, were racing through the streets toward the Angel of Death.

The younger men kept pace with the rebbe, but the older ones lagged behind as the congregation stretched into a frenzied black stream that only a volcano or some vent in the earth's surface could spew forth in such elemental, fiery fury. When this frenzied behemoth of charging bodies burst into the marketplace and saw the yellow-orange flames eating through the roof of the grand building, it emitted a collective gasping groan that echoed across the square as a massive roar.

The Krimichak goyim, pacifically enjoying the blaze with good-natured enthusiasm, turned to find themselves, if not the target of this black, minatory rush, at least an imperiled object in its path. This dark, impassioned flood must certainly overwhelm them. Instinctively, they retreated by several paces.

Some goyim suddenly discovered the serendipitous presence of honest farm implements that could be mustered in defense of their lives. Others were delightfully surprised that the cudgels and clubs upon which they happened to be leaning could, in an emergency, be used to protect themselves. Feeling very much the aggrieved party, they anxiously observed the frenzied hasidim, led by an unfamiliar man, charge toward them. As he drew closer, they noticed that neither he nor his followers wore shoes. The stocking feet stimulated a tinge of curiosity that lessened the goyim's fear.

When the black swarm came within several meters of a thunderous encounter, the delirious leader, suddenly ignoring all of Krimichak, raced up to tug on the front door of the burning synagogue. Even by pulling with all his might, however, he could not budge the heavy oak doors. The rebbe stepped back and frantically waved over some of the husky young hasidim, but their joint efforts proved equally unsuccessful. The rebbe then spun toward the goyim and pointed to someone with an ax.

"You, with the ax, open those doors immediately!" he demanded in a tone of absolute authority.

Not only did the designated man respectfully step forward but so did two others, axes in hand.

"Immediately!" the rebbe commanded.

As they raced toward the doors, they cursorily nodded in respect to the rebbe. With a wave of his arm, he encouraged them.

Like metal tongues whose appetites are never sated, the axes bit into the wood, spitting chips with gusto. With several blows, the handles and locks had been chopped out. The rebbe removed his black caftan as the axes knocked out the metal chocks that pinned the doors to the threshold.

Reb Yechezkal, panting from his sprint, ran forward to grab the rebbe's arm. The rebbe tried to push off the larger man. Their task complete, the axemen turned to the rebbe for instructions.

"Don't go in there!" Reb Yechezkal cried. "It's death!"

"Let go!" the rebbe snapped in fury.

"Let me do it!" Reb Zelig volunteered.

The rebbe turned to Reb Zelig and commanded, "Get him off of me!" Promptly taking Reb Yechezkal into his powerful grasp, Reb Zelig liberated the rebbe.

"Open the doors! Open the gates of righteousness!" he screamed at the goyim.

They quickly hooked the doors with their axheads and pulled them open. The blistering wave of heat that burst out was only a harbinger of the crackling flames that promised to incinerate any creature who dared enter. The hot gases escaping the inferno bit at the flesh and licked the eyes that were already blinking from the dazzling veil of shimmering flame itself. Shielding their faces, everyone but the rebbe dropped back. He just squinted with his hazel eyes, searching for the path that he knew must exist through that glittering destructive splendor. Behind him, even the goyim were yelling, "No! No!" He sensed that his one hope was to the left; there the fire seemed less dense. Digging his stocking feet into the dust for a good start, he could hear nothing, and the alarmed spectators could barely hear themselves; for further inside some of the roof beams had thunderously hurtled down in an incandescent shower of sparks. The conflagration sucked oxygen in a deafening, gluttonous roar.

The rebbe dashed forward and felt the severe increase in heat before he had completed his first step. Through the open doors he perceived an area in the wall of flames that was less bright; it appeared to the rebbe as a shadow of dark flame on the brighter flames. Focusing on that relatively dark patch—it glimmered with the gleam of lesser combustion—the Krimsker Rebbe pictured himself racing through it and into the synagogue toward the holy ark on the innermost wall. And, indeed, squinting as he was from the blinding surfeit of light, he could see a shimmering figure that flickered in shadowy silhouette. Initially the rebbe interpreted this as a prophetic guide whom he must follow through the hellish oven, but as he approached the doorway, he perceived that the ethereal figure was rushing forward to meet him. He understood at once that this was the Angel Gabriel, who has dominion over fire. No mere guide, Gabriel would shield him in his heavenly embrace as he had Daniel and Abraham in infinitely hotter furnaces. Not wanting to delay his rendezvous with the archangel, the rebbe surged forward. Not until he planted his foot upon the stone step before the doorway did he notice that the angel was protectively clutching something in his arms. The rebbe suddenly straightened up in miraculous greeting and reached out in a welcoming embrace.

# CHAPTER THIRTY-ONE

AFTER YECHIEL HAD CLIMBED OUT THE WINDOW OF the Angel of Death, Grisha had stealthily smoked a cigarette, cupping his hand over the red glow so that no chance passerby could possibly see anything. While smoking, he thought about Yechiel. He very much wanted the young scholar to join the Leninist group. Yechiel seemed at least as bright as Trotsky, that other precocious Jewish boy, whose real name was Bronstein—what would Katzman become? . . . But Grisha knew that he was letting his personal feelings cloud his scientific, revolutionary judgment. Yechiel was too contemplative. Such a talmudic mind lacked the decisiveness to be a party theorist. The Krimsker Rebbe himself could be an excellent party theorist; he was bold, brilliant, and incisive. Do not underestimate evil! Grisha could build some fiery revolutionary harangues around that pithy statement. What a shame that such a treasure of a man as the rebbe should be wasting his time as a mystical mentor for a few families in this backwater.

In preparation for sleep, Grisha carefully extinguished

his cigarette. If he set out at dawn, he could cover enough distance to permit a comfortable rest during the burning midday hours. His revolutionary senses and discipline in good order, he carefully closed the window and slept under a bench to avoid detection by a passerby in case he should oversleep.

Grisha did not oversleep. Knowing exactly where he was, he opened his eyes as the dull but increasing light told him that it was exactly dawn. He lay quietly and listened intently. Hearing nothing, he sat up and looked around warily. All was still.

He crawled out from under the bench and stretching, sat up. It was stuffy inside the closed building, and he knew that outside the air would be at its coolest and freshest. He quickly reached for his knapsack and raised himself off the floor to sit on the bench while organizing his departure. All he had to do was put on his cap, take his knapsack to the window, open the window, flip the sack through, following after it himself, and close the window, and he would be on his way.

Suddenly his revolutionary discipline, riveted on the future, flagged for a moment; exploring his past, he looked around to see where he had spent the night. He was surprised at the chamber's vast size and equally impressed by the solid, rich woodwork. Following the oak beams, his glance swept upward to catch the dull, sinuous gleam of the massive brass chandelier. His first impression was of a leafy, heavenly vine. Examining it more carefully in the hazy light, he realized what it was, and as stuffy as the Angel of Death was, he broke out into a cold sweat and gripped the back of the bench to keep from falling. Steadying himself, he looked up again to be sure that he had not imagined anything. No, he had not; the massive brass chandelier radiated into a myriad of branches like a man-made sunburst. Although Grisha knew with fearful certainty where he was, he had to confirm and reconfirm the obvious but awesome facts.

He stared at the chandelier that seemed capable of lighting the entire sky. Nothing could be more real than that mass of metal; yet nothing could be more unbelievable. Plagued by reality and in search of believability, he began crawling quickly toward the elevated stage at the front of the chamber. When he got close enough to examine the blue velvet hanging covering the ark of the law, he gasped, "God of my fathers!" The donor's name stitched in gold letters boldly confronted him. He listlessly dragged himself to collapse on his bench.

So all of his revolutionary activity and nocturnal underground flights had brought him here! Grisha would have liked to dismiss it as mere coincidence, but he was overwhelmed by this heartless remonstrance of fate. Everything seemed to have conspired toward this conclusion, from the last party convention to Yechiel's little brother's knock on that crippled coward's door.

Throwing caution to the winds, Grisha lit a cigarette and began pacing up and down the center aisle. Each time he approached the velvet hanging, he reread the dedicatory names. After several cigarettes, and more than several trips to the holy ark, he began to reassert his self-control. Although continuing to smoke furiously, he sat back down on the floor between the benches and continued to calm himself. Yes, he had been startled and frightened by the remarkable coincidence, but bourgeois superstitions must not rule him. They were not what Marx had meant by "historical necessity," and it was by the Marxian concept that he meant to lead his life.

Snuffing out the cigarette on the floor, he looked up at the gargantuan expanse of chandelier. There was nothing for him to fear. Determined to leave, but equally determined to prove that he was not running away, he decided upon an act of revolutionary boldness. Knowing exactly where he was, he must now sleep in the synagogue. He had sufficient provisions, and Yechiel had said that no one would come in on Tisha B'Av. Even if it would delay him a half day, the test would temper him into a stronger, more self-reliant servant of the revolution. Having taken this decision, he lit one more cigarette and slowly nursed it in an effort to relax sufficiently to sleep.

Lying down under the bench, he found himself squirming as his earliest memories of childhood assaulted him, as though the bourgeois devil himself were flinging images into his head. This continued for a long time. He heard the hasidim going to the beis midrash and watched the day grow bright and hot, but Grisha was determined to have his way, and after several fruitless hours he managed to fall asleep. Even in sleep the pictures of childhood mercilessly pursued him with a poisonous sweetness and warmth. When these finally ceased, they were replaced by horrendous, violent scenes in which the massive brass chandelier ripped from its moorings on the great beams and fell, crushing and maiming scores of worshipers, including Grisha himself. And in the screaming and moaning panic and pain no one could hear a thing. Again the scene was reenacted, but this time at night, when the hundreds of lit candles set fire to everyone and everything—the books, the building, even the holy Torah itself. The smoke seemed so real that Grisha awakened; he even sat up to be sure that the clouds of smoke were a figment of his disturbed imagination. Feeling very tired in the stuffy, hot building and knowing that the sun was broiling hot by now, he lay back down and returned to his fitful, dream-infested sleep.

When the clamorous mob from Krimichak shattered the windows, the noise resounded like the one he had heard in his dreams. The heavy flaming torches spewed smoke no more acrid than that which had already falsely awakened him. But the fire set by the mob continued to burn. The bone-dry wood, so rich and heavy, seemed to seize the flames as only perfect kindling can. Since Grisha lay on the floor, he was awakened by the heat and noise before he was overcome by the smoke that had already begun filling the upper spaces of the synagogue. His first thought was that his carelessly extinguished cigarette must have caused the blaze; now the fire had progressed far beyond control. He grabbed his knapsack and turned to flee through the window, but between him and the windows, where the torches had landed, danced a wall of fire that he dared not cross.

He reversed his direction and followed the bench to the center aisle on his way to the large windows opposite, but a parallel conflagration barred his path. In a flicker of awareness, he realized that this was an odd way for a fire to have spread; he must have flicked yet another lit cigarette over there while pacing. How else could fire be climbing the two opposite walls? And the fire was relentlessly scaling the walls, sweeping onto the low roof along the side walls that served as the floor of the horseshoe-shaped women's balcony. Grisha glanced up into the towering central space to see the monstrous chandelier reflecting the flames' flashing brilliance. Reflexively, he drew fearfully back down the aisle toward the elevated platform and ark of the law. Away from the murderously heavy fixture, he stared up at the creature's fire-bright reflections, which peeped through the swirl of smoke, mocking him and his Marxian concept of historical necessity.

Coughing from the smoke, he turned toward the elevated stage and saw his father's gold-stitched name consumed in a blaze of incandescent brilliance, then, still intact, fall as a glowing ash onto the floor.

No, it can't end here like this, he thought. But with fire everywhere his fate seemed sealed. By some deep, perhaps atavistic instinct, he leaped onto the stage and flung open the ark, whose base was already licked by the ubiquitous flames. Inside, he found a scroll of the law adorned in matching blue velvet. He seized it and, clutching it to his breast like life itself, turned to gaze upon a congregation of glowing flames shimmering in every pew, crowding the walls, and creeping into the aisle. The adherents of light had just joined hands across the back of the synagogue. Beyond that must be an anteroom that had locked doors, but Grisha prayed that it might have low windows through which he could escape. If not, he, too, would die with his father's Torah, but not, please God, struck by that hideous chandelier! He leaped into the aisle and, bending low, dashed down toward the flames without hesitating for a second, since he feared most the outstretched patricidal tentacles that hung in the smoke above.

As he safely traversed the long aisle, he heard a horrendous roar behind him, but he didn't have a moment to savor his hair-raising escape from the chandelier and falling roof, for he had already burst into the low, flickering flames. Instinctively he turned toward the small vestibule door to his right; the one to the left was already collapsing in sparks. By the time he reached the doorway on the right, he had learned with all his soul to fear the fire itself. Burying his face in the Torah scroll, he still felt the heat slapping his face in merciless, deadly insults. The portion that remained exposed felt as if it were already on fire. The air was so hot he could no longer breathe, and his searing, oxygen-starved lungs seemed on the verge of bursting. With a desire for life that defied the burning within and without, he entered the vestibule and through his one squinting eye thought he saw the light of day and of life. With a last explosive effort he propelled himself toward the opening. During his final moments in the blazing inferno he imagined that he saw a short bearded figure rushing toward him, and for a moment believed that it was, after all these years, his father greeting him in death, but then he was on the threshold of the world and life itself, and as he felt hands touch him, he realized they were cool with life.

# CHAPTER THIRTY-TWO

RUNNING FULL TILT, GRISHA DASHED INTO THE KRIMSKER Rebbe's arms. The rebbe tightly grasped both the holy Torah and its bearer in an ecstatic embrace. Since Grisha was leaning to one side behind the scroll, his tremendous momentum carried them careening wildly around in circles to safety away from the building. Had not both men been clinging to the holy Torah for dear life, certainly one or both would have been flung to the ground; instead, they balanced one another around the Torah and slowly came to a stop, like a spinning windborne seed whose symmetrical wings cradle between them the germ of life.

"It's the devil himself!" said one of Wotek's cohorts, who had flung the second torch.

"The devil himself," echoed the murmuring goyim in fearful incredulous agreement. "The devil for sure. Just look at him!"

Grisha did look like a visitor, if not an inhabitant, of infernal realms. Singed by the fire, his hair stood out in short bristles like a rusty wire brush, and the smell of it was sharp and repulsive. His exposed eyebrows and eyelashes had largely disappeared, and half his face was red and swollen and covered with black and gray soot. The arms holding the Torah were soot-streaked and covered with black and white ash. His shirt had been scorched in a dozen places until it looked like a burnt spiderweb. The bottom of his pants had been burned away—indeed, they had glowed as red as embers when he was whirling about with the rebbe. His charred shoes left black footprints on the ground as if the fiery devil himself had passed by.

The hasidim stared dumbfounded at this strange apparition, but the rebbe seemed oblivious to the man himself. The Krimsker Rebbe, as still as stone, clung to the Torah with the blissful ecstasy of a lover whose beloved, feared dead, has been miraculously restored to perfect health. His embrace, more expressive than any words, articulated the lover's newfound appreciation and increased love for the beloved as well as the irrational, passionate rapture of the moment: never must they be separated again, ever.

"Only the devil himself could survive that hell," stated Wotek with a nasty edge to his voice, as if he had been both made a fool of and cheated.

Releasing the Torah suddenly, the rebbe turned toward the goyim.

"The devil?" he repeated quietly but clearly, as one who is incredulous at what he has heard. "The devil?" he mused more loudly, as one who most certainly has misunderstood something.

"The devil?!" he screamed in amazed consternation. Then he shouted in triumph, "An angel! This is an angel!"

Springing back to Grisha, he took the Torah and held

it high above them as if he were going to smash it over their heads.

"Fools, you tried to burn something that cannot be burned! Letters of fire!"

The Krimichak men who wore hats quickly removed them. All crossed themselves in fearful reverence.

"You have not burned what cannot be burned, and you cannot drown what cannot be drowned. Go, now! Go before the devil does arrive and the Angel of Death enters the waters! Run! Flee!"

The mob momentarily cowered before the rebbe, then all broke for home in a disorderly rout. In their haste to escape, they threw down all their staves and cudgels, even some scythes and pitchforks, and raced, babbling and shouting, toward the bridge. Each thinking only of his own danger, they kicked and stepped on one another, continuously knocking each other down. Those sent sprawling into the dust quickly regained their feet and scampered away after the crowd. Even those who suffered sprains or breaks hobbled off as fast as they could, and no one looked back for fear of finding either the devil or the angel of death himself breathing down his neck.

The sequence of events was too overwhelming for the Jews to cheer the rout of the goyim. Some murmured "Thank God," but even that was hushed. Who was to say that the goyim wouldn't return tomorrow, or a month from tomorrow? An angel's continued presence—he had not disappeared immediately the way the magic frog had hopped back into the pond the night before—raised uneasy suspicions that the unnatural sequence had not ended. Respectfully curious, they pressed within several feet to examine the angel, who looked the worse for wear. No one had heard of any angel described like this, and no one had ever seen him before. Almost no one.

"Grisha, is that you?" Yechiel asked uncertainly.

The young scholar pushed his way to the front of the crowd and stared studiously at the apparition, trying to discern who was under all those disfiguring ashes, soot, and scorches.

"Grisha?" the Krimsker Rebbe repeated quietly but clearly in a tone of wonder. "Grisha?" he mused again more loudly.

The rebbe walked past Yechiel directly to Grisha and peered into the discolored face.

"No," he said, "this isn't Grisha." His voice rose triumphantly. "This is Hershel Shwartzman. Hershel, the son of Chaim Shwartzman, may he rest in peace!"

The older hasidim shook their heads and rolled their eyes in speechless disbelief. The younger ones turned to their fathers, uncles, or grandfathers for an explanation. Yechiel, who had not taken his eyes off Grisha, knew that the rebbe was right. At the rebbe's pronouncement Grisha's mouth dropped open in frank amazement, and he blinked in astonishment, just as he had when he saw his father's name stitched in gold on the blue velvet hanging.

Yechiel turned to Reb Zelig, who was standing next to him. "Who was Chaim Shwartzman?"

"May he rest in peace, Chaim Shwartzman was the wealthy lumber merchant who built the Angel of Death," Reb Zelig said in a normal tone. Then he continued in a whisper, "And he died in it blessing the Torah on the first Sabbath, when the chandelier fell on him."

Reb Zelig had thoughtfully lowered his voice, not because he feared the evil eye, but because he did not want to embarrass Hershel. As he stared at his late employer's son, tears streamed down his face.

Yechiel approached Hershel-Grisha, who looked faint from his ordeal. "Grisha, are you all right?"

"Of course he's all right," the Krimsker Rebbe answered, irritated by the silly question.

"He was in the fire, wasn't he?" Yechiel said simply, explaining his inquiry.

"Of course he was in the fire," the rebbe said impatiently. "Today he received the Torah on Mount Sinai, and the Torah was given in black fire on white fire."

The rebbe held the Torah close to his chest. "Receiving the Torah is difficult, but understanding what to do with it once it is in your hands is even more difficult. Our holy Hershel saved his father's Torah today and gave it to the children of Israel—something his father could not do—and that is why he stands covered in holiness. The Evil Inclination has been burned away, and the ashes that remain are holy."

The rebbe then turned to address Hershel directly. "My child, if only the holy sparks could remain as bright as they were today. Even now they cool into cold ash, but we must try, for we are a holy nation. We must try! I will give you my pure daughter Rachel Leah as your wife."

Then the rebbe called, "Sexton!"

Reb Yechezkal stepped forward.

"Take my future son-in-law to my house. The rest of us must escort the Torah he gave us to the beis midrash, where it must rest before beginning its journey."

As the rebbe turned to lead the procession, an agitated, tall young man with bold, square features stepped out of the crowd and into the rebbe's path. Unlike most of the other hasidim, he wore a short jacket, and his beard was closely trimmed; he had a modern, aggressive, self-confident look.

"Forgive me for speaking. I do not mean to embarrass the rebbe, but the rebbe seems to have forgotten that Rachel Leah has been promised to me. We are to be married after the feast of Succos. Reb Yechezkal himself promised her to me in your name."

Reb Yechezkal's face flushed red with shame, and he stared down at the ground. The Krimsker Rebbe, however, looked up directly into Yitzhak Weinbach's face with no expression of emotion whatsoever.

"What Reb Yechezkal did, he did in good faith, but he did not have my authority. I am not bound by his words. I am sorry if you are disappointed, but I have only one daughter and she must marry Hershel."

Unlike the rebbe, Yitzhak flushed with embarrassment and anger. He was not one to surrender what he believed was rightfully his.

"You can't do this to me!"

The Krimsker Rebbe flicked his hand impatiently, but Yitzhak refused to terminate their discussion.

"Who is he? He saved the Torah, but who is he?" he asked indignantly.

"That's who he is," the Rebbe answered. "He is the Jew who stood on Mount Sinai and saved the Torah. I'll tell you who you are, Reb Yitzhak. You are the Jew who made the fire."

"What is the rebbe saying?" Yitzhak asked in genuine ignorance.

"Look," the rebbe said, pointing to the ground.

Between them and the burning synagogue lay a box of matches that bore the distinctive red letters of Weinbach and Company. The rebbe began to step around Yitzhak, but the match manufacturer turned to confront him.

"I'm responsible for all my matches?" Yitzhak asked quizzically, uncertain that he had understood the rebbe's intent.

Calmly, with a tinge of reflective melancholy, the rebbe said, "Reb Yitzhak, if a man does not judge himself, all things judge him, and all things will become messengers of God."

Yitzhak heard the rebbe's words only too well and was frightened by them. Because he was frightened, he desperately wanted to deny them.

"That box is empty. Someone just threw it away. There aren't any matches in it, and there haven't been since it was discarded," he said with heretical, brazen scorn.

To prove his point, he moved to pick up the box, but the rebbe casually extended one of his arms that had been cradling the Torah and pointed directly at the red-lettered object, which burst instantaneously into a chemically fueled ball of brilliant flames. Yitzhak stopped short and leaped away. Later he was to claim that the heat from the burning building had ignited the matches, but at that moment he wondered whether the rebbe had miraculously saved him from sticking his hand into an explosion of matches.

Yitzhak protectively and reassuringly rubbed his still-healthy right hand. The rebbe turned to leave.

"Sexton!" the rebbe called.

"Yes?" Reb Yechezkal answered.

"No, not you. The one I'm taking with me." The rebbe glanced around until he found Reb Zelig. "Oh, there you are. Come here."

Reb Zelig stepped forward.

"Listen carefully, what I am going to tell you is very important. Stay close to me now. I don't want you to leave this Torah alone. You are going to stay with it day and night until we bring it to America."

Reb Zelig nodded, and together they turned toward the beis midrash. They had taken only two or three steps when the wall of the Angel of Death collapsed inward in a massive cracking of burning timber and an accompanying crashing swirl of sparks and smoke. Neither the Krimsker Rebbe nor his new sexton, Reb Zelig, turned back to watch. His eyes on the Torah, Reb Zelig was already conscientiously executing his rebbe's orders. The Krimsker Rebbe's gaze was turned inward, but his eyes sparkled in concentration and discovery. The rebbe was observing a scenario with perfect clarity: the great Napoleon was crossing the River Nedd at Krimsk on his way out of Russia!

# THE BRIDGE

CROSSING THE RIVER NEDD AS HE DEPARTED KRIMSK, the rebbe had the visionary experience of treading in the footsteps of Napoleon. Looking down at the water, he saw a cloud reflected as a pyramid and knew that Napoleon had crossed the river like a modern, steadfast pharaoh. The knowledge that he was emulating mighty pharaoh gave the rebbe confidence that he was traveling in the correct direction, for he understood that Israel's post-Temple exile had not gone far enough. To ensure that it would, the Krimsker Rebbe wanted to imitate the Shekinah, the glory of God's presence, by burying himself in the depths of exile and thus spreading the messianic redemption. On the throbbing steamship that crossed the Atlantic Ocean to the demonic Other Side, presentiments of diaspora impurity encouraged him.

A glance at the map told the rebbe that the city in which previous Krimsker immigrants had settled—and promised help—was the correct place. Saint Louis, buried in the middle of the continent, sat astride a river. These similarities with the old home comforted him and held the promise of a new Krimsk. In contrast to the simple Nedd, the new river had such an astonishing name, the Mississippi. On the train west, the rebbe eagerly anticipated crossing the Mississippi, in the belief that this initial encounter would inspire the same prophetic talents that his departure from Krimsk had. Repeated inquiries elicited the response from the conductor that the train was on schedule and would approach the river at sunset. To the rebbe's surprise, they did not get off the train. The train itself began to climb onto a massive masonry and iron bridge, which carried it across the river. And the river? Yaakov Moshe rushed to the window, leaning close to the pane, to examine the Mississippi in mystic intimacy, but the Eads Bridge was so high that he could barely see the barges floating impossibly far below. The river, like an ocean, stretched away as far as the eye could see. The rebbe ran across the car to the window on the opposite side, and the Mississippi stretched away even farther and grander. Suddenly he realized that the seemingly small chains of barges lost on its mammoth surface could hold all of Krimsk, Krimichak, and the pond in between. Seeing his terrified amazement, the conductor came over to announce with unbounded American pride that the American Mississippi River is greater than the Nile in ancient Egypt.

The rebbe turned back to the unbelievable sight. In the interim the setting sun had shifted slightly, and the great majestic Mississippi reflected the red dying rays; the rebbe gazed upon a boundless stream of blood like pharaoh's lesser Nile during the ferocious first plague. Yaakov Moshe turned away from the window and fell into his coach seat.

Reb Zelig, clutching the redeemed Torah, leaned toward him to ask if they should recite the blessing upon seeing a wonder of nature. The rebbe leaned forward and kissed the holy scroll's blue velvet cover, which was the color of real life-giving water and not the bloody life-depleting crimson that drained a continent through the empty void beneath. With tears in his eyes, he turned to the sexton and said, "In America there is no Sabbath, only magic," but Reb Zelig could not hear him because the bridge echoed and reechoed the metallic clatter of the wheels, mocking any attempts at speech.

# ABOUT THE AUTHOR

ALLEN HOFFMAN was born in Saint Louis and received his B.A. in American History from Harvard University. He studied the Talmud in yeshivas in New York and Jerusalem, and has taught in New York City schools. He and his wife and four children now live in Jerusalem. He teaches English literature and creative writing at Bar-Ilan University and is the author of a collection of stories, *Kagan's Superfecta.*